THE BANKER'S SECRETS

INSIDE ADVICE FOR CANADIANS ON SECURING CREDIT,
AVOIDING BANK CHARGES, MINIMIZING TAXES,
NEGOTIATING A MORTGAGE, BUILDING PERSONAL WEALTH

THE BANKER'S SECRETS

INSIDE ADVICE FOR CANADIANS ON SECURING CREDIT,
AVOIDING BANK CHARGES, MINIMIZING TAXES,
NEGOTIATING A MORTGAGE, BUILDING PERSONAL WEALTH

ANDRÉ FRAZER

MACMILLAN CANADA
Toronto

Canadian Cataloguing in Publication Data

Frazer, André
  The banker's secrets

Includes index.
ISBN 0-7715-7461-4

1. Finance, Personal—Canada.   I. Title.

HG179.F72   1997   332.024'01   C96-932490-1

1 2 3 4 5 MDM 01 00 99 98 97

Cover design by Sharon Foster Design

Macmillan Canada wishes to thank the Canada Council, the Ontario Ministry of Culture and Communications and the Ontario Arts Council for supporting its publishing program.

This book is available at special discounts for bulk purchases by your group or organization for sales promotions, premiums, fundraising and seminars. For details, contact: Macmillan Canada, Special Sales Department, 29 Birch Avenue, Toronto, ON M4V 1E2. Tel: 416-963-8830.

Macmillan Canada
A Division of Canada Publishing Corporation
Toronto, Ontario, Canada

Printed in Canada

TABLE OF CONTENTS

Wealth—An Objective Within Anyone's Grasp

I F I SAY THE WORD *WEALTH*, WHAT COMES TO YOUR mind? Is it the idea of owning a yacht or a couple of thoroughbreds? Does it mean three vacations a year? Or how about a wardrobe of expensive clothes? Or perhaps a villa in Spain? You might say it's all of these things. Then again, it might be none of these. That's the problem with wealth. It's tough to define in terms that don't refer to specific items or possessions—just as in those TV ads that try to sell you lottery tickets on the premise that you'll set up residence at a Swiss spa and hobnob with the jet set.

But let me propose a definition—one that is broader and more abstract and that conjures up notions of freedom and peace of mind. To me, wealth is this: to have the ability to pursue your true interests in life. No doubt you can fit a whole lot into this definition. And what you fit into it is up to you. I'm no psychologist, but I can tell you with certainty from having worked for years in the financial services industry that, when it comes to defining wealth, there is one universal element: the desire to be independent—to not have to worry about working for a living and to have enough capital to live life to the fullest.

Although attaining such a goal may seem out of reach for most people, trust me—it isn't. Indeed, wealth is a possibility for just about all of us. Over the years, I've had the opportunity and good fortune to help Canadians of every stripe and every walk of life with their financial well-being. And sure enough, what each of these clients believed were the tangible parts of wealth—the boats, the vacations, the lazy afternoons at the cottage while the rest of the world toiled away—was as varied as their attitudes and personalities. But what also set them apart was their determination to achieve their individual notions of independence. That's where *you* come in. You see, whatever your occupation, lifestyle, personality or level of education, the one thing that will help you achieve the independence you desire is the willingness to learn and apply some of the principles of wealth building that have brought freedom to others—the sort of freedom you want!

Believe me when I tell you that among my independently wealthy clients, none had any mystical strategies for building their wealth. Rather, they amassed their wealth by making sure they understood a few fundamental financial principles and by following some simple, yet powerful, investment strategies—strategies that I will share with you in this book.

You'll have to take these strategies and rules to heart. It will take time and dedication to follow them all with regularity. But with practice, eventually you will train yourself and your family to maintain the habits that will enable you to achieve wealth. As long as you earn a decent wage or salary, you'll be able to do it. But always remember that what matters in the end is not so much the size of your paycheque but what you do with the money you earn.

Never forget, either, that, with a banking background, I'm not about to sell you crazy ideas or pie-in-the-sky, get-rich-quick schemes. That's not my forte. What I do best, rather, is help people like you become financially independent with a plan that is simple, safe and easy to understand.

What I've done in my book is to compile the vital money-making techniques you will need to achieve your dreams of independence—the techniques that make the difference. You'll find worksheets throughout that will enable you to get started today, as well as tables that will explain to you why one strategy is better than the next. You will also reap the benefit of my years in the banking industry, with tips on how to deal with banks, how to get the best financing and how to cut the cost of investing your money.

Throughout the book, I will refer to what I consider to be the seven golden rules of wealth building. Learn to follow them religiously. In Chapter 1, I will cover the basic principles of finance that will help you understand how money can grow faster than you could ever have imagined. And I will add to these principles in every other chapter so that by the end you will feel comfortable with the logic of finance.

In Chapter 2, you will learn one of the golden rules: eliminating your debt. Indeed, you can't expect to build your wealth if you're constantly strapped with bank loans and credit card balances. After you've read this chapter, I promise you'll never look at credit the same way again.

In Chapter 3, you'll learn how to make a budget, the subject of another golden rule. Budgeting is vital to your financial well-being; you need to know where your money goes before you can think about investing it.

After learning how to get your financial house in order, you will be ready for Chapter 4 and your first taste of investing. In this chapter, we'll deal with a subject that is a perennial dilemma for most investors: whether to rent or buy a home. You'll learn everything about mortgages, including how to get the best rates from your bank and how to reduce the long-term costs of paying off your house. This chapter will be an especially good test of your knowledge of some of the principles covered in Chapter 1.

In Chapter 5, you'll learn another golden rule and discover what has to be one of the most incredible tax breaks in the world: the registered retirement savings plan (RRSP). In fact, after reading this chapter, I know you'll be convinced that RRSPs are essential to your future financial well-being and that they are indeed the best guarantee that you will be able to retire at all. They make up the foundation of your nest egg—they're that important. You'll also learn the concept of "paying yourself first": you need to save at least 15 percent of your annual income to build wealth. Don't worry. After you see the numbers in black and white, you'll never go back to your old ways.

Chapter 6 should be an exciting journey. In this chapter, you'll get to figure out exactly how much wealth you'll need before you can retire. You'll be able to see right there on the page that good financial planning may mean retiring at 50 while poor planning may mean not retiring at all. Most of all, you'll see that it is within your grasp to achieve financial independence. Of that, I know you'll be convinced.

Chapter 7 will explore the nitty-gritty of your financial investment strategy. You'll learn another golden rule: diversify your investments. Of particular importance in this chapter will be mutual funds, the ultimate diversified investment vehicle, which can protect you from high risk and still earn you solid returns.

Chapter 8 will cover the more conservative side of your portfolio. Smart investing is safe investing. In this chapter, you'll learn how bonds, term deposits, gold and income-generating real estate can help you make money while playing it safe.

Chapter 9 will be a quick, though very important, chapter. Since you'll have learned all about your investment options, I'll teach you how to decide where to put your money, based on your own assessment of how much risk you're willing to take. Risk is everything in investments, and I will cover the topic at various times throughout the book. But in Chapter 9, you'll get to test your mettle.

Taxes will be the subject of Chapter 10: how to reduce them, how to reduce them, how to reduce them. I'll show you how different investments receive different tax treatment, and I'll give you a slew of tips (legal, of course) on how you should organize these investments to keep Revenue Canada away.

Chapter 11 will discuss three golden rules, those involving insurance, emergency funds and wills. I've joined these topics together because they have one thing in common. They are all related to protecting your wealth while it's in your hands and the hands of your family. Wealth takes work to accumulate, but it can be lost in a very short time.

Finally, in Chapter 12, you'll see some of the strategies at work: I'll describe how one typical couple, on a decent wage, can amass enough wealth for their retirement.

And you won't want to skip the appendices. This section is as indispensable as the rest of this book. Among other things, you'll learn how to get financial advice on the Internet and how to choose a professional adviser. The mathematically inclined, meanwhile, will find all the financial formulas to suit their fancy.

Before we jump in, I want to say it one more time: becoming wealthy and achieving your financial independence is not only for other people—it's for you, too! The important thing is to get started *right now*. It's never too late to start. All you need is the will to learn and a plan of action. I can help you with the plan; you'll have to provide the persistence.

I know it will take you a bit of time to get started on your plan. And I also know that on occasion you will slip up. But that's okay. As long as you're patient and willing to apply some of the strategies in this book, in the long run you'll come out far, far, far ahead of where you would've been. Guaranteed! Take it from a banker.

CHAPTER 1

Financial Principles First

BEFORE SPEEDING ONTO THE ROAD TO FINANCIAL independence, you might do well to make a pit stop to ensure that you feel completely at ease with the most basic building block of finance: the power of compounding. Once you understand this fundamental principle—that reinvesting, rather than spending, the returns on your investments will make you wealthier faster—you should be able to grasp the logic of just about any concept a financial expert might throw at you.

Perhaps the easiest way to see the power of compounding at work is to examine the effects of inflation. We're all familiar with inflation: it's that annual increase in the cost of living that ensures the money you leave in your pocket today will be worth less one year from now. That money will have less spending power. For instance, if a loaf of bread costs $2.00 today, and a whiz-bang economist predicts that inflation will be 3 percent during the next year, then the loaf will cost 103 percent of $2.00, or 6 cents more, one year from now.

So far, so good. Now, let's complicate matters a little. Let's say our economist predicts that this annual rate of inflation of

3 percent will endure over the next ten years. We already know that over the next year the price of the loaf will increase by 6 cents, to reach $2.06. The following year, the price will again increase by 3 percent—but by 3 percent of $2.06 (not $2.00), or 6.18 cents—to $2.1218. (I've left in the extra decimal places to make the illustration more precise.) Let's look at a couple more years. The next jump in price will be 3 percent of $2.1218, or 6.37 cents, to raise the price to $2.1855. The year after that, the price will increase by 3 percent of $2.1855, or 6.56 cents, to $2.2511. One more year and the price will go up 3 percent of $2.2511, or 6.75 cents.

You can see the pattern already. In the first year, the increase is 6 cents. But that level of increase is short-lived; by the fifth year, the increase has reached 6.75 cents. In other words, every year the increase gets bigger, and as a result, the price of the loaf of bread gets bigger. Indeed, while the price of the loaf will have increased to $2.32 after five years, by the end of the tenth year it will have reached $2.69. Compare the increase of 32 cents in the first five years (that is, $2.32 minus $2.00) with the increase of 37 cents in the next five years (that is, $2.69 minus $2.32). As you can see, increasing the price of an item by a percentage every year doesn't make the price grow by a fixed amount each year. Not at all. It makes the price grow faster and faster over time—faster than if the price increased by only a fixed amount. In the case of the loaf of bread, had its price increased by six cents per year, after ten years the total increase would have been 10 times 6 cents, or 60 cents, to bring the cost of the loaf to $2.60. In reality, however, the price will reach $2.69—9 cents more.

It is this 9-cent difference that we can attribute to the power of compounding. By continuously increasing a number by a percentage, and including the previous increases in a new total, you are compounding the effect. And the bigger the percentage increase, the bigger the effect over time. Just think of the out-rageous inflation rates in some developing countries. Imagine if your $2.00 loaf of bread increased in price at 10 percent per year. Next year, it would cost you $2.20; the year after that, $2.42. In five years, at a 10 percent increase per year, the loaf would cost you $1.22 more, or $3.22, and after ten years, yet another $1.97 more, or $5.19!

As you can see, when it comes to inflation, the power of compounding works against you. The objective of wise financial planning, on the other hand, is to make compounding work *for* you—to invest in such a way that you will not only compensate for the negative effects of inflation, but also make money. In other words, you want to beat inflation by as much as possible to build wealth.

A woman once walked into the bank where I worked, carrying what turned out to be a brown paper bag stuffed with money—$50,000 in cash, to be precise. This woman had never trusted banks and for a number of years had chosen to store her savings at home. Fortunately, a relative had finally convinced her that keeping her money at home might be riskier than putting it in the bank vault. So here she was with her loot in a brown paper bag. She wanted to make sure her money was safe, she told me. She didn't want it to suddenly disappear from her home. I told her that for reasons of safety I thought she'd made the right decision. I didn't have the heart to tell her the obvious: that over the years inflation had eroded her wealth to a fraction of what it had once been.

Clearly, if only for the sake of protecting your wealth against the ravages of inflation, you need to find ways to make your money grow. Every year. Day by day. The lesson is simple: the money you have right now is worth more today than it will be in the future if you simply stick it under your mattress. That's because time doesn't stand still, and over time your money will buy you less and less if you don't keep up with inflation. My job in this book is to teach you how to build up the value of your money by using the power of compounding as a guide—not merely to balance the effects of inflation, but rather to beat inflation by as much as possible. I want you to think of that $20 in your pocket as being worth "$20 plus." The plus is what you could earn on your money if you invested it, just as that woman could have built up her $50,000 over the years had she invested it.

In financial terms, you might want to get used to thinking of the value of your $20 today as its present value, as what it could buy you right now. But considering that you purchased this book to learn how to make your money grow in the future, you might also get used to thinking of your money in terms of its future value. That's right. Future value is what that $20 in your pocket will be worth in the future once you've tacked on the returns you will make from investing it. What you should always remember is that ultimately the difference between the present value and the future value of your money will determine whether or not you're successful in reaching your financial goals. The more you can expect to make from investing your money, the greater that future value will be. And isn't that your objective, after all?

Compounding is the way to reach that objective. Indeed, compounding is a cornerstone of wealth building. I remember first becoming aware of compounding when my father explained to me that the longer I kept money in my bank account, the more interest I would earn and the more money I would have. Unfortunately, I wasn't much of a saver, and I never was able to build up much of a bank account. Then again, I was six at the time. What six-year-old can resist the temptation of spending money? Years later, when I was about 21, I was at an exhibition at which some financial planners had set up a booth. I looked in wonder at their charts, which showed the power of the "Eighth Wonder of the World": compounding. Alas, it still did not sink in! It took me a few more years to appreciate how powerful compounding can be and how important it is to achieving our common dream of financial independence.

Let's explore further this marvel that is the power of compounding. Let's say you have $1,000 for which you have no immediate use. Mindful as you are of the ravages of inflation, you conclude wisely that you should invest the $1,000. Moreover, rather than put the money in a bank account, which would pay a low rate of interest, you decide to invest in a mutual fund you've read about. Let's say you expect to earn 10 percent on that fund; over the next year, you will make a return of $100 on your $1,000.

The scenario is simple so far, but here comes the big question: what should you do with the $100 at the end of the year? (Let's assume for now that you wouldn't pay any income tax on it, such as in an RRSP, which I'll get to in a later chapter.) Let's rephrase the question: what do you think would happen if you spent the $100 you earned on your $1,000? You got it. You'd have made no progress in your plan to make your $1,000 grow. Sure, you would have derived some brief enjoyment from spending the $100—perhaps on the order of a dinner for two. But ask yourself this: do I want the future value of my $1,000 to be "$1,000 plus a dinner for two"? Of course not. If you did, you would never come close to financial independence. Take it from a banker: you make money by investing as much money as you can for as long as you can. For this reason, you should reinvest the returns you earn on your $1,000. And this is where the power of compounding comes in: when you compound or reinvest the returns you've earned on your money, you become wealthier faster. You earn returns on your returns! Over the medium- to long-term, this strategy can make a phenomenal difference to your wealth. Table 1 illustrates just how much you could amass over 10, 20 and 30 years if each month you invested some money in an investment that paid 10 percent per year. Again, the key here is to reinvest the returns from that monthly investment rather than to spend them.

Table 1: The Power of Compounding

Amount Invested per Month ($)	Number of Years Invested	Annual Rate of Interest (%)	Amount Accumulated after Period ($)
100	10	10	20,484
200	20	10	151,873
300	30	10	687,146
400	30	10	904,195

And after 10 years, an investment of a mere $100 per month at 10 percent would amount to $20,484. After 20 years, that plan would grow to $75,937! I don't have to tell you that these figures are incredible. And they're achievable even for the conservative investor. Consider the alternative. Imagine if instead of harnessing the power of compounding by reinvesting your returns you decided to spend them as you earned them. Believe me, the difference is not negligible. Take the case of the monthly investment of $100, which every year would amount to a $1,200 contribution to your savings. If you were going to spend the $120 in returns that you earned on the savings for the year, the total benefit of your efforts for the year would be $1,200 saved plus $120 spent. Over ten years, that would amount to $12,000 in savings plus $1,200, which you would have spent. Not bad, you say? According to Table 1, that's $7,284 less than if you simply resisted the temptation of spending the returns ($20,484 minus $13,200)! At $400 per month over 30 years, the difference would be mind-boggling: by spending all your returns rather than reinvesting them, the benefit of your efforts would amount to just $144,000 in savings plus $14,400 in spending enjoyment, for a total benefit of $158,400. I say *just* because this $14,400 spending spree over 30 years would end up costing you $745,795 (the difference between $904,195 [see Table 1] and $158,400). Now are you convinced that you should learn to fight the temptation of spending the returns on your money?

If these calculations seem complex, I'll let you in on a clever shortcut to appreciating the magic of compounding: the Rule of 72. Divide the number 72 by the annual rate of return you earn on an investment; the answer will roughly equal the number of years it will take to double your money. The rule works only if you reinvest your returns, which activates the compounding component. So, if you can earn 15 percent on your money, you will double the initial value of an investment in only 4.8 years (or 72 divided by 15). If 7 percent is the return, then it will take 10.29 years to double your money. Here's another example: say you can earn 10 percent annually on your money. Divide 72 by 10 and you get 7.2. If you decided to make a one-time investment of $1,000 tomorrow at 10 percent, that $1,000 alone—without ever having to add to it—would become $2,000 in approximately 7.2 years. Again, to drive home the point about compounding, if you decided not to reinvest the returns, the result of your efforts after 7.2 years would be $1,000 plus $720 of returns (7.2 years of returns at $100 per year), for a total benefit of just $1,720. Once you appreciate the power of compounding you will understand how to use it to generate future wealth. But let me leave you with this thought: in my years as a banker and financial adviser, I have found that the clients who have ended up with the largest or fastest-growing portfolios have been the ones who have truly understood the wonders of compounding and who have always been prepared to implement a strategy to maximize the effects of compounding. Needless to say, the client with the brown paper bag, who disregarded or was unaware of the power of compounding, was not among them.

I have seen ordinary folk use the principles in this book to build extraordinary portfolios. They didn't do this by using get-rich-quick schemes or by making risky or poor-quality investments. Most of them had only average incomes, used conservative investment strategies, minimized their taxes, diversified their risk and invested regularly. The one thing they all understood was that time was their ally and that it would have a powerful influence on the future value of their investments.

Now that you're in on the secret, there's no reason you shouldn't be part of that club!

CHAPTER 2

Managing Credit

AVING READ THE PREVIOUS CHAPTER, YOU NOW have at least a rudimentary grasp of the importance of the time value of money. You know how money can grow if you keep reinvesting it, and you understand how inflation can work against you. But are you on sound enough footing to make investments yet? More to the point, are you in debt?

In this chapter, I want to cover an important aspect of your financial well-being: credit. This area of financial planning is vital, and before I explain the investment techniques that will secure your financial independence, you must ensure that financially your house is in order.

One of the most serious personal finance problems today is the ease with which credit is available. Department store credit cards, Mastercard, VISA, finance company credit cards, gas station cards, deferred payment plans on furniture, loans from financial institutions—everywhere you turn, someone is trying to sell you a credit plan. Just sign on the dotted line and the credit is yours; it's that easy. And guess what happens when approval for your credit is a mere formality and you have all that credit at your disposal in the form of credit cards, cheques or cash advances. That's right. You reach your credit limits without batting an eye.

In addition, when you spend on credit, compound interest, that magical tool that can help build your wealth, becomes a weapon and suddenly turns on you. Interest starts accruing on your outstanding balance and then compounds and compounds and compounds on a monthly basis, eating into your financial independence. Believe me, in my years at the bank I frequently saw customers who had opted for easy credit and lost control of their spending, not to mention all hope of ever generating any wealth.

For people who succumb too easily to the lure of credit, there is only one solution to keep your financial house from caving in: bring your credit under control. Don't get me wrong. I am not saying that credit is a bad thing; it is not. But don't take credit simply because it's there. In fact, the essential point to remember about credit is the purpose for which you need it. If you need it for practical reasons—for instance, to avoid walking around with pockets full of cash—then credit is okay. But as a form of long-term financing for items you can't afford in the first place, credit spells death for the pocketbook.

Eventually, if your liabilities become too great and the regular payments on those liabilities exceed what you can comfortably afford, your financial well-being will suffer. You will have less money to invest, and less money for essentials. And until you reduce those payments, you will continue to harm your prospects for financial independence.

Let's take a closer look at the cost of using credit cards. First, depending on the type of credit card, you will pay a variety of interest rates on an outstanding balance. Need I tell you that the most expensive types are credit cards from department stores and finance companies, which charge approximately 2 percent per month? And remember how compounding works. Two percent per month doesn't mean 24 percent per year; the annual rate would be closer to 28 percent. That's because the people who are lending you money will charge interest not only on the price of that new pair of shoes but also on the interest that will accumulate as you fail to pay your monthly bill in its entirety.

If this situation already sounds bad, consider that you are paying these interest costs with after-tax dollars. If your tax rate is, say, 30 percent, you'll have to earn about $1.40 for every $1.00 in interest you pay ($1.40 minus 30 percent of $1.40 is $0.98); in effect, you are being forced to pay about 40 percent interest on the money you borrowed. As a result, I can't emphasize enough the importance of the first golden rule: pay off your debt! You must also learn to limit other types of short-term debt, such as car loans and renovation loans.

So how do you control credit? Well, the first goal is to control your use of credit cards. You may have to store them in a safe deposit box or in a filing cabinet at home. You could do the obvious and cut them up, or you could freeze them in a block of ice and store them in your freezer! In other words, use your cards only in emergencies or under special circumstances such as renting a car or taking advantage of such features as travel miles, warranty extensions, collision damage waiver insurance on vehicles or travel insurance. But you'll have to budget carefully to pay off these purchases immediately. Otherwise, you'll just keep racking up credit charges.

But let's say you have so many high-interest credit card balances outstanding that you can't even put a dent into any of them. In this case, your best option is debt consolidation. Visit your financial institution and arrange to consolidate all of your high-interest credit card debts into one debt. Basically, the institution gives you the money to pay off your debts. You, in turn, owe the institution one bigger debt, which you agree to pay off over a specific period of time. The advantage of consolidation is two-fold. First, rather than making the minimum payments on each of your credit cards—and you should realize that these required minimum payments are so low that your balance could conceivably be outstanding indefinitely—you will now have to "retire" your debt to the institution over a fixed term. Effectively, you will have forced yourself to get rid of your debt.

But I know what you're thinking: how can I possibly retire my debt if I owe the same amount of money as before? That's where the second benefit of consolidation comes in. Because you're willing to pay off your debt over time, the institution is willing to charge you a rate of interest that is lower than what you've been paying on your credit cards. And with less interest to pay, you can now eliminate more of the debt. Once you've consolidated your high-interest debts, just be sure that you pay off your credit card balances every month should you ever use your cards again. It's vital to your future wealth.

There are various types of lower-interest credit arrangements you can make to consolidate your debts. You could obtain a line of credit, a loan or a low-interest credit card such as a Gold MasterCard or a Gold VISA card, which, depending on the prime rate (the rate at which the Bank of Canada lends to banks), could carry a rate of interest of as little as 9.5 percent per year. If you decide on a line of credit, you might obtain a very favourable rate of interest if you agree to have the line of credit "fully secured" with one of your assets, such as a bond or a term deposit. With this type of arrangement, you're telling the financial institution that you're so certain you'll pay off your debt that in the unlikely event that you fail to pay it you will hand over the asset you've pledged. For its part, the financial institution will charge you less interest because it knows that if you fail to pay your debt, it will at least have the asset that you've put up as security. Just remember: the better the security you give—in other words, the more secure you make the institution feel—the better the rate you'll be able to negotiate.

Let's look at a common example of a situation suitable for debt consolidation. A husband and wife have a total debt of $25,000, which they have accumulated by using three or four credit cards to their credit limits. This couple's minimum monthly payments on their cards total $1,000, and the average annual rate of interest they're paying on the cards is 17 percent; the total amount of interest paid is at least $4,250 per year. That's $4,250 per year before they begin to pay down the $25,000 they owe!

Now, if this couple decided to consolidate their credit card debts into one loan or line of credit, they could cut their interest costs by thousands of dollars because the interest rate payable on the loan would be substantially less than 17 percent. So, let's say the interest rate on the debt consolidation loan is 10 percent and they have to pay off the loan over a period of five years. Notice how dramatically their debt payments change with this arrangement: their monthly payment becomes $531.18, while the interest in the first year is only $2,317.40. Each year, meanwhile, as they reduce the outstanding principal portion of the loan, the interest they must pay decreases.

Obviously, when you apply for a debt consolidation of this size, the bank will want enough security to cover the entire loan in case you default. So, be ready to offer the bank assets for which the bank could get some money. In fact, if your outstanding debts are large, this situation may well be the type that calls for putting up a piece of your house as a guarantee. Yes, you'll have to pay the cost of setting up a mortgage, but these fees—legal fees, appraisal fees and perhaps an administration fee—will probably be much less than the thousands of dollars per year in interest you're currently paying on your debts. In addition, you should be able to negotiate a reduction not only in fees such as the bank processing fee, but also the interest rate the bank charges for the mortgage.

Debt consolidation sounds simple enough, and for the most part, it is. But I'm sure one question is lingering in the back of your mind: do you mean to tell me I can just walk into the bank, wearing my best suit and ask for a consolidation loan, and the bank will give it to me? Well, that depends on whether you qualify. But don't be intimidated. From my years in banking, I know that credit, to the layperson, often seems like a mysterious science; in fact, it's anything but. You simply have to know what's running through your banker's mind. And one thing that's certainly running through his or her mind is how you come across. Do you look decent and trustworthy? Do you seem serious about the business at hand? I can tell you from experience that a seasoned lender will need no more than a couple of minutes to assess whether you're the type of person who's informed about personal finances. So, I'll say this only once: you've got one first impression to make, so make that first impression a good one. Look professional and you'll be treated as such. Have your paperwork in order and a plan in mind. Know what you own and what you owe. Have your papers with you, in orderly files. You may be in debt for a pile of money, but it's amazing how far you can go if you demonstrate a responsible outlook on your own affairs.

Still, that's just a "feel" test. The lender will invariably get to a checklist. Indeed, whether you are applying for a debt consolidation loan, mortgage, credit card, car loan or general purpose loan, the financial institution will refer to a more-or-less fixed list of criteria to make sure you're worth the risk. These criteria are the Five Cs of loan approval: capacity, character, collateral, other credit risks and capital.

Capacity deals with your ablity to repay the loan. First, the lender will want to know your gross monthly income, including your spouse's, if necessary, and request permission to check with your respective employers to get the exact figures. Even so, it can't hurt to bring along a paycheque stub; you'll look that much more serious about your affairs.

The key test for the lender is to see whether your current income can cover the loan payments. Usually most lenders allow approximately 30 percent of your gross monthly income for the cost of shelter (that is, your rent or your mortgage payments plus property taxes). (Again, you can only help your cause by bringing in paperwork confirming the amounts.)

If you have any other required monthly payments, such as credit card payments or support payments, a lender will allow up to 40 percent of your gross monthly income for shelter costs and these payments. In other words,

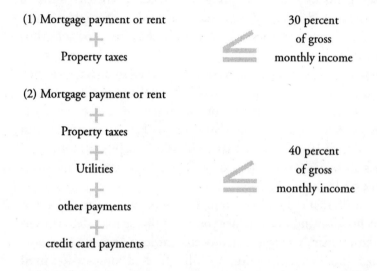

(1) Mortgage payment or rent
+
Property taxes
≤ 30 percent of gross monthly income

(2) Mortgage payment or rent
+
Property taxes
+
Utilities
+
other payments
+
credit card payments
≤ 40 percent of gross monthly income

Make these calculations before you visit your bank so that you will know what to expect. If you know ahead of time that you don't meet the 30 percent or 40 percent benchmark, be prepared to present your case. Indeed, the only way to get around these rules is to demonstrate that you are very strong in one or more of the other criteria.

When it comes to the second criterion, character, the big questions in the lender's mind are: Are you the type of person who pays debts on time? What previous loans have you had? Do your cheques bounce? Have you paid your debts as agreed between you and the lender? To obtain answers to these questions, the lender will want your permission to verify your credit record. (If you say no, you probably won't get a loan.) Verification involves checking with one of a couple of private-sector credit bureaus in North America that do nothing but gather information on people with debts. In case you're unaware, every time you've obtained credit—even a gas station card—the form you signed gave the creditor permission to release credit information to the bureau. Don't worry; this doesn't mean you're on a wanted list. In fact, since most of us use credit on a regular basis, the credit bureaus have information on just about every adult in North America.

What the credit bureau gives the lender is unbiased information, which weighs heavily in the decision to grant you a loan; this information includes details of how much you currently owe and to whom. The bureau will also tell the lender if there are any legal judgements outstanding against you. And it will give out the name of your employer, your date of birth and the name and phone number of parties to whom you have given permission in the last six months to check your credit record. This last piece of information is important, as it tells the lender whether you are currently applying for credit elsewhere. The credit bureau keeps this information for seven years. That's seven years of information on the frequency with which you seek credit. It's also seven years of details on whether you pay your debts on time, and whether you take a month, two months or even longer to pay your debts when they are overdue. Need I bother to say it? Make sure you pay all your debts on time and as agreed.

The advantage of having a clean credit record is that it may assist you in obtaining financing even if you are weak in one or more of the other lending criteria. This brings us to the third criterion: collateral. Did you know that you might have an easier time obtaining a large mortgage to purchase a house than obtaining a small debt consolidation loan? The reason for this discrepancy is that the bank sees the house as security, or collateral. In the case of a small debt consolidation, on the other hand, all you may have to offer is your signature and promise, which might not be sufficient if you test poorly on the other lending criteria.

The fourth criterion is other credit risks. This category relates to factors that may affect your reliability, such as age, level of education, marital stability and job stability. If, for example, you have a habit of changing jobs frequently and have no income between jobs, you are obviously a higher risk than someone who has kept the same job for the past ten years. Similarly, a 35-year-old with a solid credit and employment history is a much lower risk than a 21-year-old who's applying for a first loan and has just started at a first full-time job. So, if you have a sketchy work history, be prepared to answer for it, just as you would in a job interview, because you can bet that the issue will come up. Remember that in all likelihood your bank's customer service representative doesn't know you. It's up to *you* to state your case.

Finally, there's the criterion of capital. What assets do you have to fall back on should you lose your job or encounter extenuating circumstances affecting your income? Would you have to default on your loan or would you have enough savings to tide you over until you got back on your feet? Could you use your savings to pay off the loan? Could a relative lend you money? Let's face it, the bank knows you'll spend your money on food and shelter before you pay off your debt. So, having only minimal savings could work against you. Just remember that the more secure you can make the lender feel, the better your case. If someone—a relative, a generous mentor—is willing to guarantee your debt in case you default, that security might be enough.

Getting a loan depends on all five criteria. Strength in one area can help you overcome weakness in another. The bottom line is that the bank has to feel safe about lending you money.

Having covered the ins and outs of getting a loan, I should strongly advise you nevertheless to seek credit only for your mortgage or for investment purposes. In other words, if you can manage it, avoid seeking credit for purposes other than those that will ultimately make you wealthy. Don't make the lender wealthy.

Remember that charging interest on loans, lines of credit and credit cards is the way the major banks make their money. As the golden rule says: pay off your debts, especially credit card debts. You are helping no one but the bank and the finance companies when you allow your debts to get the upper hand.

CHAPTER 3

Budgeting Basics

Yes, budgeting seems to be a real snooze. It may even stir up negative emotions in you. But budgeting, the subject of our second golden rule, is a vital part of any financial plan. If you don't budget, you're liable to overspend, and not only will you likely find yourself heading towards debt consolidation, but you'll hurt your chances of achieving financial independence.

Think of yourself without a budget as being like a traveller without a map or a sailor without navigational aids. You can't plot a course, and you have no idea where you are or where you are going.

The consequences of not having such a map can be devastating. Some of the debt consolidations I've had to arrange could easily have been avoided had the customers spent a small amount of time budgeting. It's strange, but often it's the highest-income earners who spend the least time budgeting, or even attempting to control their expenses. Perhaps it's the misperception that the money will never run out that makes people act this way. In any event, I've dealt with the aftermath of excessive spending, and it isn't pleasant for anyone. And unfortunately, as we saw in the last chapter, arranging a debt consolidation isn't a cinch if you lack a good credit rating or assets to secure the loan. In other words, it's best to avoid getting into financial straits in the first place. And budgeting happens to be the best safeguard. Besides, not only does budgeting reduce the stress that comes from not knowing where your money is going, it also helps you find extra dollars to invest in your future prosperity.

A budget is nothing more than a monthly money manager, if you will. Every month, this manager tells you how much you have coming in, and limits how much you're allowed to spend. It's your control mechanism. Of course, you're the one who decides ahead of time what you can spend on each item, but it's the budget—the money manager—that keeps reminding you where you stand. For instance, if you've budgeted $200 for clothes this month, and you're about to buy yourself a pair of shoes, you'll have to check with the budget first. If you've already blown this month's $200 clothing allowance, you'll have to wait until next month.

The first step in constructing a budget involves deciding how to allocate your funds to clothing, or entertainment, or food. The answer is, work from what you spend right now. In other words, find out where your money goes every month.

This is what I propose: for two months, track all your expenses. Yes, everything—that coffee and doughnut you bought on your lunch break, the extra groceries you picked up on the way home from work, that compact disk you bought the other day. Everything. For two months. Believe me, you'll probably be surprised at all the hidden expenses.

This exercise is crucial because once you realize how much you spend and what you buy, you can decide where your priorities lie. For each expense you incur during a month, you'll have to decide whether it's essential or whether you might be able to reduce it somehow. For example, you may have subscriptions to a daily newspaper and some magazines. You'll have to decide whether you need them all. Ask yourself: do I need 48 channels on my television or could I get by with basic cable or no cable at all? The point is that you need to eliminate unnecessary expenditures, and there's no question you'll uncover plenty of those once you track your money over a couple of months. Aim to achieve a realistic budget, not a fantasy budget that you won't be able to stick to.

Let's say you know exactly where your money is going each month, and you've finished the painstaking task of deciding what's acceptable and what's not. Now it's time to construct the budget. Take a look at the sample budget worksheet on the next page and fill in the appropriate figures. (Note that the list of expenses is not exhaustive; you may need additional headings.) Use your gross pay as your income if you know approximately how much you pay in taxes each year (you'll enter your taxes farther down the sheet). If you don't know your gross income, fill in your net monthly income from your pay stubs, but leave the spaces blank for income tax and Canada Pension Plan (CPP) and employment insurance (EI) payments since your employer has deducted these already. (If you use the net income approach, any tax refund you receive from the government next year will come as an unexpected bonus!)

The idea is to budget for everything on a monthly basis. Your monthly rent or mortgage payments. Your monthly food bill. Everything. If there's a purchase or payment that you make only annually, such as home insurance, then you need to enter one-twelfth of that amount in your budget. I can't emphasize enough that to be able to stick to your budget you need to track *all* of your expenses; it's the forgotten expenses that create discrepancies between what you think you're spending and what you are actually spending.

BUDGET WORKSHEET
Based on monthly amounts

INCOME

    YOUR INCOME   _____

    YOUR SPOUSE'S INCOME   _____

    OTHER INCOME   _____

      (e.g., rental, interest, dividends)

TOTAL INCOME   _____

EXPENSES

    RENT/MORTGAGE   _____

    PROPERTY TAX   _____

    UTILITIES (gas, hydro, water)   _____

    HOME INSURANCE   _____

    PHONE/CABLE   _____

    LOAN PAYMENTS   _____

    CREDIT CARD INTEREST

      PAYMENT(S)   _____

    AUTO INSURANCE   _____

    OTHER INSURANCE   _____

    AUTO GAS & MAINTENANCE _____

    OTHER TRANSPORTATION   _____

      (e.g., cabs, transit)

    FOOD   _____

    PET FOOD   _____

    ENTERTAINMENT   _____

      (e.g., dining, movies, books)

    CLOTHES   _____

    INCOME TAX (check pay stub) _____

    OTHER TAXES   _____

      (e.g., on investment income)

    EI & CPP (if using gross income) _____

    FURNITURE   _____

    COMPUTER (hardware and software) _____

    VACATIONS   _____

PERSONAL ITEMS   _____
    (toiletries, dry cleaning, coffee)

ASSOCIATION DUES   _____
    (health club, golf club)

MISCELLANEOUS EXPENSES   _____

TOTAL EXPENSES   _____

INCOME minus EXPENSES =   _____

If this final figure is negative, then obviously you're in trouble. You need to take a close look at your finances. You'll have to either increase your income or reduce your expenses. Most likely, you got a positive figure. That's the amount of savings at the end of the month. You want to make that figure as large as possible— 15 percent of your gross income, as we'll see later in the book— because the more you have available to invest, the sooner you will be financially independent. That's why you must try to reduce your expenses in every way possible, in the same way that a business or a corporation would. Indeed, all well-managed companies have tight budget controls. They call it "zero-line budgeting," which is a fancy way of saying "don't let the final figure fall below zero." But considering that it may be difficult to achieve perfection every month, you might want to allow for overspending of up to 5 percent on each item in your budget. Just be careful not to use that leeway unless you're in a real pinch. Otherwise, your expenses will get out of hand all over again.

Once you have prepared a budget, you must learn to stick to it. You must remind yourself and your family that money is precious and that it doesn't come from a bottomless pit. If it isn't the end of the month yet and the monthly budget allowance for an item is gone, you'll need to delay some purchases or simply forgo something. The only alternative is to earn more money! I'm not suggesting you lead a miserly existence, but if you learn to control your finances *now*, over a period of years you will increase your wealth by thousands of dollars, and you and your family will be able to achieve financial independence earlier. Guaranteed!

In the nineties, being thrifty and finding ways to save money have become fashionable, and since part of learning how to budget is learning how to reduce expenses, it's time we looked at ways to cut those expenses. I'll bet that you will come up with even more ways!

Quick Money Saving Tips

- When shopping for groceries:
  - buy bulk and use coupons whenever possible
  - buy generic or house brands
  - plan ahead and shop from a list, buying only those items you need for upcoming meals
- When planning entertainment:
  - rent videos rather than buying them
  - make eating out a real treat, not something you do every day
  - quit smoking, if you can. At 10 percent annual interest, a $5-a-day habit will cost you $314,000 over 30 years
- Other ways to save money:
  - save electricity by switching off lights when not needed and switching to fluorescent or energy saver lights
  - ask your doctor to prescribe the generic version of any drugs you need
  - maintain your household goods in working order to make them last longer
  - avoid investing in stocks on a "hot tip" from a friend or relative, because it'll probably mean kissing your money goodbye. It takes sound professional management to make money on the stock market. Either you hire the advice, or you dedicate yourself to understanding the market in depth.

CUTTING COSTS

Shelter

Shelter is probably your biggest expense. I suggest that you aim to purchase a property for you and your family, since over the long term, real estate has usually proven to be the best investment a person can make. By paying rent, you are making someone else rich, since you are paying someone else's mortgage. You are also losing out on the potential capital growth of a property. Rent payments always increase over time. But with a mortgage, you have more control over your payments, since *you* choose the length of your mortgage term. Meanwhile, if interest rates are higher than anticipated when you renew your mortgage, you can make extra payments to reduce the outstanding balance of your mortgage debt. Remember, as well, that if interest rates have gone up, it is likely inflation has risen, too. And higher inflation means higher rent, adding more support to the argument for owning real estate.

But let's leave the comparison aside for a moment. Instead, let's assume you rent. Now, let's see how much you could add to your future financial independence if instead of renting an apartment at, for instance, $1,000 per month, you chose to rent one for $50 less and invested the money instead. From Table 1 (page 11), at 10 percent per year, an investment of just $100 per month amounted to $20,484 after ten years. Therefore, an investment of $50 per month would bring half that amount— still a pretty tidy sum, at $10,242. That's money for your retirement, money you could definitely use later.

Automobiles: Old vs New, Flashy vs Practical

A new automobile depreciates by up to 30 percent in the first year. In other words, if tomorrow morning you were to buy yourself a shiny new car for $20,000, it could be worth as little as $14,000 in a year's time. Don't buy a brand new automobile. Buy a car that is less than two years old. That way, you will avoid paying all that initial depreciation but will still be covered by the new-car warranty.

Cars are usually the second most expensive purchases we make. I recommend being frugal when you buy a car. An expensive car will depreciate just as a cheaper car does, but the expensive car could cost you an extra $1,000 to $2,000 per year in depreciation. And that expensive car's higher price means less money in your future financial stockpile. Ask yourself: do I need the plush leather seats, the four-wheel drive, the sun-roof? In addition, less expensive, less sporty cars are generally more fuel efficient, and their insurance rates are lower. That's more money for your savings.

"But I want a new car." Fine. Just don't buy this year's model. If you must buy new, visit your dealer when the new model comes out, and buy last year's model, which the dealer wants to get off the lot to make room for the new, higher-priced stock. Don't worry. The dealer will take an offer that is lower than usual. Discontinued or "ugly duckling" cars often go for a song, simply because the demand for them is low, even though they may be mechanically sound. And before you go shopping for a new or used vehicle, purchase a car buyer's guide that lists the best prices available on the car you want. Armed with this knowledge, you'll be in a stronger bargaining position.

On the subject of knowledge and preparation, remember that once you're in the dealer's showroom, it's too late to be doing your homework. The salesperson is a highly skilled professional, and if you don't know what you want and how you'll pay for it, or you don't negotiate properly and can't decide on options and warranties, you'll be at the salesperson's mercy. When I worked at the bank, once in a while I would receive a phone call from a client who happened to be sitting in the dealer's office. Invariably, the client would ask me a question that should have been answered ahead of time. I got questions such as "Do you think the dealer's loan rate is good?" and "Is the lease option a good deal?" Or my favourite: "do you think your bank can lend me the money to buy this little gem?" I'll be honest: phoning your banker while you're caught up in the excitement of purchasing a vehicle is not a good idea! Check with your banker beforehand to see what you qualify for, or tell the dealer you will check with your banker before you finalize any deals. If the dealer sees you're unprepared, that lack of preparation could cost you dearly.

Here's a tip that you may find useful: You are probably aware that if you trade in your old vehicle for a new one, the dealer will charge you the provincial sales tax on the difference in price between the two cars. But did you know that you're entitled to receive credit for the GST on that difference? Dealers obviously don't like to publicize this little-known fact. I myself missed out on this credit a few years ago, even though the dealer was very reputable. You see, while the dealer must remit GST to Revenue Canada on the price of the new car you're buying, he or she also gets a tax credit from Revenue Canada to equal $7 \div 107$, or 6.54 percent, of your old car. If you trade in your old car for $1,000, therefore, that's $65.40 in your dealer's pocket when it should be in yours. So make sure you ask for it. (You might also consider selling your old car through the classified ads; you will probably get a better price from an individual than from a dealer. But make sure you get a certified cheque or bank draft from the purchaser.)

Auto Insurance

If you're not the type to have accidents, agree to pay a higher deductible so that your annual insurance premium will be lower than it would be otherwise. Even if you do have a scrape, say, after three years, you'll still come out ahead.

Let me illustrate. Let's say you have two options: (1) you can pay an annual premium of $800 and have a $500 deductible or (2) you can pay a $1,100 premium and have a $100 deductible. Now, let's say you decide it might be wise to expect an accident of some sort after three years. If you took option (1), your total cost after three years would amount to three years of premiums plus one deductible or 3 x $800 + $500 = $2,900. Under option (2), however, your total cost would be 3 x $1,100 + $100 = $3,400. In other words, you'd be $500 ahead with option (1). And if you could manage to avoid an accident for more than three years, you would save yourself even more money by taking the option with the higher deductible.

To Lease or Not to Lease...

As new-vehicle prices continue to soar, leasing is becoming a more and more popular method of "purchasing" a vehicle these days. When you lease a vehicle, you pay a fixed monthly amount for a specified period of time, at the end of which you usually have an option to purchase the vehicle.

In the short term, leasing often seems more attractive than buying because the monthly lease payments are lower than the monthly loan payments you'd have to make if you had bought the car. But leasing has its downside. For one thing, when you lease, you have to maintain the vehicle to the dealership's standards. If you don't, you might have to pay a penalty when you return the vehicle. A more important problem with leasing, however, is that you don't own the vehicle; the dealer does. And if you do decide you'd like to own it at the end of the lease—usually after 24 to 48 months—you'll have to make one big payment equivalent to the vehicle's market value. Because of this final payment, your total outlay will be greater than if you had borrowed the money to buy the car, even though the monthly lease payments until that point would be lower than monthly loan payments. You see, with a lease you are paying for the depreciation on the vehicle, as well as the finance company's profit. With a loan, by contrast, you may be paying interest every month, but you're also reducing the principal balance outstanding on the loan. Besides, with a loan, you own the car, and you can do with it whatever you wish.

Here's an example. Say you want a new $20,000 car. If you leased the car, your monthly payments might be $370, and at the end of 48 months you could buy the car from the dealer for $10,000. Now, let's say you decided to borrow the $20,000 instead and pay off the loan in 48 months in equal monthly payments. At an annual rate of interest of 10 percent, your monthly payments would amount to $507. As mentioned, you are indeed paying $137 per month more to borrow the money than if you leased the car ($507 − $370). But look closely. If you lease, your total outlay over four years would be $17,760 in monthly payments plus $10,000 as a final payment, or $27,760. Borrowing, however, would cost you $24,336, or $3,424 less. Add to that the cost of maintaining the leased vehicle, which could be high if the dealer does the maintenance, as well as the per-kilometre cost of driving more than your allotted kilometres each year. Suddenly, borrowing the money to buy a car seems much more attractive.

But let's not short-change car leasing: it does have its advantages. First, there's the convenience. The dealer will bend over backwards to convince you to sign a lease and to make your life easier, once that lease is up, to persuade you to lease another vehicle. A second advantage relates to taxes. If you use your car for business purposes, obviously you can deduct expenses under either a lease arrangement or a loan arrangement to the extent that you use your car to earn an income. Monthly lease payments are fully deductible. However, only the depreciation and interest portions of loan payments are deductible; (that is, the portion of the loan payment that you pay to increase your ownerhip of the vehicle is not deductible.) As a result, you can deduct more from your income by leasing.

Yet another advantage of leasing, if you can call it that, is the element of "prestige" or "sophistication." Indeed, leasing is one way to drive around in a car that you probably can't afford! If you must lease, do take a close look at the make of car you choose. Some luxury and Japanese imports depreciate more slowly than do North American cars, and this could make for comparatively favourable leasing conditions. And if you do lease, read all the small print carefully. Some provinces have introduced legislation to ensure that lease contracts are in plain language. In any case, here's a list of items you should look out for:

- The residual value of the vehicle (at the end of the lease period).
- The amount of the monthly lease payment, the number of payments and details of all fees associated with the lease.
- Your options at the end of the lease.
- The down payment you are required to make.
- The number of kilometres you can drive per year and the cost of additional kilometres.
- The required maintenance schedule.
- Your responsibilities if the car is stolen, destroyed or in an accident.
- Geographical restrictions (can you drive the car outside Canada?).
- Restrictions on who may drive the car.
- Penalties if you need to cancel the lease agreement.

Overall, you're still probably better off buying a vehicle than leasing one, even if you have to borrow the money. A financial planner or accountant, even a banker, should be able to calculate the difference between leasing and borrowing. (Again, don't call for advice when you're sitting across from the car dealer.) If you want to do the comparison on your own, some computer programs can help you do the calculations. Once you enter the necessary figures (monthly payments, length of lease, final payment, and so on) the program compares the rate of interest that you'd be paying on a lease versus a loan. But take my word— the rate on a lease will probably be substantially higher than that on a car loan!

Computers

The computer is perhaps the greatest innovation of the twentieth century, and by the year 2000 most North American homes will have one. Unfortunately, computers happen to be expensive—maybe not in terms of the initial outlay, but certainly once you add the cost of all the software that you'll need to make your computer run.

The trouble with computers is that they become obsolete as soon as they leave the store—there's an endless cycle of innovation at work. You must resist the temptation to get caught up in that cycle. For most people, a good computer should be useful for at least three to four years. The computer itself won't wear out; rather, eventually it won't have the capacity to deal with the new bells, whistles and software that hit the market each year. Ask yourself if you need those bells and whistles. For instance, if you use your computer strictly for word processing, and it still does the job, you might think twice about upgrading your system. Consider the benefits of keeping a computer as long as you can and of not buying every new piece of software. Let's say that over the next 20 years you expect to spend an average of $2,500 per year on your computer rather than investing the money at 10 percent. Because of the power of compounding, you would end up forgoing savings of $143,187! But if you spent $2,500 only every three years, the total cost over 20 years would come to $59,934—a savings of $83,253.

There's no question that computers are on their way to becoming the new consumer product of preference—not yet replacing the automobile, but getting there. Like cars, computers are essential, yet expensive. Fortunately, you can substantially reduce your costs. One way to save money is to check with your employer. Companies often have to upgrade their systems in the name of efficiency, and end up selling, or even giving away, their older equipment to their employees.

Another way to save money is to look for outlets selling so-called obsolete computers that previous owners have traded in for the latest model. Sometimes these computers are leftover stock from retailers who needed to make room for new models. Giant discount retail chains often advertise these older models in their circulars to lure you into their store. Once you are inside the store, however, the salesperson provides you with a litany of reasons why you shouldn't buy the older model and why the latest, higher-priced equipment is better. Expect the sales pitch to be peppered with the word *obsolete*. But don't fall for that pitch if you know that last year's model is fine for your purposes. If you've done your research and you know precisely what you intend to use the computer for, there's no reason you should wind up buying a machine that can launch a small satellite when you only want to do some word processing and send the occasional e-mail.

And finally: Get the Most Out of Your Bank

- Obtain a brochure detailing the types of accounts the financial institution offers and their service charges. Ask the staff which account would work best for your purposes. If you write a lot of cheques, or make a lot of withdrawals or electronic debits, open an account that does not charge for each transaction. Sometimes paying a monthly fee can be the best deal. Some institutions also offer lower fees if you keep a minimum balance in the account. In this case, even though you may not earn much interest on a bank account, you can save a lot in service charges.
- If your account charges you for each transaction, withdraw some money every time you go into the bank to make a deposit or perform some other transaction. That way you'll incur only one transaction fee.
- Use your bank's automatic teller machines (ATM), which sometimes cost less to use than going to a teller. Avoid using the machines of other institutions, which charge up to $2 for the privilege.
- Rather than writing cheques, which cost you a processing fee each time, pay for your purchases by cash, direct payment or credit card. If you use your credit card, the time between the

date of the purchase and the date you have to pay your credit card balance could be up to two months. In effect, you are getting an interest-free loan for two months! But this practice is advantageous only if you pay off your credit card balance in full by the due date.

- Don't let cheques bounce. One non-sufficient-funds (NSF) cheque could cost you up to $30. If you're worried that on occasion you might write a cheque that your chequing account won't cover, arrange for overdraft privileges. For a minimal cost, your bank will either "cover" for you or transfer funds from another of your accounts or from money market funds.

- If you have substantial dealings with one bank, and you feel you have been charged a service fee unfairly, speak to a bank official to see if the bank will cancel the charge. Remember, you're the customer.

- Keep any account you may have opened a long time ago, as its service charges might be lower than those of new accounts. One account that I opened in 1978 doesn't charge me for withdrawals, regardless of the number of transactions or the balance in my account. (I won't name the bank for fear it will realize that it isn't making any money on me!)

- Shop around for your bank account, bank loan and credit cards. Since the competition among banks is brutal, many offer low rates and low service charges.

- If you travel outside Canada, rent cars or carry a large balance on your credit cards, apply for a low-interest Gold VISA or MasterCard. Even though the annual fee may be $100, you'll more than make it up with the money you save on travel insurance, rental collision waiver deductions and the lower interest rate.

As a closing thought, let me repeat: cut your expenses and stick to your budget, and you will reap the rewards down the road!

CHAPTER 4

Do You Want to Buy
a Home?

YOU ARE FLIPPPING THROUGH THE CLASSIFIEDS OF your newspaper when an ad suddenly jumps out at you. "This gem of a house can be yours," says the ad. There's a picture of the house, and it's just the sort of house you'd like to live in. And then you read the unusual details of the offer: you can either buy the house for $200,000 with a $50,000 down payment or rent it for $1,400 per month.

So you take out your calculator and your mortgage tables and start doing some figuring. Let's see. If you put down $50,000, you'll need to get a mortgage for the balance of $150,000. At a 10 percent interest rate over 20 years, the monthly payment will be $1,428. Since the ad also tells you that property taxes are $120 per month, your total outlay per month will be $1,548, if you buy. That's $148 more per month than if you rented the house. What should you do?

At first glance, renting might be the better option. In fact, putting aside this difference of $148 for a moment, renting has its advantages, many of them qualitative:

- When you rent, you can move on relatively short notice. If you don't like your location, you can relocate fairly easily.
- Renting is usually cheaper than buying, on a monthly basis. You don't have to pay condominium fees or maintenance fees, among other charges.
- Although you have to come up with the rent each month, the stress involved is not as high as if you had to come up with the monthly mortgage payment. You could lose your home, your good credit rating and much more if you were to default on a mortgage!
- If you or your family expects to relocate frequently, you are probably better off renting, since the costs of selling and purchasing a home are substantial.
- Renting ties up less of your money. If you've put your money into a business or other investments, you may prefer to rent.
- If you rent an apartment, it is your landlord who's responsible for the care and maintenance of your building.
- Rental units may have more recreational facilities than private homes.
- Property values fluctuate. And if you purchase a property at the peak of a real estate cycle, its value may go down, as many people in Toronto and certain parts of Alberta found out during the recession in the early 1990s. In some cases, property values went down so dramatically that mortgages exceeded the value of the property. In other words, these home-owners were stuck in a negative equity situation. They owned more on their properties than the properties were worth.

Still, deep down, you think you might like to own a house. So you review the advantages of pursuing that option.

- There is tremendous pride in owning a home.
- You are your own master. You make the rules. You can renovate, decorate and landscape to your heart's content.

- Usually, real estate goes up in value over the long term; as a result, it is considered a low-risk investment. So your capital should be very secure.
- You have more control over your destiny. You cannot be forced to relocate by rising rental rates or changes in building management or zoning.
- There are excellent tax benefits to owning a home. Any increase in the value of your home (that is, capital gains) is tax free! Thus, if your home increases in value by $20,000, that money is yours; the government will not take it away from you.

Let's return to your dilemma of whether to rent or buy the property listed in your newspaper. You're still torn between the two options. By renting, you wouldn't have to deal with the headaches and the risks that owning a property entails. But you're undaunted. And to make your final decision, you'd like to analyze a few more numbers. So you decide to base your comparison on your financial status ten years from now. For starters, you check with your financial institution or use your financial calculator to figure out that if you bought the house, the amount owing after ten years on your original $150,000 mortgage would be $108,402. You also estimate that the house would increase in value at 3 percent per year (compounded, of course). Over ten years, that rate of increase would bring the value of the house to $268,783. If you sold the house at that time, you'd receive $160,381 (the selling price of $268,783 minus the $108,402 you would still owe on your mortgage). And since you would have paid a deposit of $50,000, you would net $110,381 by investing in your home.

Now, let's see how well you'd fare by renting. Obviously, if you rented, you could invest your $50,000 deposit. So, let's say you were optimistic and wise, and you figured you could earn 10 percent on that money. After ten years of reinvesting your returns at 10 percent, your $50,000 would be worth $129,687, an increase of $79,687. A very good return, indeed. Unfortunately, that increase is $30,694 less than you'd have had if you had bought the home. In fact, the return on your $50,000 investment could be even less since you would probably have to pay tax on your returns. By contrast, your capital gain from owning the house—the difference between the price at which you sold the house and the price at which you bought it ($268,783 − $200,000 = $68,783)—would be tax free if you kept the house as your principal residence.

Slowly, and based on your assumptions, you're beginning to realize that owning the house might be a better proposition, financially at least, than renting it. And you haven't even accounted for rent increases over time! If your rent increased as fast as the value of the house, at 3 percent per year, after ten years you'd probably be paying more than $1,800 per month in rent. In other words, that $148 benefit from renting that you calculated above would quickly disappear. In fact, the rent would probably turn out to be greater than the total cost of the mortgage plus property taxes after only four years!

Clearly, over a long period of time, it is usually better, financially, to own rather than rent your home. But home ownership doesn't have to be your sole objective in life. As long as you regularly save a portion of your earnings and follow my investment guidelines, you should be secure in your later years.

MORTGAGES

No chapter on the subject of buying a home would be complete without delving into the fine points of mortgages. For most people, a mortgage is their biggest lifetime expense. Yet, surprisingly few of us bother to explore some of the very simple methods of reducing that expense.

First, let's look at how a mortgage works. When you purchase a property, you usually have to borrow money from a financial institution. (For argument's sake, let's make this institution a bank.) The bank will provide you with a lump sum of money that you will add to your own money to buy the property. The mortgage will carry an annual rate of interest, which is what the bank charges you for the money. Put another way, the interest is what the bank wants to earn from its investment in you. The monthly or bi-weekly payments you make on the mortgage are not just interest; they are a blend of both interest and principal; by the end of the mortgage period, you will have paid off the principal of the loan. The house is yours!

Moreover, this blended payment is fixed: you make the same payment at regular intervals. Now, this is the interesting part about a mortgage: if you were to analyze what this blended payment consists of, you would notice that over time the proportions of interest and principal change. In Table 2, I've broken down, for the first ten payment periods, the interest/principal blend on a $90,000 mortgage that is payable every month over 25 years at an interest rate of 8.25 percent per year.

Table 2: Blended Monthly Payments on a $90,000 Mortgage

Payment number	Payment amount ($)	Principal ($)	Interest ($)	Balance of Principal ($)
1	701.31	92.93	608.38	89,907.07
2	701.31	93.56	607.75	89,813.51
3	701.31	94.19	607.12	89,719.32
4	701.31	94.83	606.48	89,624.49
5	701.31	95.47	605.84	89,529.02
6	701.31	96.12	605.19	89,432.90
7	701.31	96.77	604.54	89,336.13
8	701.31	97.42	603.89	89,238.71
9	701.31	98.08	603.23	89,140.63
10	701.31	98.74	602.57	89,041.89

In the Payment Amount column, you'll notice that the amount is fixed; every month, you pay the bank $701.31. But that's the only amount that remains constant. Notice in the Principal and Interest columns that the amounts change every month: the principal keeps increasing and the interest keeps decreasing. That's because, with each payment, you're paying back a little bit of the principal. And every time you pay back some of the principal, you owe the bank less money, and you own that much more of your house. In turn, if you owe the bank less money from one period to the next, the interest you owe on that debt will also decrease from payment to payment.

The Balance column, meanwhile, shows your running tab, or the declining principal amount owed to the bank. If we were to expand this table to include 300 payment periods (25 years times 12 payment periods per year), the balance at the end of the 300th period would be 0. And since the amount of principal you pay every month increases over time, while the amount of interest decreases, the final payment will consist mostly of principal, with very little interest.

By now, you have probably noticed that in the early payment periods your contribution to the principal is very small. Indeed, in the early years of a mortgage, most of your blended payment consists of interest, which, though it declines over time, adds up to a huge amount over the life of a mortgage. In fact, in the above example, you would pay $120,389 in interest over those 25 years! Imagine. You've borrowed $90,000 and it ends up costing you $90,000 plus $120,389. The point is that the longer you take to pay off your mortgage, the more interest you will pay. Now consider a completely different situation: you agree to pay back the $90,000 after one month in one payment, rather than after 25 years in 300 payments. At an annual interest rate of 8.25 percent, your total payment for that month would be $90,608.38. Only $608.38 in interest! Clearly there is a trade-off between the size of your regular payments and the length of time you make them.

Obviously, it's to your advantage, if you can afford it, to pay off your mortgage as quickly as possible. I will discuss ways of doing this, but first I should clarify a couple of concepts regarding mortgages. You might be aware that a mortgage always has a term as well as an amortization period. Once upon a time, when interest rates didn't fluctuate as much as they have in recent years, banks used to give out 25-year mortgages. You made your blended payments every month—just as in the table above—but you made the same payment for 25 years. In other words, the interest rate never changed. These days, however, banks are unwilling to give out 25-year mortgages; it's too risky. Consider how the bank works.

INVESTOR → Money invested in term deposits → BANK → Money invested in mortgages → MORTGAGE CUSTOMER

As you can see, to lend you money for your mortgage, the bank has to get the funds elsewhere. Trouble is, for the bank to lend you money for 25 years, someone must be willing to lend money to the bank for 25 years. And getting that money from an investor costs too much; in an environment in which interest rates are volatile, investment opportunities change all the time, and investors are unwilling to "lock in" for so long. The bank would have to pay the investor a very high rate of interest, and you'd have to pay an even higher rate of interest on your mortgage. In the end, nobody would be willing to take out mortgages.

Today, the longest-term mortgage you'll get from a bank is ten years. You'll notice I've used the word *term:* that's the length of time over which the bank will lend you money at a certain rate. It is not the period over which you must pay off the mortgage. All it means is that after ten years you'll have to renegotiate your mortgage—the interest rate, in other words. But the term could be six months, one year, two years or five years, depending on the length of time you choose. Just remember that the longer the term, the more you'll have to pay in interest.

Amortization also refers to a period of time, but this period has a different purpose. While the *term* refers to the duration of your loan contract, the *amortization period* refers to the length of time that you actually use in your calculations to determine how much you'll pay each month. When the banks used to give out 25-year mortgages, the term and the amortization period were the same. Not anymore. Yet, you will still plug into your calculations the amortization period—for instance, 25 years— as if you had a 25-year mortgage and as if you could renegotiate your mortgage on the same conditions over and over again for 25 years. In reality, you will have to renegotiate your mortgage sooner than that. If in two years, for instance, you sign a new agreement at a different interest rate, your monthly payments will be different.

But why, you wonder, do you have to use the amortization period in your calculations when the term is much shorter? Why not match the two periods? Well, consider what would happen if you had, say, a five-year mortgage with a five-year amortization. How big would your monthly payments be? Not $701.31, as in the example of the $90,000 mortgage. In fact, at an annual interest rate of 8.25 percent, you would have to pay $1,830 per month! Certainly, you'd end up paying less than $20,000 in interest over the five years, but can you afford $1,830 per month *before* property taxes and utilities? Would your bank even lend you the money?

As you can clearly see, a longer amortization period means smaller monthly payments and, therefore, greater affordability. But the downside remains that the longer the amortization period, the more interest you end up paying. In the end, it's a question of balance between trying to pay off your mortgage as soon as possible and making sure you can afford the payments. One solution is to set your amortization period to 20 years instead of 25. The monthly payments will be slightly higher— about $50 more in our example of the $90,000 mortgage—but you'll save five years of interest payments.

Or you might choose to match the amortization period to the number of years left before your intended date of retirement. For example, if you wish to retire at age 55, and you are now 32, make sure the amortization period on your mortgage is 23 years or less. If you move to a new house in the meantime, increasing the size of your mortgage, be sure to keep the remaining amortization period constant. Obviously, this decision will also be a lifestyle choice, since if you move to a more expensive home and take on a bigger mortgage, you'll have to make larger payments. If you cannot afford the payments, the mortgage will have to carry past your retirement age.

One especially good way of paying off your mortgage sooner is to increase the frequency of your payments. For instance, imagine if instead of paying $701.31 once a month, you paid half of it, or $350.65, every two weeks. In all likelihood, this practice wouldn't change your ability to make your payments. But consider how much money you could save. Look at Table 3.

Table 3: Blended Semi-monthly Payments on a $90,000 Mortgage

Payment number	Payment amount ($)	Principal ($)	Interest ($)	Balance of Principal ($)
1	350.65	70.37	280.28	89,929.63
2	350.65	70.59	280.06	89,859.04
3	350.65	70.81	279.84	89,788.23
4	350.65	71.03	279.62	89,717.20
5	350.65	71.25	279.40	89,645.95
6	350.65	71.47	279.18	89,574.48
7	350.65	71.70	278.95	89,502.78
8	350.65	71.92	278.73	89,430.86
9	350.65	72.14	278.51	89,358.72
10	350.65	72.37	278.28	89,286.35
11	350.65	72.59	278.06	89,213.76
12	350.65	72.82	277.83	89,140.94
13	350.65	73.05	277.60	89,067.89

After the first 13 bi-weekly payments (in other words, 26 weeks or six months into your mortgage), the balance owing on your mortgage would be $89,067.89. Now, if you refer to Table 2 (page 43), in which you were making monthly payments of $701.31, you'll notice that your balance owing after six months was $89,432.90. By increasing your frequency of payment, you would have decreased your balance owing by $365.01. That amount doesn't sound like much, but you will end up saving a total of $27,557 in interest and pay off your mortgage five years sooner!

Most financial institutions will gladly let you make payments every two weeks. Just be sure that this payment is half of the monthly payment and that you make 26 payments per year. You see, if instead of paying every two weeks you decided to pay twice a month, you would end up making 24 payments per year instead of 26. And it's those two extra payments per year that make a huge difference over the long run. In effect, you're making an extra month's payment each year. Now, if you were to combine this payment option with an amortization period of 20 years instead of 25, you would make drastic savings without much effort.

Obviously, any extra payment you can make towards your mortgage will save you money. And in the early years, especially, every dollar you put against the mortgage will save you more than a dollar in interest. It's amazing but true! Therefore, whenever you have extra cash, and if your mortgage agreement permits it, make a payment towards the remaining principal of the mortgage. Or you could increase your regular payments by a comfortable amount that meets the bank's guidelines. But remember: when you have extra cash, pay down your debts in order from highest to lowest interest rate. As such, you would pay off your credit card debt before you reduced your mortgage. It makes no sense to pay down an 8.5 percent debt when there's a 28 percent debt hanging over your head.

This focus on interest rates brings us to the fine print of your mortgage and dealing with your financial institution. Banking has become so competitive in recent years that the typical bank, trust company or credit union has a lot more to offer today than it did even five years ago. And you can bet it's doing its utmost to keep its clients happy and to attract clients from its rivals. Your financial institution is primarily interested in what is called "relationship banking"; it wants not just a part of your personal banking business but all of it. And for this business, it's willing to give you some special deals, including a reduction in your service fees, as well as higher rates on your term deposits, RRSPs and RRIFs (Registered Retirement Income Funds). And, yes, reduced rates on loans or mortgages.

Indeed, having worked for a decade in the banking industry, I have had the benefit of learning all the unwritten rules and secrets of the typical financial institution. And one secret is that banks will often discount their advertised mortgage rates for their best customers. In fact, it should be fairly easy to get a discount of at least one-quarter of a percent of the posted rate if you do all your banking at a particular bank. On a mortgage of $100,000 or more, that discount may be as much as one-half of a percent.

I say "fairly easy," but you might have to work a little for it. More precisely, you might have to negotiate. If you feel intimidated by that thought, all I can say is, "Don't be." Given the competition for your business, your banker actually expects you to negotiate the best deal you can. If you don't, the next customer will!

When you first apply for a mortgage, or if your mortgage is up for renewal, ask what rate your bank is willing to offer you and then check with the competition. Tell your banker you want to negotiate a better deal, otherwise you'll transfer your business to the competition. If your banker won't negotiate, go somewhere else, but explain why. If you're a good customer, he or she will almost certainly reconsider. For effective bargaining, you need to be coming from a position of strength, when you're not locked into a mortgage.

Remember, not all mortgages are created equal! For instance, usually, if you pay off your mortgage before the end of the term, you are liable for one of two penalties: (1) you must pay an amount equivalent to three months' interest or (2) you must pay an interest-rate differential penalty, which is the difference between the interest rate you've been paying on the mortgage and the interest rate at which the bank could reloan the money you no longer need, over the number of months remaining. Now, some banks, to ease the burden of your penalty, allow you to pay down a certain amount of the principal before you pay off the mortgage. But one way to avoid any penalties in the first place is to ensure that your mortgage is either "portable" or "assumable." If it's portable, you can take it with you from one property to another. If it's assumable, someone—the buyer of your house, for instance—can assume the mortgage in your place.

In summary, the issues to consider when you negotiate your mortgage include –

- **The frequency of payments.** Can you make payments every week or two weeks?
- **Size of payments.** Can you increase the payments and if so, by how much?
- **Additional payments.** Can you make extra payments against the principal of the mortgage? If so, how many? Most banks allow for principal reduction of at least 10 percent of the original mortgage, while some trust companies allow for 15, even 20 percent. Some credit unions go as high as 25 percent.

You'll also want to keep in mind the fees that usually accompany a mortgage. Here's a list of tips:

- Shop around for special offers that include free legal packages, free appraisals and rebates. If you are buying a property or increasing your mortgage, and the bank has to do an appraisal, you can probably persuade the bank to waive the appraisal fee since it is usually less than $150.

- Some banks actually charge a mortgage application fee. Make sure the bank waives this fee or take your business elsewhere.
- Ask about renewal fees on the mortgage and make sure your bank waives those, too. After all, why should the bank charge you to renew your mortgage when it benefits from the renewal?

Remember that these items are always negotiable, at least to the extent of the amount of business you do with your bank. Again, if you have a mortgage at a bank, you should be able to negotiate better rates on all your business, and you should receive reduced service charges on your main banking account.

Finally, here's a tax tip about your mortgage. If you plan to rent part of your property, you'll obviously have to declare the revenue on your tax returns. But you'll also be able to deduct part of the interest on your mortgage; you can claim up to the proportion of the property that the rental unit represents. Basically, if you borrow for investment purposes, and a rental unit constitutes an investment, Revenue Canada grants you a tax deduction for the borrowing costs on that investment. However, once you sell the property, you might have to pay tax on the capital gains you will have made on the investment part of your property.

CHAPTER 5

Registered Retirement Savings Plans

B Y NOW, YOU'VE LEARNED WHAT IT TAKES TO GET your financial house in order. You've also learned how to manage debt and how to budget, and I hope you've grasped the logic behind the basic tools of finance that will help your money grow. Now you're ready to learn how to accumulate wealth, how to make that financial house grow.

At this point, the most important golden rule comes in: save 15 percent of your gross earnings. Not 6 percent, not 12 percent, but 15 percent. Minimum.

Many financial advisers stress the importance of saving at least 10 percent of your gross monthly income to protect your wealth and secure your financial future, and in many respects this is excellent advice. By signing up for a forced savings plan of some sort and contributing 10 percent of your income to diversified investments, you definitely will be further ahead at retirement than the person who does none of those things!

But in my professional opinion, and from my experience, 10 percent is not enough. It's not enough for those of us who want to secure our financial independence at an earlier age or who want to ensure we have enough for an enjoyable retirement. Ten percent is only a marginal amount of your earnings, and I believe that the results of such a plan will be only marginal. You see, the barriers to financial independence are large. And they are numerous: the ravages of inflation; occasional emergencies; increases in taxation and cut-backs in government programs and expenditures; increases in medical costs and municipal taxes; user fees for a broad range of services at all levels of government; increases in the percentage of your paycheque that goes to CPP and EI; and increases in energy costs above the inflation rate.

The point I am making is that in a perfect world the 10 percent solution might work, but in reality you need more. You need to save a minimum of 15 percent of your gross income; that figure should be your benchmark. This level of savings, along with a financial plan and successful investment strategy, will ensure your financial independence. And it is realistic. In some ways, the long-touted 10 percent solution is a passive attempt to secure your financial independence. It's a last resort. It is not a proactive, aggressive strategy for overcoming the barriers to achieving wealth.

Let's look at the difference between the impact on your wealth of saving 10 percent of your gross income and the impact of saving 15 percent. Two investors, both earning a gross income of $50,000 per year, deposit their savings monthly into an investment plan. While Investor A saves 10 percent of the $50,000, Investor B saves 15 percent.

For the first example, let's assume both investors earn an 8 percent return on their savings, and that every year they re-invest, or compound, their returns at the same rate. (Let's also assume, for simplicity, that neither investor will pay income tax on the returns.) Over various time periods, their accumulated savings will look like this:

Table 4: Comparison of Savings on $50,000 Income at an Annual Return of 8 Percent

Savings Period (years)	Investor A's Savings (10%) ($)	Investor B's Savings (15%) ($)
5	31,006	46,508
10	75,951	113,927
15	141,992	212,986
20	239,026	358,537
25	381,602	572,399
30	591,093	886,633

Notice how the difference between a 15 percent savings rate and a 10 percent savings rate grows over time. That's the effect of compounding. Now, imagine if you could earn more than an 8 percent return. Table 5 illustrates the effects of a 10 percent and a 12 percent annual return on investment.

Table 5: Comparison of Savings on $50,000 Income at Annual Returns of 10 and 12 Percent

Savings Period (years)	Investor A's Savings (10%) ($)	Investor B's Savings (15%) ($)
	10% Annual Return	
5	32,572	48,858
10	84,358	126,537
15	167,760	251,640
20	302,080	453,120
25	528,403	777,605
30	866,795	1,300,193
	12% Annual Return	
5	34,210	51,315
10	93,766	140,649
15	198,723	298,045
20	383,694	575,541
25	709,675	1,064,513
30	1,284,166	1,926,249

Clearly, as the annual rate of return on investment increases, the difference in impact of the two savings rates becomes more and more pronounced. But don't limit yourself to 15 percent! If you and your family are especially good at saving and can save more, *do it*. The higher the percentage you save, the earlier you will reach financial freedom. In fact, the higher your earnings, the greater the percentage that you should be able to save. Use Table 6 as a guide.

Table 6: Savings per Income Level

Gross Earnings ($)	Proportion of Income Saved (%)
0–54,999	15
55,000–59,999	16
60,000–64,999	17
65,000–69,999	18
70,000–74,999	19
75,000–79,999	20
80,000–84,999	21
85,000–89,999	22
90,000–94,999	23
95,000–99,999	24
100,000+	25+

By now, I hope you're convinced of the wisdom of saving at least 15 percent of your gross income each year. The next big issue is: What should you do with your savings? Should you invest it in bonds, term deposits or mutual funds? Well, the short answer is that you should invest in all of these. But it's the method by which you put your money in these investment vehicles that can make a world of difference to your future wealth.

Let's say tomorrow morning you decide to put some of your savings in a mutual fund, but six months later you want to get out of the fund. And let's assume you make money on your investment over those six months. Obviously, the following spring, the government would expect you to pay income tax on your returns.

Returns are income, after all. But what if you could find a way to make the investment, earn the returns and not pay income tax on those returns? Even better, what if you could deduct from your income the amount you originally invested in the mutual fund? That's right. Never mind whether you earned even a penny on your investment, what if you could deduct what you put down? Well, you can—by making your investment through what is called the Registered Retirement Savings Plan, or RRSP for short.

You see, when the federal government realized some years ago that people couldn't rely on the CPP or corporate pension plans for their retirement anymore, it created the RRSP. The objective was to allow Canadians to "shelter" their investments from the effects of taxation until the day they retired. And sure enough, for many Canadians today, RRSPs are the foundation of retirement wealth building.

The mechanics of an RRSP are simple. Basically, whenever you make an investment through or inside your RRSP, the government lets you deduct from your annual income an amount equivalent to the investment you've made (up to a contribution limit). You can choose from a wide variety of investments, the most popular being term deposits, interest-bearing savings accounts and mutual funds, of which there are dozens of varieties in themselves.

Let's see how this investment strategy works. You deposit $6,000 in a bank account through your RRSP. You will be entitled to deduct the $6,000 from your taxable income. If your taxable income is $41,000, your net income for purposes of determining how much you owe the government in taxes will be $35,000. In other words, you'll pay taxes on an amount that is $6,000 less than if you hadn't invested through your RRSP. The more you contribute, obviously, the more you can reduce your taxable income (again, to a contribution limit).

As you've probably ascertained by now, the higher your tax bracket the more you can benefit from an RRSP. For instance, if you fall into a marginal tax bracket of 30 percent and you invest $1,000 through your RRSP, you will save $300 (30 percent of

$1,000) in income tax the year you make the investment. But if you fall into a 50 percent tax bracket, you will reduce your taxes by $500!

What's more—and this is the beauty of an RRSP—if you reinvest your returns in the investment vehicle itself rather than take them out (in other words, if you keep re-investing), those returns will also be tax exempt. In theory, you could leave your money in an RRSP investment indefinitely and never have to pay tax on any of it, including any of the growth. And that money would continue to grow. It's incredible. Not only do you pay less in income tax by contributing to an RRSP, you also earn more on your investment because your returns are tax sheltered.

Unquestionably, RRSPs are the best tax break the government has to offer. And to open an RRSP, you only have to visit your financial institution. You can even open more than one. So it's imperative that you make use of RRSPs if you want to build up the maximum in retirement dollars, or indeed if you want to have retirement dollars at all!

Of course, the government isn't ready to let you enjoy your tax-free investment forever. Indeed, one day you will have to start paying tax on your RRSP nest egg. And that will be the day that you start taking money *out* of the RRSP. But presumably you will withdraw money only when you retire, at a time when your high-income earning years are behind you and your tax bracket is lower.

But even if you were to have a change of heart on the day of your retirement, and you decided to keep working, you would still have benefited immensely from having reinvested your money through an RRSP. That's because your returns would have kept growing over the years, without ever having suffered the erosion of taxation. You would have been compounding the full amount of your returns.

Let's look at an example of this incredible benefit. Two people each invest $5,000, Investor A through an RRSP and Investor B outside an RRSP. Both investors earn a return of 12 percent, and both fall into the 30 percent tax bracket. Investor A, by virtue of the sheltering effects of the RRSP, manages to avoid paying 30 percent tax on any returns, while Investor B has to pay tax. After one year, Investor A has earned $600 (12 percent of $5,000) and reinvests all of it in the RRSP. Investor B has also earned $600, but must pay taxes of $180 (30 percent of $600). That's $180 less for Investor B to reinvest—not a small amount, but not overwhelming either. But that's only one year. Over 30 years, the difference would be huge. Investor A would have accumulated $149,800, while Investor B would have a comparatively small $56,215—a difference of $93,585! And that's only the difference in the returns over 30 years. This comparison doesn't consider what would happen if Investor A decided to invest the $1,500 tax refund (or tax deduction) from investing $5,000 in an RRSP in the first place! (Remember that you get a tax deduction, 30 percent in Investor A's case, merely by investing the money, whether you ever earn a return or not.) The difference between the investors' nest eggs, in that case, would be much greater. To calculate the difference, let's use the Rule of 72, which we learned in Chapter 1. Recall that if you divide 72 by the rate of return, you will get the approximate number of years it takes to double a one-time investment. So if you divide 72 by 12, you get 6; it will take six years to double your money. After another six years, you will double it again, meaning that after 12 years your $1,500 will be worth four times as much. After 18 years, it's up to 8 times, at 24 years 16 times and at 30 years 32 times the original amount. As such, according to the Rule of 72, your $1,500 after 30 years would be worth 32 times $1,500, or $48,000. (The exact value would be $44,940; remember that the Rule of 72 is an approximate shortcut.) You can see that investing your tax refund could make you a good deal of money. And if every time you put money into your RRSP you also made sure to invest your tax refund, the positive impact on your wealth would be absolutely immense. For this reason, I must impress upon you the importance of investing at least 50 percent of your tax refund in an RRSP. Make it a rule!

At this point, you might conclude that the wisest course is to invest in an RRSP every last penny you can get your hands on. But I must caution you on two points. First, for reasons of financial flexibility and diversification, you should limit your RRSP investments to two-thirds of your annual savings (or 10 percent of your savings if you save the minimum 15 percent per year). Second, even if you wanted to invest as much money as possible in an RRSP, the government wouldn't let you; after all, it doesn't want to give away the entire store.

Consider first my suggestion that you limit your RRSP contributions to two-thirds of your savings. Again, the reason I'm making this suggestion is to ensure you have maximum flexibility and control over your nest egg as your financial situation changes over the years. After all, not every investment meets the government RRSP eligibility requirements. By having all your money in an RRSP, in effect you would be limiting your investment opportunities. Moreover, what if the government were to change the rules and RRSPs suddenly became less desirable? Or what if you needed funds because of an unforeseeable event? Don't misunderstand me: RRSPs are the best way to make money. But my philosophy is: don't put all your eggs in one basket!

The second precaution has to do with the limit the government places on your contribution. I caution you because if you overcontribute, the penalties can be stiff. Nevertheless, Revenue Canada will allow you to contribute up to $2,000 more than your limit without penalty, for use in future years. To find out your contribution limit, check your income tax notice of assessment from Revenue Canada, or contact the department directly.

You might also find it useful to calculate your limit yourself. For the years 1996 through 2002, the government has set the maximum RRSP contribution at 18 percent of the previous year's earned income minus your pension adjustment, or $13,500, whichever is less. So, if last year your earned income was $40,000 and your pension adjustment (which your employer keeps track of) was $2,500, you can contribute the lesser of 18 percent of $40,000 ($7,200) minus $2,500, which equals $4,700, or $13,500. Therefore in this case you can contribute $4,700 to an RRSP for that earnings year. You may also have unused amounts from previous years.

As you might have deduced, by setting a $13,500 limit the government has decided that $75,000 is the cut-off income level for putting 18 percent of income into an RRSP (18 percent of $75,000 is $13,500). At income levels higher than $75,000, the $13,500 limit will represent a smaller and smaller percentage of income. In effect, the government has determined that people with an income level of more than $75,000 per year need the benefits of an RRSP less than those with lower income levels. But the $13,500 limit will increase eventually. In the year 2003, it will increase to $14,500, and in 2004, to $15,500. That year, the cut-off income level for contributing no more than 18 percent of income will be $86,111 (that is, 18 percent of $86,111 is $15,500). However, if you earned $86,111 in 2004 and follow my investment advice, you would not reach the $15,500 limit. Let me explain. If you followed Table 6, on page 55, which shows minimum savings rates for different income levels, then at an income level of $86,111, you would want to save at least 22 percent, or $18,944. And if you followed my rule that you should limit your RRSP contribution to two-thirds of your savings, you would end up putting $12,630 into your RRSP—$2,870 less than the allowable amount. In fact, for the year 2004, only if you earned more than $96,875 and matched the savings rate of 24 percent from the table would two-thirds of your savings equal the contribution limit. However—and this is important—the government will allow you to contribute, in any year, not only that year's limit, but also any allowable amount you haven't claimed in past years. As such, even if your income were to rise above $100,000, you'd probably still have enough unused contributions to invest two-thirds of your income in your RRSP.

POWERFUL TECHNIQUES FOR MAXIMIZING YOUR RRSP

If you make a lump sum contribution each year, make it at the beginning rather than the end of the year, since our friend The Power of Compounding will make a huge difference over time in the final value of your RRSP.

This is one instance of the early bird catching the worm, in this case, extra earnings on the RRSP. Again, let's consider the example of two investors. Each year, Investor A makes a $3,000 RRSP deposit at the start of the year, while Investor B makes a $3,000 deposit at the end of the year. Both investors earn 10 percent on their investment. As you can see from the graph below, making your deposit at the start of the year rather than at the end will leave you much better off after 25 years. In that period, you will have made one extra payment, one extra $3,000 deposit, compounded annually at 10 percent. That's a $32,500 difference.

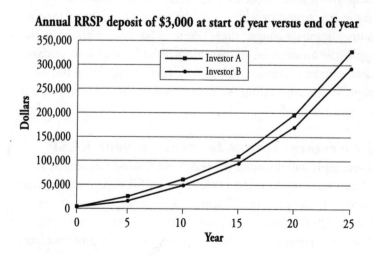

Annual RRSP deposit of $3,000 at start of year versus end of year

Yet, most of us persist in waiting until the last minute to make our deposit. In fact, because Revenue Canada allows us to make our deposit up to 60 days into the following year (by

March 1, or February 29 in a leap year), most of us keep wasting all that compounding power. Believe me, I used to see this at the bank every year. Without fail, on that 60th day the bank would stay open late, staffed to the hilt like every other financial institution and ready to accommodate the stragglers. At least these folks were making an RRSP deposit, but it would be much better if they had arranged to pay their deposit in bits over the course of the year!

Set up a spousal plan.

While I strongly urge both you and your spouse to contribute as much as you can to your respective plans, you should still set up a spousal plan. This plan allows you to contribute to an RRSP in your spouse's name but claim the tax deduction yourself. Either spouse can make a contribution in the other's name, although the obvious point here is to ensure that the spouse in the higher tax bracket contributes to the other's plan. For one thing, the initial tax deduction from the contribution will be that much bigger. In addition, if the status of the lower-income spouse doesn't change, then when he or she withdraws the funds, the amount of tax payable will be lower. However, you cannot make a contribution to your spouse's RRSP in the three calendar years preceding the withdrawal of the funds; if you do, you will be taxed!

If necessary, borrow to invest in your RRSP.

An example will illustrate the reasoning behind this advice. Let's say you want to deposit $3,000 in an RRSP, and your marginal tax rate is 30 percent. If you make the deposit, you get to deduct $3,000 from your income and receive a tax refund of $900 (30 percent of $3,000). There's only one problem: you don't have the money. However, don't simply dismiss the matter; borrow the money for a year instead. You see, if you borrowed $3,000 for one year at, say, 9 percent annual interest and agreed to make equal monthly payments to pay back the loan, each payment would be $262.35. For the year, those payments would amount to $3,148.20. In other words, borrowing the money for the year would cost you only $148.20. (Don't be misled into thinking that a 9 percent interest rate would cost you $270 in interest. That would be true only if you paid back the whole principal and interest in a lump sum at the end. If you paid back the loan in equal instalments, you would be paying some principal every month, as well as interest on a declining outstanding debt. The situation is the same as that of a mortgage except the term is only one year long!)

So, by borrowing the money to make your $3,000 RRSP investment, you're paying out $148.20 for the year, but you're also taking advantage of a $900 tax break. You will have made $751.80! Not a bad deal. Furthermore, in January and February each year, most financial institutions offer RRSP loans at very competitive interest rates. And these institutions even allow you to wait 90 days before having to make your first payment. The idea behind this offer is to give you enough time to receive your tax refund before you have to start making the payments. Of course, with this type of loan arrangement, instead of making 12 monthly payments during the year, you make nine or ten larger payments starting from the third or fourth month. Then, once you have your tax refund, retire as much of the loan as possible. This pushes forward the date of repayment of the loan, reducing the amount of interest you pay. Shop around for the best rates on the RRSP and the loan because the market is extremely competitive! Another point about RRSP loans is that they will not necessarily affect your ability to get other loans (as long as you can afford the payments) since lenders see RRSP loans more as a savings plan than a repayment of a debt. In fact, lenders often do not include RRSP loan payments when they calculate debt service ratios (that is, your ability to pay your debts).

That said, do try to avoid taking out a loan for your RRSP. Instead, start a preauthorized deposit plan to put money into your RRSP on a monthly basis, which I'll discuss in a minute.

Get ahead of the game and you'll not only save interest on the loan but you'll also benefit from the earlier compounding effect of the deposits.

Every year new RRSP products become available. Some products with the highest rates are available from credit unions. If you see an advertised rate that is higher than the one your financial institution offers, take a copy of the ad to your bank. Your bank will probably be able to offer a similar rate, even though its advertised rates are lower. If you're dealing with one of the larger institutions, the higher rate may have to be authorized by the branch manager or by someone with even greater authority. But it's worth the hassle.

Make RRSP contributions through a regular purchase plan to coincide with your pay deposits, if possible.

To ensure that you contribute on a regular basis to your RRSP, make arrangements for your bank, trust company or mutual fund manager to take funds automatically out of your bank account and deposit them into your RRSP.

You might also ensure that the amount of these deposits is fixed. The fancy term for this approach to investing is "dollar cost averaging." Whether your chosen investment vehicle is a term deposit or mutual fund, by dollar cost averaging, you are investing the same amount at set intervals throughout the year—$50 every two weeks, for example.

The concept is simple enough, but what's so great about dollar cost averaging? For starters, investing regularly at a fixed level is a good habit. Equally important is that by taking the discretion out of the "how much" and "when" of investing, you reduce the amount of risk to which you expose yourself. Let's say the market for a particular mutual fund has been volatile lately (the price of funds can change weekly, even daily), and rather than make regular deposits to your RRSP you've decided to make one lump sum investment. No doubt you can see that this is a gamble: you could be blessed with the right timing, or you could live to regret your one investment this year. By making many and smaller deposits, with dollar cost averaging, you can cover yourself. It's a conservative strategy, but as long as the value of your investment keeps increasing over the long run (and you can bet that a mutual fund manager's job depends on positive returns), you will have something to show for your efforts in the end.

Let me illustrate by referring to Table 7:

Table 7: Dollar Cost Averaging in a Mutual Fund

Date of Deposit	Price per Unit ($)	Number of Units for $50	Units Owned	Cumulative Value ($)
Today	13.55	3.69		= 50.00
in 2 wks	13.86	3.61	+ 3.69	= 101.14
in 4 wks	13.31	3.76	+ 3.61 + 3.69	= 147.21
in 6 wks	13.77	3.63	+ 3.76 + 3.61 + 3.69	= 202.29

Let's say you decide to make a deposit of $50 every two weeks and that today the price of one unit of a particular mutual fund is $13.55. If you make your $50 deposit today, you will be able to purchase 3.69 units of the fund (that is, $50 ÷ $13.55 = 3.69). Now, say in two weeks the unit goes up in price to $13.86. You will then be able to purchase only 3.61 units for your $50. But your 3.69 units from two weeks earlier will now be worth $51.14, for a total accumulated value of $101.14. If two weeks later the unit price drops to $13.31, you will be able to buy 3.76 units for your $50, though the total value of all the units you will have bought until that point will be $147.21. Admittedly, that's a 1.9 percent loss on the $150 you will have put up so far. But imagine if you'd invested the entire $150 on the day that the price stood at $13.86. You'd have 10.82 units. But two weeks later, when the price hit $13.31, your units would be worth $144.05, representing a 4.0 percent loss. So, you see, dollar cost averaging minimizes the risk of loss. Again, if the mutual fund increases in value over time, you will make money. For instance, if the price per unit should bounce back up, from $13.31 to $13.77 in the subsequent two weeks, you will be able to buy 3.63 units at that moment and your total units will now be worth $202.29, giving a 1.1 percent return on your investment in six weeks.

People who earn an irregular income, of course, may have difficulty making regular deposits to their RRSPs. I'm thinking in particular of people who work on commission or who receive irregular paycheques for whatever reason. For them, setting up an automatic savings plan is a legitimate problem, since there are times when there might not be enough money in the bank account to cover a transfer to a mutual fund or other investment. Here are some solutions:

- If you are paid only once a month, for instance, arrange to have 15 percent of your average monthly salary withdrawn from your bank account and deposited in your investment account, with two-thirds of it to your RRSP. But make sure there is a buffer for when your earnings are slightly lower than average.
- Make the investment yourself when you receive a paycheque. This approach requires more willpower and a little more effort, but as I keep stressing, it's the long-term consistency that will build your future financial independence.
- Arrange for the automatic withdrawal of smaller amounts on a more frequent basis. For example, if you usually receive a paycheque about every month, arrange for 3 percent of your pay to be withdrawn from your account weekly. Again, ensure there is a buffer to avoid a shortfall.

WHICH COMES FIRST? YOUR MORTGAGE OR YOUR RRSP?

The answer to this commonly asked question depends on your financial situation. In short, priority is determined by which "investment" offers a higher return.

Let's say you suddenly have $2,000 in hand, and your marginal tax rate is 30 percent. You decide to pay down your mortgage by $2,000. What you will gain is the reduced amount of interest you have to pay on the mortgage, or $200 each year (10 percent of $2,000). But consider if you invested that $200 every year in your RRSP. You would then benefit every year from a tax refund of $60 ($200 x your marginal tax rate of 30 percent). After ten years of making an annual investment of $260 and compounding at, for instance, 8 percent, you would have $3,766.51.

Now, let's say you chose instead to deposit your $2,000 in your RRSP. In the first year, you would receive a one-time tax refund of $600 because of your tax bracket. If you reinvested the refund, for a total investment of $2,600, and earned 8 percent on this amount, after ten years you would have $5,613.20. That's $1,846.69 more than if you paid down your mortgage.

Of course, the investment period and the rate of return affect the difference between the two options over time. Over 20 years, for instance, paying down the mortgage and investing the savings on interest in your RRSP at 8 percent would give you $11,898.11. But putting your money straight into your RRSP, meanwhile, would give you $12,118.49. Eventually, the advantage of paying down the mortgage would overtake that of the RRSP investment option. However, this process might take longer than the time remaining on your mortgage, in which case you might consider putting your money into your RRSP. But beware: the lower the rate of return on the RRSP investment, the less attractive that option becomes. In contrast, the higher the return, the more favourable the RRSP option is. Similarly, if mortgage rates soared at the time of your renewal, you would save much more from paying down your mortgage, because of the reduction in interest payments.

All in all, while putting your money into your RRSP does seem to be the more attractive option, you can never predict what mortgage rates will be in five or ten years; as a result, to some degree it's important to reduce your exposure to the risk of mortgage rate fluctuations. Ultimately, you would do well to follow my philosophy of not putting all your eggs in one basket, and use at least your tax refund from your RRSP investment to pay down your mortgage.

So far we've been talking about 8 percent and 10 percent returns on RRSP investments, and eventually we will have to deal with the million-dollar question: what is the best investment inside the RRSP? Since that topic constitutes a couple of chapters in itself, for now, suffice to say that the government has a fixed list of eligible investments, ranging from low-interest savings accounts to certificates of deposit and mutual funds. But before dealing with specific investments, let's turn to the subject of how much money you will need to retire.

CHAPTER 6

How Much Will You Need To Retire?

O VER THE YEARS, I'VE HAD A GREAT VARIETY OF clients—some better savers than others and some more daring than others. And to each of these clients, retirement has meant different things. But in every case in which these clients met their retirement objectives, they diligently stuck to a program.

Some of my wealthiest clients, though not yet 50 years of age, managed to accumulate a wealth base in the hundreds of thousands of dollars—and that base didn't even include their house! These clients were living proof of how quickly you can amass wealth. They used many of the principles I've covered in this book, and though they didn't have a thorough understanding of all the techniques I discuss, they were successful. That's why, armed with your new knowledge, you truly have a great opportunity to assure your future financial freedom.

Always remember that the strategies in this book are a means to an end. What that end is, however, is up to you. It depends on your needs. As a result, it's important that you learn to figure out how much you'll need before you can consider yourself financially independent and, consequently, free to live the life you want.

To begin, once you terminate your employment you will have cut off your major source of income. Granted, you might have a pension coming to you, but you might have to wait several years before you are eligible to receive it. Regardless, on its own, your pension probably won't be enough; in all likelihood you will have to rely on your assets for support. Indeed, the point of this retirement planning exercise is to figure out how big those assets will have to be to generate enough income for your lifestyle. So, we'll have to make some predictions, using some of the financial principles we've covered.

And when I say *assets,* I mean assets free of debt—in other words, what you own minus what you owe. One of your objectives in achieving your financial independence should be to pay off all your debts, including your mortgage, before you retire. You will recall that in Chapter 4 we discussed matching the amortization period on your mortgage to the number of years remaining until your retirement. It's a wise strategy because you don't want to be saddled with big payments when your main source of income, your employment, has been cut off.

I should also comment on the undue importance that some people attach to their home as a source of retirement income. Somehow these individuals figure that if they sell their home at retirement, they'll be able to invest the proceeds and generate enough income to support their lifestyle and cover the cost of alternate shelter. They not only expect it, they depend on it. This approach is unwise. I'm the first to argue that real estate, in the long term, is a great investment, and I stick by that assertion. I also realize you might be thinking that if you're going to predict how much your portfolio of assets will be worth in 25 years, you might as well predict what the value of your house will be. Regarding this approach, I have two points to make.

First, you can probably weather the storm if, say, the value of mutual fund X, in which you have $20,000, suddenly starts to slip on the day you retire. Your many other assets might be growing fabulously. But your house is a big asset, probably bigger than any other single asset in your portfolio of investments. And if on the day you plan to retire, the housing market where you live is stuck in a deep rut, you'll be sorry you relied on that one asset for your financial independence.

Second, no matter what your retirement plans are, you'll still need a place to live. The cost of shelter is an expense you simply can't eliminate. Consequently, if you sell your house and place your capital elsewhere, a part of your income stream will still have to go to shelter—possibly rent. Of course, you might generate enough income from the capital to cover your rent and have some left over. But how much will that leftover be? Five hundred dollars a year? A thousand dollars? Will it be enough to justify making your financial future dependent on the value of your house? Or consider the possibility of "trading down"—selling your house for a less expensive one. Not a bad idea. But, again, will the difference in value be so great that you should attach so much importance to it? If you are now planning to pay off your house by the time you retire, stick with your plan. You will have eliminated the worry of paying for shelter. In other words, you should consider your house's future value as a bonus. In the meantime, concentrate on building up the value of your other assets, such as RRSP investments. And if you do decide to sell your house when you retire, and move into smaller quarters because you and your spouse want to travel the globe for a few years, you'll have that much more income from your added capital to put toward your trips.

So, how do you figure out how much income you'll need at your retirement and the age at which you will be able to retire? Let's say you and your spouse are currently earning a total of $60,000. Morever, let's assume that at your retirement you would be content to have the lifestyle that you're presently enjoying. In other words, if at this very moment you had enough capital or savings stashed away to guarantee that you could sustain your current lifestyle, you'd quit your job tomorrow morning. But presumably you don't have that kind of capital yet, and our task is to determine how long it will take you to amass it.

But before we do that, we need to resolve one issue: if you retired tomorrow morning, would you still need an income of $60,000? The answer is no. Think about it: once you stop working you won't have to spend all that money on work clothes and business suits anymore. You'll have eliminated the cost of travelling to and from work. In addition, getting rid of a second car should save you at least $3,200 per year, given a conservative estimate of depreciation and maintenance of $2,000 and insurance costs of $1,200. Meanwhile, you will have just finished paying off your mortgage. And if your children move out at that time, your expenses for food and clothing will be lower. In total, these savings can amount to thousands and thousands of dollars. Thus, as a general rule, I estimate that from the day you retire you should need no more than approximately 65 percent of your and your spouse's combined gross salary.

Of course, you'll probably have greater expenses for vacations, as well as for health care and insurance. But if you don't plan to drastically change your spending habits, 65 percent of $60,000 should be plenty for maintaining a lifestyle that is as good as, if not better than, the one you enjoy now.

So, let's calculate 65 percent of $60,000. The answer is $39,000, which is the amount you will need. The question is, where will it come from? It could be pension money, from the government or your company pension plan, but you might not receive it until you reach a certain age. Back in the good old days, many employers used to have structured pension plans that would pay you a fixed percentage of your final salary until you and your spouse passed on, minus any other pension plan payments, such as CPP and Old Age Security (OAS) allowances. If you're lucky enough to have such a pension plan, you might nearly be set for your retirement. As for all that extra capital you will have saved up by following the strategies I've outlined in this book, it will be like very thick icing on the cake.

Alas, most of us don't have that kind of guaranteed income to fall back on. Most likely, we'll be relying only in part on income from CPP or OAS and only once we reach a prescribed age. For 1996, the monthly CPP and OAS rates are, respectively, $727.08 and $399.91. These are the maximum amounts payable at age 65.

The government adjusts these rates to stay in line with the Consumer Price Index (CPP on an annual basis and OAS on a monthly basis). It is important to note that you can receive your CPP payments as early as age 60, but that your allowance will be less than what you'd receive at age 65. The reduction amounts to 0.5 percent for every month before your 65th birthday. For example, if you take your CPP at age 62 and are eligible for the maximum, you will receive only 82 percent of what you would receive at age 65 [100% − (36 months x 0.5% per month) = 82%]. If you retired at age 60, each month you would receive 70 percent [100% − (60 months x 0.5% per month)] of $727.08, or $508.96. This amounts to $6,107.52 per year.

As you can see, in all likelihood your pension won't come close to meeting your financial needs and might make up a mere 16 percent of the income you'll require. And even then you won't receive it until you reach the appropriate age.

But you might have other forms of income, such as rental income, small business income or disability income. For argument's sake, let's say you expect to receive $9,000 per year from various sources. Then, in our example, you'll need to build up your savings over the years—to generate an income of $30,000 per year: Final gross income: $60,000 Required retirement: 65% x $60,000 = $39,000 income. Subtract any sources of income = $9,000 (estimate) e.g. employer's pension plan, rental income, disability income, part-time business income, etc. Amount of annual income required from savings = $30,000.

So far, so good. Now that we know just how much income (in today's dollars) you will need to retire, it's time to work out how much savings or "capital" you will require to generate this income starting the first day of your retirement. Let's be on the conservative side and assume that in your retirement days you will earn a return of 8 percent per year on your capital. In other words, since you'll no longer have a job to fall back on, you won't want to make risky investments of the sort that could earn you high returns in a favourable market, but that could also break you if the market soured. You want to play it safe, and 8 percent is a reasonable expectation.

We're now ready to calculate how much capital you'll need. To do that, divide your required level of income by the rate of return: $30,000 divided by 8 percent equals $375,000. In other words, an 8 percent annual return on $375,000 will give you $30,000 per year.

Table 8: Savings Required to Produce Various Levels of Retirement Income at a Rate of Return of 8 Percent

To produce retirement income of		You need savings of
$20,000	———>	$250,000
$25,000	———>	$312,500
$30,000	———>	$375,000
$35,000	———>	$437,500
$40,000	———>	$500,000
$45,000	———>	$562,500
$50,000	———>	$625,000

Let's take another example from the table above. Let's say you wanted to produce an annual income of $40,000. At an 8 percent rate of return, you would require a capital base of $40,000 divided by .08 = $500,000.

Now, you should realize two things about these amounts. First, by taking 8 percent of $375,000 to generate an annual income of $30,000, you are assuming that you won't ever touch the capital. In other words, it will exist in perpetuity. It will out-live you! (If you have no intention of leaving money behind, the best approach is to set up what is called an annuity, which I'll get to later in this chapter.)

Second, you probably have realized by now that inflation will erode your fixed annual income over time. Indeed, $30,000 in your first year of retirement will probably buy you a good deal more than in your 15th year. As such, at an annual inflation rate of 3 percent, for instance, you will require an income of $30,900 in your second year, $31,827 in your third year, and so on.

Where, then, will that extra money come from? One possibility is to dip into your capital every year to compensate for inflation. Be aware, however, that since the capital base will shrink, so will 8 percent of it; as a result, every year your income will get smaller. To compensate, you'll have to withdraw more of your capital, and over time, your capital base will decrease faster and faster. In fact, you will have depleted your entire capital within 20 years! If you retire at 50, that approach might not be the best one.

A better approach would entail saving a minimum of 3 percent of your income each year—though 5 to 7 percent would be ideal. After all, if until the day you retire you have managed to save 15 percent or more of your annual income, there is no reason you shouldn't be able to continue setting aside some savings. In your retirement, these savings could be important if inflation starts to rise.

With this matter aside, let's deal with the issue of how long it will take you to accumulate the $375,000 capital base that you'll require to generate $30,000 per year. Since you will accumulate your capital base at some point in the future, you'll need to adjust that capital for inflation. You see, if today you need $375,000 based on your current income, in one year you'll need more. At a 3 percent rate of inflation, for example, you'll need $11,250 more. And in several years, you'll need even more. Take a look at Table 9 on page 77. For various levels of required retirement income in the first column, you will find in the second column the corresponding capital base that you would need if you retired today. In subsequent columns, you will find the corresponding capital, compounded at 3 percent, required at a given point in the future. For example, in 25 years, to produce the equivalent of a retirement income of $50,000 in today's dollars, you would require $1,308,610 in capital. Similarly, to produce a retirement income of $30,000 in today's dollars, you would need, in 20 years, a capital base of $677,292. (Of course, if you already have savings, you can retire independently wealthy earlier on.)

This table is useful because it allows you to figure out in a given number of years what your total savings should be; if they fall short of your required capital, at least you know ahead of time that you'll need to work longer before you can retire. For instance, if you need $30,000 per year to retire, and you determine that in 20 years your total savings will have amounted to only $500,000, you'll know that 20 years is too optimistic as a retirement target date, since at that point you would require $677,292. But don't worry. Since you can expect to earn returns that are greater than the rate of inflation, you'll catch up soon enough! And that's the key: at what point will your capital or savings match or surpass the amount of capital, adjusted for inflation, you'll need to generate your retirement income?

Now that we have an idea of the future capital requirement for various levels of income, let's look at the second half of the equation: your accumulation of savings into the future. You'll recall that we assumed you could earn 8 percent on your capital after you retire. We chose that conservative figure because you would likely be averse in your retirement to taking the risks that could earn you more. In the years leading up to your retirement, however, you are probably prepared to take more risks because you are employed. As such, let's assume that in your working years you will be able to achieve a return on your investments of 10 percent per year. (A rate of return of 10 percent is still fairly

Table 9: Capital Required in Today's Dollars and in Future Dollars for Specified Retirement Income Levels

Annual Retirement Income ($)	Capital Required in Today's dollars	Capital required in Future (3% inflation rate, 8% rate of return)					
	Today	5 years	10 years	15 years	20 years	25 years	30 years
20,000	250,000	289,819	335,979	389,492	451,528	523,444	606,815
25,000	312,500	362,273	419,974	486,865	564,410	654,305	758,519
30,000	375,000	434,729	503,969	584,238	677,292	785,166	910,226
35,000	437,500	507,182	587,963	681,611	790,174	916,027	1,061,930
40,000	500,000	579,637	671,958	778,984	903,056	1,046,888	1,213,634
45,000	562,500	652,092	755,953	876,357	1,015,938	1,177,749	1,365,338
50,000	625,000	724,546	839,948	973,730	1,128,820	1,308,610	1,517,042

conservative for high-quality mutual funds, and you may indeed be able to earn substantially more. But to be safe, we'll consider 10 percent.) Moreover, we'll consider that you expect your current gross income of $60,000 per year to grow at the same rate as inflation. If that's the case, then your savings will also grow at the rate of inflation. After all, if this year you expect to save $9,000 (that is, 15 percent of $60,000), next year you can expect to save 3 percent more, or $9,270, because your $60,000 income will have risen by 3 percent, to $61,800, 15 percent of which is $9,270.

So, then, let's see what will become of your savings in the future, at various levels of income, if you keep putting aside 15 percent of your income, and if these savings grow at three percent per year. Take a look at Table 10.

As you can see, if your current income is $60,000 per year, your savings this year will be $9,000. After 20 years of compounded interest, you will have $712,278, and after 25 years $1,255,062! These figures may sound unbelievable, but they are anything but fictitious. They're simply the result of the power of compounding. Let me explain the logic with a five-year illustration. Let's say your income is $60,000 per year, and you have just finished saving $9,000 (or 15 percent of your income). This is what your accumulated savings will look like over the next five years:

- In one year, your $9,000, invested at 10 percent, will have become $9,900. Meanwhile, your savings over the next year will be $9,270, as they will have grown at a rate of 3 percent. Therefore, your total accumulated savings one year from now will be $9,900 + $9,270 = $19,170.
- In two years, your accumulated savings of $19,170 will have grown to $21,087 at 10 percent, while your new savings for the year once again will have grown by 3 percent to $9,548.10. Total accumulated savings at the end of Year Two, therefore, will be $21,087 + $9,548.10 = $30,635.10.

Table 10: Accumulation of Savings at Different Income Levels

Current Income ($)	Amount Saved ($)	Savings Accumulated in the Future based on Income Growth of 3% per year (15% of income) ($)					
		5 years	10 years	15 years	20 years	25 years	30 years
30,000	4,500	37,126	94,438	192,231	356,139	627,531	1,073,203
35,000	5,250	43,313	110,166	224,256	415,471	732,077	1,251,355
40,000	6,000	49,500	125,904	256,308	474,853	836,707	1,430,937
45,000	6,750	55,689	141,642	288,347	534,210	941,296	1,609,803
50,000	7,500	61,874	157,380	320,386	593,567	1,045,884	1,788,671
55,000	8,250	68,063	173,118	352,424	652,923	1,150,473	1,967,538
60,000	9,000	74,251	188,856	384,462	712,278	1,255,062	2,146,405
65,000	9,750	80,437	204,594	416,501	771,637	1,359,649	2,325,272
70,000	10,500	86,626	220,332	448,539	830,993	1,464,238	2,504 139
75,000	11,250	92,815	236,070	480,578	890,349	1,568,826	2,683,006

- In three years, invested savings = $30,635.10 x 1.1 = $33,698.61. New savings = $9,548.10 x 1.03 = $9,834.54. Total savings = $43,533.15.
- In four years, invested savings = $43,533.15 x 1.1 = $47,886.47. New savings = $9,834.54 x 1.03 = $10,129.58. Total savings = $58,016.05.
- In five years, invested savings = $58,016.05 x 1.1 = $63,817.65. New savings = $10,129.58 x 1.03 = $10,433.47. Total savings = $74,251.12. If you check Table 10, you'll find the $74,251 figure at the five-year column along the $60,000-income row.

Now that we know how your savings will grow, let's see how long it will take you to retire. Look at the row for a current income of $60,000 in Table 10. If you follow it across to the ten-year column, you will find that in ten years you will have accumulated savings of $188,856. Now turn back to Table 9. You'll recall that we determined that if you now earn $60,000 per year, you'll need $30,000 per year once you retire. So follow the row from the retirement income of $30,000 to the ten-year column. The figure you find is $503,969. In other words, you'll need $503,969 in ten years if you want to retire at that time with a $30,000 income. Evidently, you won't be financially secure in ten years; you'll have only $188,856. So you'll have to keep working. Let's check, then, under the 15-year column. In Table 9 you'll notice that you'll need $584,238. But from Table 10, at your current $60,000 income, you'll have only $384,462. You'll still be short. So, let's keep going. Check 20 years. From Table 9, you'll need $677,292, and from Table 10, you'll have $712,278. Which means that within 20 years you'll have enough to retire on. So, if you and your spouse are now 30 years of age, you could be financially free before age 50! (Forget Freedom at 55 for you two!)

Here is another example. First, let's spell out the assumptions: currently, you earn $40,000 per year. You decide that in your retirement you'll want a higher standard of living, concluding that 65 percent of $40,000, or $26,000 per year, minus whatever other income you might have, will fall short of your needs. You figure that you'll need $45,000 to retire on. To see how long it will take you to accumulate the necessary savings, again look at Table 9 and follow the row across from a retirement income of $45,000 to, say, the 25-year column. As you can see, in 25 years you'll need $1,177,749 in capital to generate $45,000 in income. From Table 10, however, you realize that at your current $40,000 income, you will have saved only $836,707 in 25 years. So you will have to keep working and saving. But 30 years from now, you will require $1,365,338 (from Table 9) while your savings will amount to $1,430,937 (from Table 10). As you will have noted, there's always a point at which you will be able to retire. But in some cases, it will take longer for the power of compounding to work its magic.

A word of caution about these calculations: they are based on assumptions, and individual situations will vary tremendously. Inflation will vary, as will the earnings on your money. Our assumptions might even be too conservative. For instance, you may already have some savings, or you might be able to earn more than 10 percent on average per year on your investments. And certainly, as your income rises, you should be able to save more than 15 percent of your gross income. Indeed, these examples are meant to give you some idea of how much money you can accumulate over an extended period of time, if you save and invest wisely. For a more accurate assessment of your financial needs for the future, or if you feel intimidated by tables such as these, have a financial planner or retirement specialist do a financial assessment for you. (You'll find a useful table in the appendix describing the strengths and weaknesses of consultants such as lawyers, planners, bankers and so on.)

As I noted earlier in the discussion of the effect of inflation on your retirement income, even after you have entered the financially free retirement zone, you should continue to save a portion of your money—albeit a smaller percentage than during your working days. Again, I suggest that saving between 5 and 7 percent of your gross income in retirement is a sound strategy.

Finally, you'll recall that in calculating your retirement income, we assumed that the capital base would remain untouched. You would live off the returns and leave the capital behind. But what if you decided you wanted to take it all with you? Not only do you want to spend the returns, you also want to spend the entire capital?

The best way to do this is to set up an annuity. Basically, an annuity works the same way as a mortgage does, except that the roles are reversed. While in the case of a mortgage the *bank invests money in you* with the understanding that you will pay it back in equal amounts over a set period of time, in the case of an annuity it is *you who invests in someone* with the understanding that the recipient will pay you back in equal amounts over a set period of time. With a mortgage, you owe nothing after making your final payment; with an annuity, you are owed nothing after receiving the final payment. Obviously, the period of repayment you choose will be crucial. After all, you'll be in your retirement years, and you wouldn't want to run out of income.

Let's look at an example: you have saved $300,000 for your retirement, and you can earn 9 percent on it. Moreover, you have no other source of income. In that case, your annual retirement income will be $27,000 ($300,000 x 9%). However, if you set up an annuity lasting 25 years, (that is, its value will be zero at the end of that time), you would receive $28,020 per year, or nearly 4 percent more than a straight $27,000.

Table 11: Payments on a $300,000 Annuity

Payment Period	Annuity ($)	Principal ($)	Interest ($)	Balance ($)
Present				300,000
1	28,020	24,478	3,542	271,980
2	28,020	24,159	3,861	268,438
3	28,020	23,812	4,208	264,577
25	28,020	—	—	0

Now, let's say you're certain of needing no more than $27,000 per year in your retirement. By setting up a 25-year annuity, you would need only $289,078 in savings instead of $300,000. You could extend the length of the annuity to 29 years if you started off with the full $300,000. You could retire four years sooner!

The variations are endless, and these calculations do require the use of a financial calculator or a financial software program for your computer. But for the keeners among you, the appropriate formula appears in Appendix D.

Hopefully, I have shown you in this chapter that building wealth required to make you financially independent doesn't take that long, assuming that you earn a reasonable income and are committed to attaining financial freedom. And at the risk of sounding like a broken record, I'll say it again: the sooner you start saving, the better!

CHAPTER 7

Diversify Your Investments: Don't Put All Your Eggs in One Basket!

H OW MANY TIMES HAVE YOU HEARD SOMEONE say "Don't put all your eggs in one basket"? Hundreds of times, I'm sure. You've heard it from me on a couple of occasions already! That's because in the business of financial planning, it's an expression that carries a lot of weight; in fact, it's one of my golden rules. The reason for this popularity is that this saying sums up the best way, over a long period of time, to maximize the growth of your portfolio. In other words, when you invest, make sure you diversify. Put some variety into your investment portfolio.

Yet, people seldom follow this advice. I've seen it over and over again: investors put all their money in just one type of investment and later regret it. I've had customers, for instance, who insisted on investing only in guaranteed investment certificates (GICs). Why? Because that's what they'd always done and because they considered GICs to be risk-free. They liked knowing ahead of time exactly what they would earn on their investment. Admittedly, investing in GICs made sense in the late seventies and through most of the eighties because interest rates were very high. And locking into high, long-term rates did benefit an awful lot of people. But the nineties have played out differently, and those people who continued to insist on GICs have paid the price with plummeting interest rates at a time when the TSE 300 and the Dow Jones Industrial Average, which measure the performance of the Toronto and New York stock exchanges, respectively, have increased in value dramatically. If these GIC investors had diversified their portfolios, they would have reaped the rewards of a soaring stock market in the last few years!

But just as I've seen GIC-obsessed investors regret putting all their money in one place, so too have I seen stock-obsessed investors kick themselves the morning after a stock market crash. The point is that you can never predict how any particular investment will perform. And if you can't make that prediction, why would you want to put all your money in one place? Consider what happened to interest rates in 1996. Who could have predicted they would be the lowest in 40 years? Certainly, these rates were a boon to anyone who needed a mortgage to buy a house. But if all your money was sitting in a bank account, those rates cost you dearly. I don't mean "cost" in the sense that you lost money. Rather, you suffered an "opportunity cost": you easily could have found an investment opportunity with better returns than a low-interest bank account. Similarly, if you locked all your money in a GIC just before a jump in interest rates, you would have forgone the opportunity of earning a higher rate—if only you'd waited a little.

Opportunity costs can be as devastating as out-of-pocket costs because you're always saying to yourself, "What if I'd done this?" or "What if I'd done that?" "I'd have more money by now." Possibly. Then again, you could have less money. You can agonize to death over the possibilities. As a result, I propose that the best way, the only way, to reduce the amount of risk to which you expose yourself, not to mention the stress-inducing second-guessing, is to diversify. Don't put all your money in GICs or bond funds or equity funds or mortgage funds or real estate. Rather, put a bit of money in each of these. If you hear, for example, that over the next few months the price of gold will increase rapidly because of fears about inflation (gold has long been a safe haven from a weakening dollar), don't put all your money in gold. Consider increasing slightly the percentage of your portfolio invested in gold, but don't go overboard. There is no guarantee that the price of gold will go up. You could, in fact, lose money.

And suppose you did invest a bit in gold and lose some money? In this situation, diversification would serve you well. Indeed, while the value of one of your investments might be going down, the value of another could be going through the roof. What you earn is the net result. This point is very important. Think of your investment portfolio as a unit, a single investment with many components. Each component may be doing well or poorly at any given moment, but it is the overall performance of the whole that should concern you. Over a long period of time, this overall performance should be better than what you would achieve if you constantly shifted your money between investments, exposing yourself to greater risk. Take it from me, diversification works. Better than that, take it from world-renowned finance theorists who have proven that diversification, over the long run, produces better returns.

MUTUAL FUNDS

Now that you know about the wisdom of diversification, what should your diversified portfolio consist of? While in the next chapter I will discuss GICs, stocks, bonds and real estate, for now I'll stick to the one type of investment that should play a big role in your investment strategy: mutual funds.

If I happen to be partial to the use of mutual funds as a cornerstone of a sound investment strategy (after all, I am devoting an entire chapter to the topic), it's because not only are they eligible for RRSP tax sheltering, but they also have, by their very nature, precisely the one element that I've been arguing should be your guide in constructing your portfolio: diversification. Indeed, a good mutual fund is itself a portfolio of investments in a large number of stocks or bonds, or both. Some even include investments in mortgages and real estate. In other words, when you buy 100 units of a mutual fund, you are buying 100 units of an instrument that someone else—a mutual fund manager—has already diversified for you and other investors like you. And that's a further important distinction of a mutual fund: by definition, it is a fund, or pool of money, that is "mutual"—that pools the dollars of many investors.

"Fair enough," you say, "but why do I need someone else to do the diversifying for me, particularly since I'll surely have to give a cut of my earnings to whoever manages the fund?" Well, you're right to conclude that investing in a mutual fund will cost you some sort of management fee. But bear in mind that mutual fund managers are experts at finding the right investments. In all likelihood, they know more about the potential returns of a particular investment than you do—than I do, for that matter. And that expertise translates into better returns for the investor.

Moreover, because of this pool of money, the fund can buy into a range of investments that is far wider than those you could buy on your own. For instance, while your limited resources might restrict you to investments in a few companies, the fund can invest in dozens of companies. Because of this broad diversification, the value of a fund will fluctuate less than would a portfolio of only a handful of investments. And less fluctuation means greater security for you. (Remember, however, that the diversified nature of mutual funds still does not justify putting all of your money into them. They are merely one type of investment vehicle and should be one component in your portfolio.)

Fund Fees

When you buy into a mutual fund you might have to pay a "load" fee. This fee goes to the salespeople who have sold you the fund. It will be either a "front-end" load fee or a "back-end" load fee, depending on whether you pay when you first invest or when you withdraw from the fund. Increasingly, nowadays, funds are charging back-end fees that decrease over the life of your investment, eventually to zero. Many funds that you can buy through banks, trust companies and credit unions charge no fee at all. They are "no-load" funds. Another fee, one that is unavoidable, is the fund management fee. After all, someone has to compensate the fund's managers for their salaries and for the costs they incur in running the fund (just as you would pay an employee, agent or personal adviser). But you won't actually have to pay the management fee out of your pocket. Rather, every year, the managers take out of the fund a fee that can vary from 1 to 3 percent of the total value of the fund. (You can expect the higher-performing managers to charge top rates.)

Because of their attributes, mutual funds have become an investment of choice, with more and more Canadians buying into them each year. In fact, between the spring and fall of 1996 alone, Canadians increased their holdings in mutual funds to $187.5 billion from $160 billion. This level of excitement, of course, was all but nonexistent in the late eighties. Consumers, at the time, were content earning high interest on their guaranteed-return investments and daily-interest savings accounts. The banks, trust companies and credit unions, meanwhile, were content selling these instruments without having to expend any effort. No question about it, investing was much simpler back then.

But then the financial climate started to change. Interest rates started to come down, consumers started to be choosy and baby boomers started to age, becoming concerned for the first time about their financial well-being. By 1992, more and more investors who traditionally had invested only in fixed-term investments were starting to diversify into a whole range of mutual funds. And the more variety they wanted, the more the market-place was willing to accommodate and innovate; today, there seems to be no limit to the mix of investments that mutual fund managers can put together.

As for types of funds, there is, of course, the basic "meat and potatoes" mutual fund, which appeared earliest in the evolution: the equity fund. A fund of this type concentrates on investing in the stocks of various companies—sometimes 100 or more different stocks. Other types of funds include bond funds, which invest in a variety of bonds, such as government (federal, provincial, municipal) and corporate bonds; mortgage funds, which purchase pools of mortgages from financial institutions (yes, possibly your own mortgage); money market funds, which consist of government treasury bills and commercial paper; balanced funds, which are a mixture of stocks and bonds; and international funds, which invest in equities worldwide. And the list goes on. (In the appendices, you'll find a handy list of dozens of mutual fund companies, which offer hundreds of different types of funds.)

So how do you go about choosing among these different types of funds? To a great degree, that decision has to do with your "risk tolerance"—how much risk you're willing to take or how comfortable you'll feel if the value of a fund fluctuates regularly. The value of any mutual fund can vary yearly, monthly, even daily. On paper, at least, this fluctuation will affect the value of your investment. But some mutual funds vary more than others and by greater percentages. For that reason, they are in effect "riskier," because it is more difficult to predict how they'll perform from one day to the next. The mutual funds with the lowest risk are generally the money market funds and mortgage funds, because the investments that these funds make are relatively secure. A money market fund, you'll recall, consists of government treasury bills and commercial paper, instruments on which the return is fixed and virtually guaranteed. Mortgage funds consist of mortgages on which the returns (that is, the payments of mortgagees) are equally predictable.

Next up the risk ladder, at a medium risk level, are the balanced funds, which consist of a mix of stocks and bonds. Bonds may be almost risk-free, but as soon as you throw in some stocks, the risk increases. At the top of the ladder are such high-risk mutual funds as equity funds and international funds. There simply is no guarantee—as there is with a treasury bill, for instance—what kind of returns you'll make on the stocks of companies, whether they're local companies or foreign ones. (Still, as risky as these funds may be, by being diversified, they're still less risky than putting all of your money on a single company's stock.)

Obviously, the potential pay-off from a fund depends on its riskiness. The greater the risk, the greater the potential return or loss. Therefore, how you go about choosing the right fund depends on your risk profile. In Chapter 9 I'll show you a sophisticated way of determining roughly how much risk you should be willing to take in building your investment portfolio. For now, it should suffice to say that you should invest, not in one type, but in several types of mutual funds. In other words, just as to reduce risk you should diversify your portfolio across a range of investment types, you should also diversify *within* the investment category of mutual funds. The reason for this further diversification is "market risk." Consider the stock market crash of 1987. That fateful day in October, widespread panic led to the selling of shares at stock markets around the world, causing stock prices to plummet. Even if you had a well-diversified stock fund at the time, there was no escaping the carnage; too many of your stocks in that fund had lost value.

However, had you invested some of your money in a less risky type of mutual fund, such as a mortgage fund, bond fund or money market fund, you would likely have been able to counteract the decline in your stock fund. In fact, you probably would have made money since many investors who'd lost their shirts on the stock market were looking elsewhere to park their own money. The lesson here is that market risk is very difficult to eliminate in one particular type of mutual fund. Make sure you diversify your mutual fund holdings!

So why bother putting any money in equity funds, which expose you to the risk of big losses? Well, there are two reasons. First, there's the issue of inflation. Imagine if the rate of inflation suddenly shot up at a time when all your money was in low-risk mutual funds. You would find that your already-low returns on these funds would suffer a dramatic erosion in value, as would the value of your funds. But while inflation was eating up the purchasing power of your returns, it might also be increasing the profits of a slew of companies: higher prices can lead to higher profits, and higher profits mean higher stock values, and the value of a good equity mutual fund could increase substantially as a result.

Second, consider the effect of interest rates. If you had all your money in low-risk mutual funds and interest rates suddenly shot up, what do you think would happen to the value of the mortgages and government and corporate bonds in your funds? It would go down. Think about it: if the marketplace were suddenly offering new, low-risk bonds and mortgages that paid a higher rate than your low-risk investments, no one would want to buy your investments unless you offered a discount to compensate for your lower returns. Of course, if interest rates plummeted, investors would want your investments and be willing to pay more for them. The question is, can you predict, with certainty, which way interest rates will go? Of course not. Clearly, your best bet is to invest in a range of mutual funds. (If you happened to have a disproportionately large investment in low-risk bond funds or mortgage funds at a time when you anticipated interest rates would go up, you might want to transfer your investments, only for the short term, to a money market fund, which is less sensitive to changes in interest rates. Once rates seemed to have finished rising, transfer your money back into bond or mortgage funds. Obviously, timing is everything in this type of manoeuvre, and you might have to do some research. Just make sure to watch the Bank of Canada rate, which influences most other interest rates. Also, check that your mutual funds allow transfers at minimal or no cost; most do, on 24 hours notice.)

Ultimately, it is precisely because economic conditions change continuously that you should not only diversify your mutual fund holdings across a range of funds, but also invest in funds over the long term to give them a chance to prove themselves. And when I say *long term*, I don't mean six months to a year; I mean five years, ten years or preferably more. Only by staying the course will you be able to weather fluctuations in the unit value of the funds.

Unfortunately, all too many mutual fund investors allow short-term fluctuations to influence them. Invariably, these individuals are unable to resist the temptation of taking their money out of a fund the minute its value starts to slide. What they fail to realize is that a low-priced mutual fund holds the promise of substantial future growth.

Without a doubt, thousands of impatient investors of mutual funds have lost money that could have been recovered had they only waited for the funds to "turn around." Such a situation occurred with the slow-down in 1994 of Canadian bond and equity markets. Until that time, bond and equity mutual funds had been performing like gangbusters, registering three-year average returns of 13.6 percent and 11.2 percent, respectively.

But in 1994, the Canadian bond and equity gravy train ran out of steam. The average return on equity funds for the year plummeted to 2.4 percent, and bond funds lost 2.3 percent. That year, I realized firsthand that a bit of uncertainty and some paper losses (losses on paper only) can quickly conspire to send otherwise rational people into a frenzy! Some clients, mainly newcomers to mutual funds, panicked. And rather than stick to the long-term view, these investors chose to turn their paper losses into actual losses and sold off their holdings, many of them scurrying back to the safe haven of GICs and certificates of deposit.

What a shame. Within one year, the average return on Canadian equity funds was back up to 12.2 percent. Bond funds were back up to 14.1 percent. If only these investors had given the market more time. But, as often happens in the cyclical world of mutual funds, the public ends up buying at the peak, or very near the peak, of a cycle, only to retreat as soon as there's a market correction. Invariably, many of the victims never return to mutual funds.

The lesson here is clear: don't be an investor who tries to perfect the art of buying high and selling low. This fate befalls all too many new mutual fund investors despite their best intentions of buying for the long term. Ultimately, if there's a way to avoid the fall, it's to remember what we discussed in Chapter 5: avoid making large and infrequent transactions. Instead, stick with your program of dollar cost averaging—of buying mutual funds frequently and in small, fixed amounts.

Extra Tips on Picking Funds

✓ Before investing in a fund, carefully analyze the fund's annual report and prospectus to learn about its past performance and investment focus. Check the one-, three- and five-year average annual returns to see if the fund has consistent returns; find out what the investment holdings of the funds are to see if they match the asset investments you are seeking; and read what the investment strategy of the fund is. In the prospectus you should review details on the administration of the fund, including the applicable sales charges and management fees.

✓ Some equity funds specialize in a sector of the stock market, such as resources, consumer products or industrial products. This specialization could affect your returns. During a period of economic growth, for instance, the demand for, and price of, raw materials will increase, causing an increase in the share prices of the resource companies producing these raw materials. If a fund puts a lot of its money in these companies, it might do well in such a climate.

✓ Some funds base their investments on the size, or capitalization, of companies (that is, small, medium or large "cap"). When you first invest in funds, focus on well-diversified blue-chip stock funds, bond funds or balanced funds. The larger, more diversified funds will fluctuate much less in price than the funds loaded with smaller "cap" companies. As your knowledge of, and feel for, mutual funds increases, you might consider small- or medium-sized companies' funds, which, though more risky, offer higher potential returns.

✓ Consider foreign investments as a form of diversification: a foreign economy might be faring better than Canada's economy, while a weakening Canadian dollar could boost the relative value of your foreign holdings. The government will allow you to invest only up to 20 percent of an RRSP account directly in foreign mutual funds. But you can increase this percentage by investing in Canadian funds that have strong holdings in foreign stocks. It's perfectly legal.

LABOUR-SPONSORED VENTURE CAPITAL CORPORATIONS (LSVCCS)

In recent years, a new type of investment vehicle with the potential of paying out incredible returns has hit the market: the labour-sponsored venture capital fund. Most provinces have their own version of this fund, which resembles the mutual fund in that it is a pool of money. But there are differences. A labour-sponsored fund invests mostly in young companies, many of them privately owned. And since the mission of these funds is to support Canadian companies and develop Canadian industry, governments across the country are prepared to give you, the investor, huge tax benefits. These benefits include tax credits on the federal government's labour-sponsored funds and the provincial employee venture capital fund. On top of that, this investment qualifies for your RRSP! In total, you could save as much as 75 percent of the cost of your contribution. If you bought $2,000 of a particular fund's shares, for instance, and you happened to be in the top marginal tax bracket, you could reduce your taxes by up to $1,500.

Of course, as with all investments, there are drawbacks. For one thing, because the funds usually focus on companies that are still in the early stages of their evolution, such as a company developing a new drug, the risks are greater; such companies are more susceptible to failure than are older, established firms. Then there's the question of the lock-in period: you'll have to keep your money in the fund for eight years as required by the 1996 federal budget, which extended the lock-in period. This period will also give the fund's investments a chance to pan out (a drug company at the start-up research stage could still be five or even ten years from the commercial stage.)

Before venturing into this type of investment, do your homework. Obtain a copy of the prospectus. Check to see who manages the fund (it can be a mix of industry professionals and labour leaders), what type of research the fund managers do before they invest in a particular company and what type of companies the fund is looking to invest in. Ask yourself: do the companies seem too risky for my portfolio? If need be, consult a financial adviser or a professional who sells such a fund.

In light of the above considerations, I suggest that you place only a small portion of your RRSP investments in these funds, despite their excellent tax benefits, since they are high risk. But don't ignore them as an investment vehicle. The combination of tax breaks and long-term returns on the funds could be well worth the investment.

One final note about funds. After a few years of researching funds, of learning about their peculiarities and of picking or rejecting them for your portfolio, you might find yourself wanting more control over your nest egg. Rather than continue handing over much of the decision making to fund managers, you might decide that *you* want to make all the decisions. At that point, you may want to set up a "self-directed" RRSP. As the name implies, it is you who will choose the particular RRSP-eligible stocks, bonds, mortgage-backed securities, treasury bills and what-nots that will constitute your portfolio. And by taking complete control over your future wealth, you'll save yourself the management fees!

But I must caution you. While you can open a self-directed plan with only a small amount of capital, as a rule you should wait until you have a very large portfolio, worth at least $50,000, before you venture into such a plan. You see, unless you have acquired enough investment experience and have the time, energy and resources to devote to this enterprise, your returns will be no better than if you invested in quality mutual funds and paid the fees. A difference of a couple of percentage points in your returns can push back your retirement by several years. Remember, you want to protect your wealth, not gamble it away.

CHAPTER 8

The Low Road to Wealth Building

I F YOU'VE BOUGHT THIS BOOK AND YOU'RE STILL with me three-quarters of the way through, it's probably because you want to take a measured, sensible approach to your investments. You don't want to rush into things. Instead, you're looking for a strategy that won't place your money at risk needlessly. In other words, you're appealing to your cautious, conservative side.

Caution is a good thing. Experience in safe, sound financial management I have; tips on how to bet at the racetrack I haven't. In my years in the financial industry, I've seen too many people blindly back investments that were all hype and no legs. These people were looking to race their way to financial independence, gambling their money on long-shot deals as they went.

I don't need to tell you what becomes of such investors. And I know that if you've read this far, you are not, and will not become, one of them. Therefore, I want to discuss investment opportunities that are safer and more conservative than, say, investing directly in the stock market. Your portfolio, after all, should cover a range of investments; I think I've emphasized enough that diversification is the best strategy. And short of leaving your money in a bank account, there are indeed investment vehicles, such as income-generating real estate, that will satisfy the conservative part of your portfolio while earning you decent returns.

BONDS (RRSP-eligible)

You can't get much more conservative than time-honoured, mom-and-apple-pie Canada Savings Bonds (CSBs). (You can also buy provincial bonds, which carry a little more risk but pay out slightly more interest than do CSBs.) CSBs carry virtually no risk because returns are guaranteed by the government; as a result, they don't earn huge returns. But they still offer a measure of protection against inflation. More than that—and this is the main attraction—CSBs are cashable, without penalty, at any time after three months. (You will forfeit your interest if you cash them within the first three months.) This cashability is convenient because it gives you flexibility in the event of interest rate fluctuations in the market-place. For instance, you may find another investment in the market-place that carries only slightly more risk but pays much higher returns. Such a situation would occur if banks suddenly increased their rates on term deposits. Then you might choose to sell your bonds and transfer your money into term deposits. But the government is all too aware that investors might take advantage of this cashability. Consequently, to avoid a widespread cashing of its bonds, in this situation it will usually increase the interest rate on the bonds to one that is competitive, for a specified period of time. In effect, this move cuts your opportunity cost. One more thing. It is best to cash CSBs on the first of the month, in order to get the previous month's accrued interest. If you cash them mid-month or at the end of the month, you're not entitled to receive any more interest.

Note that CSBs are available each year over a two-week period from the last week of October to the first week of November. (CSBs became even more attractive to buyers in 1995 when the Bank of Canada sold them in RRSP form for the first time.)

GICs and TERM DEPOSITS (RRSP-eligible)

When interest rates are low, it can seem impossible to maximize your investment return without having to resort to stocks. But stocks are always risky: if the market is overheated (rising quickly), it may be due for a downward correction in value.

Of course, you can always lock some of your money into a regular term deposit, which, over a fixed period of time, will pay you a higher rate than if you left your money in a bank account. But let's say you want flexibility with your higher returns. One relatively new product that financial institutions have been touting in recent years is the "flexible" or "variable" guaranteed investment certificate (flexible GIC). As the name implies, the main attraction of the GIC is that it guarantees a minimum rate of return, over the course of its term, without tying you down to that rate. If interest rates rise during the term of the GIC, it is your prerogative to reinvest your money at a higher rate. There are many variations on this theme, and each financial institution has its own name for its product. Some flexible GICs, for instance, now have their returns tied to the performance of certain stocks; in other words, if over a fixed term the stocks increase in value, you get a higher return. With flexible GICs, you truly get the best of both worlds: a good interest rate to begin with and an even better one if market rates go up. All you need to do is keep your eye on the current market rate and follow the appropriate procedure for switching to the higher rate.

A wise strategy when you invest in GICs and term deposits is to stagger their maturity dates. That way, if one instrument matures at a time when interest rates are comparatively low, you can renew for only a short period of time until rates turn around. Meanwhile, if another instrument matures in an environment of high interest rates, you can renew at the higher rate for a longer term. The goal is to earn the highest rates possible for the longest period of time.

However, GICs are not always the investment of choice. In recent years, they have been a good hedge against inflation (as have bonds, for that matter), offering rates that have far surpassed increases in the cost of living. But in days of high inflation, GICs are not the best way to high returns. Equity will offer higher returns because inflation brings with it the potential for higher profits in industry, boosting the value of a company. Therefore, to make an informed decision, it is important to analyze carefully the health of the economy, as well as your own risk profile and investment portfolio.

Here's a final tip about GICs and term deposits: a good time of year to buy them is during the CSB season because financial institutions will be competing for investors' money. You'll find all kinds of deals at this time, and you should be able to get rates that are one-quarter to one-half of a percent better than the usual rates. RRSP season, which runs from mid-January to the end of February, is also a good time of year to buy, as financial institutions wage battle for your business. But while I do subscribe to the idea it's better to invest in an RRSP than not, I strongly urge you not to wait until the end of February to make your previous year's RRSP contribution. Remember what I showed you in Chapter 5: the earlier you make your RRSP contribution, the greater will be your benefits from compounding.

DIVIDEND REINVESTMENT PLANS
(RRSP-eligible)

If you want to play the stock market, but still want a measure of safety, you can always invest in blue-chip stocks; these are stocks of big companies whose value fluctuates very little and whose potential returns are consequently low. Alternatively, you could invest in a mutual fund of blue-chip companies, which, of course, will cost you management fees. Yet another option is investing in a company's preferred stock. This type of stock guarantees you both a fixed dividend and, as its name implies, preference of payment (that is, you will receive dividends before the holders of riskier common stock do).

In all of the above cases, you will have to pay a transaction or management fee. But there is one way to invest safely in blue-chip companies without the added expense and with a discount on top of that. It's called the dividend reinvestment plan. (And, incidentally, it's a great way to use dollar cost averaging.)

This is the way the plan works: first, you buy shares directly from a blue-chip company that has such a plan or through a transfer agent who administers a company's plan. Then, on the day the company pays out a dividend, rather than give you your dividend in cash, the company reinvests your dividend for you into more shares of the company. For example, if you bought 100 shares of ABC company, and, soon after, ABC issued a dividend of $2 per share, your dividends would amount to $200. But rather than give you the $200, the company would buy $200 worth of shares for you. If the stock is trading at $50 per share, you'll have four more shares to your name. The benefit of this plan is that you pay absolutely no transaction fees because there is no agent to pay. Some companies will even give you a 5 percent discount on the shares bought with the dividends! The Low-Cost Investment Program, set up by the Canadian Shareowners Association, allows you to invest, without paying brokerage costs, in a large number of Canadian and American companies, including Alberta Energy, BC Gas, Royal Bank of Canada and Wendy's International. You can contact the Canadian Shareowners Association at (519) 252-1555, or write to 1090 University Avenue West, P.O. Box 7337, Windsor, ON N9C 4E9.

GOLD

Gold is an investment that has truly stood the test of time. There are three reasons for this: it is a thing of beauty, used in jewellery, vases, sculptures and other items; it is difficult to find and therefore only limited quantities are available; and its physical properties make it valuable as an industrial material for coins or very high-quality conductors.

Indeed, gold has proven to be a solid hedge against inflation and the effects of international turmoil. In times of international crisis and risk, world markets have often turned to gold as a stable investment. And it is because of this stability that you, too, should consider investing a small portion of your portfolio—3 to 7 percent—in gold. But what form should this gold come in? Follow these tips:

- When purchasing jewellery in your day-to-day life, remember to look for quality and purity, not some fancy design. In other words, don't buy a $1,000 piece of jewellery containing only a quarter ounce of gold, because in a time of crisis it won't be the designer of the ring or chain that will matter, but the gold content.
- Purchase gold bars directly from a chartered bank.
- Invest in a mutual fund that consists of mainly gold stocks, such as TD's Green Line Precious Metals Fund, the Royal Trust Precious Metals Fund, the Scotia Precious Metals Fund, Dynamic Precious Metals or Universal Precious Metals Fund.

INVESTMENT PROPERTY

Land ownership has probably made more fortunes than any other type of investment. The reason? The law of supply and demand. Land is in limited supply, but a continuously increasing population wants to own it. Over time, this pressure can only push the price of real estate upwards, particularly in the more desirable areas. However, if you plan to invest in real estate, you need to adopt a long-term view. Indeed, while real estate in the Western world soared in price throughout much of the seventies and eighties, recently it has suffered a downturn in many regions. But over time the trend always seems to be upwards. Consider Table 12. In spite of both increases and decreases in the average price, the average annual percentage change is +6.80%. That is, the price generally rises.

Table 12: Average House Price in Toronto from 1979 to 1995*

Year	Average Price ($)	Annual percentage Increase/Decrease
1979	$70,830	
1980	75,694	6.87
1981	90,203	19.17
1982	95,496	5.87
1983	101,626	6.42
1984	102,318	0.68
1985	109,094	6.62
1986	138,925	27.34
1987	189,105	36.12
1988	229,635	21.43
1989	273,698	19.19
1990	255,020	−6.82
1991	234,313	−8.12
1992	214,971	−8.25
1993	206,490	−3.95
1994	208,921	1.18
1995	203,028	−2.82
Average compound annual percentage increase: 6.80		

*Information provided by the Toronto Real Estate Board.

As I discussed earlier, owning a home is arguably the best investment you can make because after some time you will reduce your shelter costs to a negligible amount. And not only will you likely make a profit if you sell it, but this profit will be tax free.

But besides home ownership, there's another way to make money from real estate: invest in an income-generating property. Let me illustrate this with the example of a personal real estate investment of mine, on which I started to make a profit almost as soon as I bought the property.

The investment in question was a condominium priced at $69,000. Because of a special government program at the time, I was able to put down only 5 percent, or $3,450. So I had to take out a mortgage for the balance: a $65,550 mortgage at 8.75 percent for a term of five years, amortized over 20 years. My monthly payment on the mortgage was $572.35, which initially consisted of $469.12 in interest and $103.23 in principal (you'll recall that while the payment remains the same over time, the interest portion decreases and the principal portion increases.) I also had to pay property taxes of about $58 and condo fees of $100, making the total cost per month $730.35. But, this amount wasn't my true cost because the principal portion of my monthly payment was money in *my* pocket. (Although I will not receive this money until I sell the property, it is still mine.) Therefore, my real cost in the first month was only $627.12 ($730.35 − $103.23 in principal). And since the principal portion of my payment has increased over time, I have effectively paid less and less per month. For argument's sake, let's take $625 as my monthly cost.

Now for the rental income side of the equation. I started by renting the condo at $585 per month. I made sure to charge a little less than the going rate for similar condos to keep tenants for a long time and therefore minimize turnover and advertising costs. So, with $585 coming in and $625 going out, my shortfall every month was roughly $40. Bear in mind, of course, that since this was an income-generating property, this "commercial enterprise" of mine was subject to income tax. But just as the revenue is taxable, so are the expenses deductible. I could thus apply my loss of $40 per month, or $480 per year, to any other income I had. In other words, initially at least, I was losing less than $40 per month. But I can hear you say: "Yes, but you were still short some money." True, except that within a year my $69,000 property had increased in value to $85,000! What's a few dollars per month when you're sitting on that kind of profit?

Even if the property had not increased in value, it still would have been a good investment because of the decreasing interest portion of my monthly payments. After five years, or 60 payments, the interest per month will have decreased to $415 from $469.12. And if the $158 I initially paid in property taxes and condo fees increases at an inflation rate of 3 percent per year (to reach $183 per month after five years) my real cost per month will be $598 ($415 + $183). But the rent will have also increased at 3 percent per year, to end up at $678 after five years. In other words, I will be earning $80 per month (taxable, of course), and this net income will keep growing. Meanwhile, I will own more and more of the equity in the condo. Never mind the increase in my net worth from the property's increase in value!

Eventually, when I've paid off the mortgage, my only expenses will be maintenance, condo fees and property taxes. Without the mortgage payment, my rental income will provide a nice cash flow. You'll notice I brought up the subject of maintenance. As a landlord, you have to maintain the property, which is money out of your pocket. But the cost of maintenance is tax deductible. Also deductible is depreciation, or capital cost allowance (CCA). You see, the government lets you assume that over time your rental unit (but not the land on which it sits) will decrease in value because of wear and tear. So it allows you to deduct an allowance for this depreciation. This deduction will help reduce the taxes you have to pay on your income from the property. (But be aware that you can't use the CCA deduction to reduce your net income to a negative number.)

As you can easily see, owning a rental property can be a wealth-building proposition. And as a bonus, mortgage interest on investment properties is deductible; in fact, even if the interest on the mortgage is greater than your income from the property, you should be able to deduct it from your other business income, making your investment property an even sweeter prospect!

Of course, one of the reasons for these benefits is that, since you are using other people's money, you have "leverage." Basically, the bigger your leverage, the higher the value of the property you can buy. Imagine a lever on a fulcrum, like a plank of wood on a boulder, which you would use to lift a big weight. Think of the asset you're trying to buy as the weight you're trying to lift and the force you have to apply to the plank as the amount of ready money you have to invest.

Obviously, the smaller the force you apply to the plank, the greater the length of plank you'll need on your side of the boulder to lift the weight. Conversely, the greater the force you apply, the shorter the length of plank you'll need. The length of plank that you need on your side is the size of the loan or mortgage you'll need to buy the property—it's your leverage.

Let's apply this concept of leverage to an investment opportunity and see how it can affect your returns. Let's say you have $75,000 to invest. You decide to buy a $200,000 house as an investment property and you expect it to increase in value by 15 percent, to $230,000, in three years, giving you a $30,000 profit. Consider what your return would be under two different scenarios: in the first, you invest $75,000 and borrow $125,000, while in the second you put down $50,000 and borrow $150,000. Now, notice the effect on your returns from the property. In the first case, you would earn a $30,000 profit on a $75,000 personal investment, while in the second you would earn the $30,000 on a $50,000 personal investment. That's a return of 40 percent versus 60 percent, or, compounded annually over three years, 12 percent versus 17 percent. In other words, the more you borrow, the greater your return.

Of course, in both cases your interest costs and property taxes will reduce your actual returns. But the rental income from the property will increase your returns. Let's say that in the first scenario, in which you borrow $125,000, your rental income equals the property taxes and interest costs, but that in the second scenario, in which you borrow $25,000 more, your rental income covers only the property taxes (that is, you have to pay the interest every month). If you pay an average of 9 percent interest per year on your mortgage, then your total additional cost under this scenario will be $6,750 (three years x 9 percent of $25,000). Your net return for the second scenario, therefore, will be $23,250 ($30,000 − $6,750), divided by the $50,000 you put down. That's a 46.5 percent return, which is still higher than the 40 percent return in the first scenario, over three years. As an average annual compound rate, your net return would be 13.6 percent in the second scenario and 12 percent in the first.

But beware! Just as an increase in the value of your property will earn greater returns the more you borrow, so will a decrease in value bring you greater losses. Consider what would happen if the property went down in value by $30,000. In the first scenario, in which you invested $75,000 of your money, your three-year loss would be $30,000 divided by $75,000, or 40 percent (12 percent per year.) In the second scenario, however, not only would you lose $30,000 on a smaller initial investment, but you would also lose the additional cost of interest of $6,750 divided by $50,000. In other words, your total three-year loss would be $36,750 divided by $50,000, or 73.5 percent. That's a 20 percent loss per year on your investment. And let's say you managed to put down only $25,000 of your money and borrowed as much as $175,000—raising your interest costs by yet another $6,750 over three years. If the property went up

$30,000 in value, you would earn an average annual return of about 19 percent. But if the property went down $30,000, you would suffer an annual loss of 40 percent! That's the effect of leverage: the greater the leverage (or loan), the greater the risk, and, consequently, the greater the return or loss.

In light of this effect, it's not wise to borrow a large sum of money when the property market is volatile. Sure, you can make a tidy profit if the value goes up, but, considering the size of the potential loss, are you willing to take the chance? Leverage has managed to wipe out many real estate fortunes.

In the end, I would urge you to base your purchase of a property not on the chance of capital appreciation, but on the long-term cash flow that the property can generate. This approach is the best way to limit your exposure to risk. Look for residential properties with locations in high demand. That property could be a single-family dwelling, duplex, triplex, fourplex or apartment building. In a good location, this property may cost you a little more, but your risk will be minimal.

Yet a safer way to get into the income-property market with a minimal investment is to incorporate a suite in your own home. If you obtained clearance from your city's zoning department, renovated your house at a cost of $15,000, and were able to rent out the suite at $600 per month, your annual return would be $7,200 per year divided by $15,000, or 48 percent. That's a phenomenal return on investment. Even if you had to borrow the money and pay interest of 9 percent per year, although your costs would go up by about $1,350 in the first year, your return would still be 39 percent. In fact, your return would go up as your interest costs decreased over time. (Of course, your rental income would be taxable, while your property taxes would probably rise a little. But the interest you paid on a $15,000 loan would be tax deductible, as would the proportion of your property taxes that the suite represented. In addition, the government would allow you to deduct CCA on the suite.)

Numbers aside, if you decide that you want to be a landlord, treat this new responsibility as a part-time job and be as professional as possible. Ensure that you draw up tenancy agreements and screen your tenants very carefully. Keep detailed records, make appropriate repairs as required and ensure that your tenants are aware of their responsibilities. In my experience, if you treat your tenants with respect, they will regard you in the same light.

Again, do not expect to get rich quick from real estate investing. Yes, some speculators do make huge amounts of money, but these people are usually full-fledged professionals with a unique physical constitution for handling risk. Consider your properties to be long-term investments, similar to your mutual funds or retirement savings plans. In the long run, remember, the tortoise beat the hare! That's my philosophy: financial independence through small, safe and diversified long-term investments. Indeed, owning a solid rental property or two should well reduce the overall risk of your portfolio.

Before becoming a landlord, however, you would be wise to read a book or two on the subject and make sure you are familiar with the tax implications of owning income-generating property. Moreover, consider getting professional advice. As I have found with investing in mutual funds and financial instruments, it pays to have professional advice, and in the case of investment properties, it is best to work with a Realtor who is very experienced and whom you can trust. I learned more from my real estate agent when I bought my first rental property than from many books. The Realtor showed me a number of investment properties, calculated the income I would get from each one and discussed the tax implications with me.

Because they work on commission, real estate agents will do their utmost to make the sale. Use this system to your advantage. Get to know a few Realtors and have them show you a number of properties. After a while you will discover which agent is the most helpful, has the most knowledge and seems the most trustworthy.

Take your time. Don't rush into any investment before you have thoroughly evaluated the property and your resources. Check with your bank to see if it finances rental properties and find out what its policies are. Some banks allow you to use the Canada Mortgage and Housing Corporation (CMHC) to insure the mortgage if the deposit you have is less than 25 percent of the purchase price. With CMHC investment property insurance, you can make a deposit of as little as 15 percent of the purchase price of a rental property. Of course, you have to be able to demonstrate that your income from the rental property and other sources will cover the mortgage payments. Unfortunately, not every financial institution will provide a CMHC investment property mortgage. If your financial institution does not offer this option, your Realtor may be able to assist you in securing financing by connecting you with a good mortgage broker or by referring you to a banker specializing in rental properties. Just be sure to check what fees, if any, the broker will charge you, since you must minimize all of your expenses.

If you decide you want to make an offer on a property, you should also consult with a lawyer, who will help you understand the legal implications of your offer and who will do the paperwork for your purchase. Moreover, have an engineering inspection done on the property to ensure it's not in need of major repairs. If it is, make sure to list in your "offer to purchase" any repairs the vendor will have to complete. And set a completion date for the repairs. Most important, decide what price you want to pay based on your evaluation of the market and of the rental income you expect to earn. Keep in mind that the agent on the other side of the table—the one who represents the seller—will paint a glowing picture of the property, possibly inflating some figures and "forgetting" to mention a few flaws in the property. But remember, as the purchaser, you are in the driver's seat. Your offer is your only opportunity to make demands. So, be sure you feel comfortable with it, because once the seller accepts it, the property is yours.

Before closing, I must emphasize that a property investment should be only one part of your portfolio. You must still diversify your holdings. In other words, don't stake your future financial independence on real estate. Invest in mutual funds, GICs, gold and some of the other instruments we've covered. You want to not only maximize your returns but also minimize your exposure to risk.

Next chapter, we'll assess your risk profile and decide how to diversify your portfolio.

CHAPTER 9

How Much Risk Do You Want to Take?

RISK IS THE CHANCE OF LOSS, THE POSSIBILITY that an investment will turn sour. Every investment—a stock, a mutual fund, real estate—carries some risk. Everything. GICs have risk; they could lose value because of inflation (which to me is a big risk) unless they are short-term or flexible GICs. Theoretically, even a CSB has risk, except that the risk of the government defaulting on such a bond is very small, virtually non-existent. Consequently, you can't expect to make nearly as much money on a CSB as you might on a new mining stock trading on the Vancouver Stock Exchange. Certainly, if this stock does earn high returns, you could make a tidy sum, a great deal more than on a CSB. But the chances that the stock will make money are also much, much smaller than the odds that the government will pay interest on your bond. Therefore, the ultimate quandary for you, as an investor, is to decide how much risk you're willing to tolerate for the return that you'll earn. Remember, the greater the expected return, the greater the risk.

But how do you quantify risk? It's a tricky question, though economists have come up with a workable answer. Simply put, the riskiness of an investment is a function of its volatility. The more volatile the investment—in other words, the more the value of the investment changes over time—the greater the risk. While economists measure volatility in terms of an investment's "Beta factor" and "variance," suffice it to say that stocks are riskier than bonds, which are riskier than highly liquid cash instruments, such as treasury bills.

On the other hand, the returns for stocks are greater than those for bonds, which exceed those for cash. Consider one leading study, by Ibbotson Associates in Chicago, in which the authors compared the change in value of stocks, bonds and cash during the period from 1925 to 1992—a period during which inflation averaged 3.2 percent per year. The authors found that $1.00 in stock in 1925 had risen in value to $727.38 in 1992, while $1.00 of long-term government bonds had risen to $23.71, and $1.00 of treasury bills to $11.40. Indeed, the clear conclusion in study after study has been that stocks outperform bonds (or debt), which outperform cash. Meanwhile, all three forms of investment outperform inflation, which in the case of the Ibbotson study increased the cost of $1.00 of goods in 1925 to $7.92 in 1992.

No doubt, investing in something riskier than bonds and treasury bills can bring you attractive returns. But what about the risk? What if you're the type of investor who wants as little risk as possible and who's willing to forgo higher returns? Indeed, you might be the sort who'd rather eliminate virtually all risk and settle for the guaranteed returns. Yes, that would be an option. But wait! If you took that approach, you would be cheating yourself out of much greater returns for the same amount of risk. "What?" you say. That's right. You see, much research on the performance of stocks, bonds and cash has been done in the last 30 years. And what the leading studies have shown is that if you build your portfolio with a mix of risk-free cash investments, bonds and stocks, you could actually expose yourself to no more overall risk than if you put all your money in only risk-free cash investments. I know it sounds contradictory to the idea that greater returns mean greater risk. But it's true! Finance theorists call this the Modern Portfolio Theory.

As you might have realized, the lesson to be learned from this research is that diversification is the best approach to investing. In other words: don't put all your eggs in one basket! (Sound familiar?)

But how do you figure out the ideal mix for your portfolio? Well, this process can be as simple or as complex as you desire. The simplest approach would be to put all your money in a balanced mutual fund consisting of cash, bonds and stocks; your portfolio would instantly be diversified. (Then again, keep in mind that you'd also be relying on the abilities of only one group of investment managers. And that risk might be more than you care to take.) Alternatively, you could invest in a mutual fund for each type of investment.

Ultimately, however, you should know the proportion of your total investments, within a few percentage points, that should be put in cash, bonds and stocks. One way to determine this proportion is to follow the approach that most investment advisers and financial planners use.

First, let's look at what these experts have concluded is a reasonable mix of investments for an average person in different age groups (see Table 13).

Table 13: Percentage Breakdown of Portfolio Investments for Different Age Groups

Age (years)	Cash Assets	Debt Assets	Equity Assets
20–29	35%	50%	15%
30–39	15	20	65
40–49	15	30	55
50–59	15	40	45
60–64	15	50	35
65 and up	20	60	20

For example, if you are in the 40–49 age bracket, your portfolio should consist of 15 percent cash, 30 percent debt and 55 percent equity. Cash Assets include savings accounts, certificates of deposit (cashable term deposits or GICs with a term of less than a year), CSBs, money market funds and treasury bills. Debt Assets include investments in mortgage and bond funds, preferred stock and other government bonds. Equity Assets include investments in stock or equity mutual funds.

Remember, these figures are for the average investor in each age group. The obvious question is, are you the average investor? One way to find out is to assess your risk tolerance. Ask yourself this question: am I most likely to keep my money locked up in a safe or to invest only in risky VSE stocks? If you want safety at any cost, give yourself a risk factor of "1." If you thrive on maximum risk, give yourself a risk factor of "10." If you think you're right in the middle—that you're average, in other words—give yourself a "5." You could also be a "2" or a "7" or a "6"; it's up to you. Only *you* know your inclinations.

Once you've determined your risk factor, check Table 14, which shows by how many percentage points you should alter the proportions of investment types in your portfolio based on your risk factor.

Table 14: Percentage Change in Proportions of Investment Types with Risk Factor

Risk Factor	Cash Assets	Debt Assets	Equity Assets
1	(invest only in cash)		
2	+10	+ 5	–15
3	+ 5	+ 5	–10
4	+ 3	+ 2	– 5
5	0	0	0
6	– 3	– 2	+ 5
7	– 5	– 5	+10
8	–10	– 5	+15
9	–10	–10	+20
10	–15	–15	+30

Let's try an example. We'll assume your risk factor is "4." In other words, you're marginally more inclined to look for safety than you are to take risks; you're slightly more conservative than the average. Now, let's assume further that you're 37 years of age. From Table 13 (on page 114), you figured out that a good investment mix for an average investor in your age group consists of 15 percent cash, 20 percent debt and 65 percent equity. But because your risk tolerance is "4," you want to adjust these percentages. Look at the row next to "4" in Table 14. You'll want to increase your cash holdings by 3 percent, increase your debt holdings by 2 percent and decrease your equity holdings by 5 percent. Your new mix will be 18 percent cash, 22 percent debt and 60 percent equity. Notice that if your risk factor were a "5," your mix wouldn't change because the mixes in Table 13 are based on the average investor.

As you can see, the possibilities are endless, depending on your age and risk tolerance. Indeed, no two investors are exactly alike. But bear in mind that these figures are only rough estimates; your percentages can vary by a couple of points with no adverse effects.

As for the foreign content of your diversified portfolio, a good benchmark is 35 percent of your debt and 35 percent of your equity. So, if you're the average 40-year-old, with 30 percent of your portfolio in debt investments and 55 percent in equity investments, you want to ensure that 10.5 percent of your portfolio is foreign debt (that is, 35 percent of 30 percent) and that 19.25 percent is foreign equity (that is, 35 percent of 55 percent).

Finally, as you've probably noticed, these calculations don't include investments in income-generating properties or in such speculative assets as gold, jewellery or art. If you decide to make any of these investments, I recommend that you classify them as equity and limit them to no more than 10 percent of your portfolio. (In the case of an income-generating property, use the value of your net equity—the value of the property minus the mortgage.)

CHAPTER 10

"T" is for Taxes

F ACE IT. IN CANADA, TAX RATES ARE AMONG THE highest in the world. And this state of affairs probably won't change in our lifetime. That said, there is a good deal you can do to reduce the amount you pay in taxes.

First, let's go over some of the ground we've already covered elsewhere in this book, beginning, of course, with the most basic and most important way to cut down on your tax bite: make contributions to an RRSP. I can't emphasize enough how important this strategy is. Yet, only 40 percent of taxpayers exploit this tax break. By contributing to an RRSP, you can get a refund from Revenue Canada of up to 50 percent of your deposits. This plan is one of the world's most generous. Please make the most of it.

Another highly effective way to reduce taxes is to own your home. As you'll recall, any capital gains you make from selling your principal residence are exempt from taxes. So, if your house goes up $30,000 in value between the time you buy it and the time you sell it, that $30,000 is yours to keep—all of it.

That's not the case with other investments, such as stocks, investment properties or mutual funds. Let's consider stocks for a moment. If stocks that you own go up $30,000 in value between the time you buy them and the time you sell them, that $30,000 becomes a taxable capital gain, and you will have to pay income tax on 75 percent of it, or $22,500. If your marginal tax bracket is 40 percent, your total tax bill will be $9,000, not $0, as in the case of the principal residence.

What's Your Marginal Tax Rate?

It's the percentage of your taxable income (that is, not your gross income, but your income after deductions) that you would have to pay in federal and provincial taxes if you earned one more dollar of taxable income. To figure out your marginal tax rate, look first at the federal tax rates. For each range of taxable income, the federal government charges a different rate. For the 1996 taxation year:

For the portion of your taxable income that is…	You pay taxes at a rate of…
$29,590.00 or less	17%
$29,590.01 to $59,180.00	26%
$59,180.01 and up	29%

Therefore, if your taxable income is $35,000, you will pay federal taxes of 17 percent on the first $29,591 and 26 percent on the remaining $5,409. Your marginal federal tax rate, therefore, is 26 percent. But you must also pay provincial taxes, which generally amount to about 50 percent of the federal rates. Consequently, your combined federal and provincial marginal tax rate will be 26 percent plus 13 percent, or 39 percent. (Some federal and provincial surtaxes may raise that rate even higher.)

As for interest income—such as returns on mortgage funds, money market funds, CSBs, GICs and other fixed income securities—the income tax verdict is worse. Income on these instruments is fully taxable. At a 40 percent marginal tax rate, $30,000 in interest income would cost you $12,000 in taxes!

As you can see, it is better for tax purposes to have capital gains than interest. But even better than capital gains (except on your principal residence, of course, because they are tax exempt) is dividend income on stocks. You see, while you do have to pay income tax on dividend income, Revenue Canada gives you a dividend tax credit that is large enough to make dividend income attractive. The way it works is like this. You are required to "gross up" your dividend income by 25 percent and calculate federal tax on this amount. In our example, this would be $30,000, grossed up by 25 percent to $37,500. For a taxpayer in a 40 percent marginal tax bracket, the federal taxes on this grossed-up amount would be 26 percent or $9,750. This amount is then reduced by the dividend tax credit, which is equal to 2/3 of the gross-up amount or 2/3 of $7,500, which equals $5,000. Net federal taxes are thus $4,750, the $9,750 in federal taxes minus the dividend tax credit of $5,000. Finally, you calculate the total taxes, including provincial taxes you would have to pay on the $30,000 dividend, which is 1.5 times your federal taxes $4,750, or $7,125. If this seems very complicated to you, don't worry. Below is a table which will easily enable you to calculate the approximate amount of taxes on dividends you receive, without all these heavy duty calculations!

Table 15 shows you at a glance the taxes you will pay depending on which type of return you receive on your investment. It also shows the taxes payable at three different marginal tax rates.

Table 15: Taxes Payable on Different Types of Returns at 3 Marginal Tax Rates

Percentage in taxes that you pay on income from:			
Marginal Tax Rate (%)	Dividends	Capital Gains	Interest
30	approx. 13	22.5	30
40	approx. 25	30.0	40
50	approx. 34	37.5	50

Therefore, if your marginal tax rate is 40 percent and you receive $13,000 in dividends, you will pay approximately 25 percent of $13,000, or $3,250 in taxes, whereas if you made that $13,000 in capital gains, you would pay 30 percent, or $3,900. As interest income, your return would cost you 40 percent of $13,000, or $5,200. (Some mutual funds are in fact dividend income funds and are worth checking out, since they reduce your potential taxes and often invest in high-quality preferred shares.)

As attractive as dividend income is, remember that in the case of dividends on preferred stocks, which carry a fixed percentage return every year, the corporations issuing the dividends are aware that you'll get a tax credit. Often, they will offer a lower dividend to take advantage of your tax credit. So be sure to check what exactly is your effective yield, or return, on your preferred stock.

None of these tax calculations, of course, applies to investments you make through your RRSP because returns on these investments are tax free. But remember: once you take money out of your RRSP, you will have to pay tax on whatever you withdraw. In addition, you won't get a tax credit at the time of withdrawal; you'll have to pay at your full marginal tax rate.

Once you retire, however, there is a way to transfer money out of an RRSP without paying taxes, and that's to "roll" your RRSP into what is called a registered retirement income fund (RRIF). An RRIF is a tax-sheltered registered retirement plan that allows you to gradually withdraw, at prescribed minimum rates, your accumulated RRSP savings. Of course, you will have to pay tax once you take money out of your RRIF.

Another way to withdraw from your RRSP without paying taxes immediately is to set up an annuity, which turns your savings into a regular stream of equal annual payments. As you'll recall from Chapter 6, the principle is the same as with a mortgage, except that with a mortgage, you pay the bank at fixed intervals, while in the case of an annuity, you receive equal payments at fixed intervals. There are two types of annuities: the life annuity, which you can purchase through an insurance company and which pays you an annual amount for life, and a fixed-term annuity, which is available through most financial institutions and which pays you an annual amount for a fixed period of time. (Your payments will be greater under the second option, but they will stop after a set number of years.)

There are advantages to both RRIFs and annuities, but RRIFs lend themselves more favourably to protecting you against inflation because the rate of return used to compute your annuity payments will probably be lower than what you could earn by choosing the investments in your RRIF.

OTHER STRATEGIES TO REDUCE YOUR TAXES

- Place investments in the name of the spouse with the lower income. This way, the taxes owed should be lower. Ensure that there is a paper trail showing that the money came from this spouse; otherwise, the government could attribute it back to the other spouse. One strategy is to have the higher-income spouse make the mortgage payments and cover other expenses that are not tax deductible, leaving the lower-income spouse to make the investments. This way, if you had to, you could easily show Revenue Canada that the lower-income spouse did earn the investment income.

- Split your incomes. A spouse who earns $65,000 will pay taxes at a rate substantially higher than the rate of a spouse who earns $15,000. In fact, the total taxes the couple will pay will be much higher than if each spouse earned $40,000. That's because while the lower-income spouse's marginal tax rate will go up, the higher-income spouse's marginal tax rate will come down by much more. So, if you can manage to "split" your incomes, you could save thousands of dollars in taxes. But be careful! Revenue Canada doesn't allow spouses to "artificially" split combined incomes. One solution is to look at how much each of you wants to earn at your particular jobs, in relation to the time you spend at those jobs and the extra income after taxes that the job earns you. Of course, if both spouses are in business together, make sure to even out the two salaries.

- Take advantage of the "secondary income" loophole. Let me explain this loophole by telling you first what you *can't* do. Revenue Canada does not allow a higher-income spouse to transfer property to the lower-income spouse for the purpose of lowering taxes. The government will attribute the income back to the higher-income spouse in this situation. (Nevertheless, you *can* transfer the property if the transfer takes place at market value and the transferor pays taxes on any resulting capital gains.) A similar situation arises with a transfer of property to children under 18: the government will attribute any property income back to the transferor. Now, let me show you where the "secondary income" provision comes in. Let's say you're the higher-income spouse, and you transfer $10,000 in property to your spouse. If that $10,000 earns $1,000 in returns, as I noted above, you will have to pay taxes on it, even though it's in your spouse's hands. Now, let's say this $1,000 generates an income the following year; this income also ends up in your spouse's hands. However, this "secondary income" is attributable not to you, but to your spouse. That is, every year you will pay taxes on the $1,000 income, and your spouse will pay taxes on the income from the $1,000. Over time, this secondary stream of income can build up. If, for instance, the $1,000 itself earns 10 percent, and your marginal tax rate happens to be 30 percent higher than your spouse's, then every year you will save $30 in taxes. Over 20 years, that savings amounts to $1,718. And if the original transfer in question was $100,000 rather than $10,000, the total tax savings over 20 years would be $17,180. All that money saved by making a minor bookkeeping adjustment! However, again, be careful that your documentation is in order.

- Set up spousal RRSPs. (See Chapter 5)
- Pay your spouse's taxes! If your tax bracket is higher than your spouse's, *you* should be sending a cheque to Revenue Canada for any taxes your spouse owes. This way, investment income that your spouse earns on what would otherwise have gone to the government will be taxable at a lower rate.
- Set up a home business. By starting a business at home, you will be able to deduct some of your household expenses, provided that you expect your business to make a profit. For example, if you use a room as an office and that room takes up one-sixth of your house, you can deduct one-sixth of the interest on your mortgage or one-sixth of your rent. You can also deduct one-sixth of the cost of heating, lighting and home insurance, as well as one-sixth of your property taxes. (Note, however, that your home office must be your principal place of business or that you must use it exclusively for your business on a regular basis for meeting clients, customers or patients.) You can also deduct the CCA of office equipment, such as a computer, fax machine and photocopier. In total, you can deduct expenses only up to the amount you earn from the business; you cannot use your deductions to incur a loss. Keep in mind, however, that you can carry forward unused deductions from previous years.

There are many more complicated and risky tax shelters, but none of them matches the common-sense shelters and deductions I have mentioned above. Don't take chances on your tax deductions, and never base investment decisions on tax considerations alone. The investment is what makes the money; the taxes merely reduce it.

ONE FINAL LOOPHOLE

Let's say you have $14,000 invested in a blue-chip mutual fund that you don't want to touch. Since it's an excellent fund, you'd like to keep your money in it for many years. Now, let's assume as well that you have your mind set on buying a car worth $14,000 (you've followed my advice and have been checking out used cars) but that you don't have the money available to purchase the car. How can you buy the car without losing your investment?

Most people would take out a loan for $14,000 and purchase the car, paying interest on the loan in after-tax dollars. End of story. But what if you could borrow the money for the car and effectively make the interest on the loan tax deductible? You can!

Here's how: first, cash in your mutual fund and use the proceeds to buy the car. Next, go to your financial institution and arrange to get a $14,000 loan. But this loan won't be for the car, since you've already bought it. Instead, this loan will allow you to buy back into your mutual fund. (If you agree to put up your mutual fund investment as security against the loan, you'll be able to pay a lower rate of interest on the loan, a rate that is usually close to the prime rate.) Now, this is where the benefit comes in. At the end of the year, ask your bank to give you a statement of the interest you have paid on your loan. This interest, believe it or not, will be tax deductible. You see, whenever you borrow money to make an investment, the government gives you a deduction, against any income on the investment, for the interest on the loan (you enter the amount of interest in your tax return under the section entitled "Carrying Costs"). In other words, by doing a couple of bookkeeping manoeuvres and visiting your bank, you have reduced your taxes by the cost of borrowing for your car. And the higher your income, of course, the bigger your savings.

Do keep in mind, however, that since you will have disposed of your mutual fund, even for a brief period of time, you will have to pay taxes on any capital gains you will have made. (But even if you do pay capital gains tax, the result may still be to your benefit, because if in a few years you were to sell your mutual fund a second time, you would pay capital gains tax only on the difference in value between the second time you bought it and the second time you sold it. In other words, you would still have gained from taking out the loan.) Conversely, if you suffered a capital loss, you will get a credit on your taxes.

Finally, when you negotiate your loan agreement with the bank, make sure that your payments are blended, as they are for a mortgage. Otherwise, the principal amount of the loan will remain untouched, while the value of your car is depreciating. Ultimately, you'll owe the principal without an asset to show for it.

CHAPTER 11

Protect What You've Got

WHEN I WORKED AT THE BANK, CLIENTS WOULD occasionally come in to apply for loans because a sudden disability had put them out of work. The expenses were adding up, and their disability income, usually a fraction of their previous income, couldn't keep up. And while I could sympathize with these clients, as a banker I had to be concerned with their ability to meet their debt obligations. You see, without a guarantee that a client's cash flow will meet his or her debt obligations, a banker cannot grant a loan, whatever the hardship.

What if *your* spouse suddenly were to die or become disabled? How would you manage financially? You might have to dip into your life savings to survive, and the time it would take for these savings to disappear would surely be much shorter than the time it took you to accumulate them. As I mentioned before, it takes concentrated effort to build wealth, but it takes almost nothing to lose it all. Which is why before I set out to write a book about ways to achieve financial independence, I resolved to include a chapter on ways of safeguarding that independence from disaster. In my years in the financial services industry, I have often seen nest eggs frittered away because the people who'd built them had dispensed with three golden rules: insure yourself properly, set up an emergency funds account and draw up wills to keep the courts and government out of your personal affairs. Let's cover these topics one at a time.

INSURANCE

Insurance protects your family against the effects of you or your spouse suddenly dying or becoming disabled. By buying insurance, you can make sure there'll be enough money coming in to protect your family's standard of living in the event of a setback.

What kind of insurance should you buy? The possibilities are endless. But there are three particular types you should consider: disability insurance, life insurance and mortgage insurance.

Disability Insurance

What would your source of income be if you suddenly became disabled and unable to work? If you work for a company, you probably have a short-term and long-term disability plan. Check with your human resources department to see what coverage you have.

Other possible sources of disability income include employment insurance, CPP and workers' compensation. If you're lucky enough to be covered by workers' compensation, then perhaps you're all set. Many of us, however, don't have this coverage. That leaves the government. However, it's unwise to expect that the government will take care of you if you become disabled: you may not qualify, the payment period may be too short or the amount of the payment may be too small. For example, the CPP definition of *disabled* is fairly strict; it requires that physical or mental impairment be both severe and prolonged. *Severe* means that a person is unable to pursue any substantially gainful employment, and *prolonged* means that the disability is probably indefinite and likely to result in death. Under these conditions, the maximum monthly amount you can receive is $870.92—not much in today's expensive world!

Given these limitations, you would be wise to purchase disability insurance. Consider that in these days of contracting out and downsizing, many of us end up being unemployed for some period of time. Some of us change careers. Some of us— in fact, many of us—become self-employed. Who provides the coverage in those situations? No one. And even if after leaving a company you can continue your coverage, that coverage might be inadequate and expensive (in fact, continuing your coverage usually is very expensive).

So, what should you purchase in terms of disability coverage, and what details should you be looking at?

- Choose a longer elimination period if possible. The elimination period is the time that elapses from the day you file a claim until the day you start receiving your benefits. If you set the elimination period at three months or longer, your premiums will be smaller than if you required your benefits immediately. But what do you do until the first payment? If you have a group disability plan through work, you should be covered during the elimination period. Meanwhile, EI should cover you for a maximum of 15 weeks, although you will receive your first cheque only after a waiting period of two weeks.

- Take only the coverage you need. Check how much your employer's group plan will pay and figure out the extra amount you would require. But keep in mind that insurance companies will not pay amounts greater than two-thirds of your gross income because they fear you would lose the incentive to return to work. In other words, if your employer's plan already amounts to two-thirds of your gross income, don't waste money by buying insurance yourself.

- Carefully check the conditions under which you can receive benefits. For example, will the policy cover you for as long as you are unable to perform your job, a similar job or any job? Also check the policy's definition of *disabled.*
- Read all the small print and ask the insurance agent any information you don't understand. But don't let overanalysis prevent you from purchasing a policy, since it is essential to protect your family's financial independence.

Life Insurance

There are two types of life insurance. Term life insurance gives you coverage for a set term or period of time. If you die during the term, the insurance company pays the value of the policy to the beneficiary. If you live past the end of the term, the coverage ends (unless, of course, you renew it).

Whole life insurance (or permanent life insurance) is for life: once you die, the insurance company pays the value of the policy to the beneficiary.

So far, so good. But which type should you pick? Well, before I answer that question, let me remind you that the only use for insurance is to protect your family's standard of living. Consider this: let's say you plan to follow the advice in this book and expect to have enough savings in 20 years on which to retire. How much life insurance coverage do you think you'll need after 20 years? Zero, that's how much. You see, if you didn't die until you were in retirement—and hopefully you will be well into it before that happens—your spouse would probably have more than enough savings to live on. So why would you need coverage? And while you're at it, consider that at some point you may no longer have to support an entire family. If your kids moved out in ten years, why would you need as much coverage then as you do now?

You can probably see where I'm headed: if you expect that after a certain period of time you won't need the insurance anymore, then term life insurance is the right option. It is also the cheaper option, by far. You see, with whole life insurance, the insurance company has to estimate how long you'll live, based on "mortality tables." It'll work out the probability that you'll die at 60, at 70 and so on. Of course, the longer you live, the longer the company will have your money invested for its own benefit. Trouble is, the company knows that at some point, like it or not, it will have to pay out. With a term policy, on the other hand, the company can essentially gamble that you'll live past the expiration date of the policy. And if you're healthy and you don't wash windows on the CN Tower for a living, then the company can estimate with greater certainty whether you will make it past the end of the term and whether it will have to pay out on your policy. It is because of this greater certainty associated with a term life policy that the company is willing to charge you less.

When it comes to life insurance, you want coverage only for as long as you will need it. If 20 years is the cut-off, then 20 years of insurance will do. Your cut-off might be 25 years, 15 years, 30 years. But whatever your cut-off, that's the term to get.

Of course, your plans for financial independence may change over the years. You might realize at a certain point that it will take you a few extra years to complete the nest egg. To guard against this possibility, make sure you can renew the policy once it lapses. And do make sure that you can renew without having to take a further medical exam. (You don't want an illness down the road to send your premiums sky-high.) Another consideration is whether you can convert your term insurance to whole life insurance without a medical exam. This benefit is especially useful if you suddenly take on a riskier occupation or if your health deteriorates.

While I recommend that you take term insurance, there is one attractive alternative under the whole life umbrella: universal life insurance. This type of insurance is unique in that it allows you to make investment decisions; you can decide where part of your premiums should be invested. And why should you want to do this? Well, the better the return on your premiums, the higher the value of your policy. Some universal policies will even allow you to pay for part of your premiums using these returns. This benefit can be substantial because you end up paying part of your premiums in after-tax dollars, since the investment part of your policy is tax sheltered. (Choose this type of insurance only if you know enough about investments. Otherwise, you'll be better off paying lower premiums under a term life policy and investing the savings through your RRSP.)

But should you dismiss basic whole life insurance altogether? That depends. Whole life insurance can be useful for emergencies (you can use the policy's cash value for a loan). It might also be the right choice for people who are poor savers. You see, when you finish paying your premiums the policy will have the face value for which you originally bought it—as if it were a financial instrument you could sell. So, if you're a poor saver and you opt for term life insurance, you might squander the savings you will have made by taking term instead of whole life insurance, rather than investing them wisely. In that case, you're much better off letting the insurance company handle the money for you under a whole life policy. At least you'll have something to show for it in the end. (Then again, if you follow the advice in this book, you won't squander your money, nor will you need to borrow for emergencies against your policy.)

Let's look at an example to examine the difference between term life and whole life insurance. Let's say that you're 35 years old and that according to the insurance company's mortality tables you're expected to live until the age of 73. Moreover, you've figured out that you need $100,000 of coverage (we'll analyze your insurance needs below).

So, you're faced with two choices. Your first option is to purchase whole life insurance. For your indefinite coverage of $100,000 you will pay $100 per month for 15 years. In other words, in 15 years you will have no more premiums to pay but you will continue to have full coverage. Your second option is to purchase term life insurance. You decide on a five-year renewable term policy. For this coverage, you will have to pay an average of $20 per month for the first five years. If you renew, your premium will increase to $30 for the next five years and $40 for the five years after that.

Now, let's compare the two options. If you take term insurance, you will save yourself $80 per month in the first five years, $70 in the second five and $60 in the last five. At an annual rate of return of 12 percent per year, these savings will amount to $6,568 for the first five years, $5,747 for the next five and $4,926 for the last five. In other words, if you died on the last day of your policy coverage, in 15 years, your beneficiaries would receive $100,000 and have thousands of dollars in accumulated savings. Of course, neither you nor the insurance company expects you to die at that point because you'll be only 50 and you're supposed to live until 73. Does this mean you've wasted your money on term life insurance and that you should have taken whole life insurance instead? Far from it. Remember those savings? Well, in the 23 years after the term expires, and until your expected passing, these savings, invested at 12 percent per year, will amount to $480,454! (Obviously, if you still had dependants, you probably would continue your term insurance coverage until they left home. But although the premiums would eat into your savings, you'd still be much better off than if your beneficiaries ultimately received only $100,000.)

Now that you have a good idea of the type of insurance you should purchase, you need to figure out how much coverage you should buy. Of course, you might already have some coverage through your employer, though in all likelihood that coverage won't be nearly enough. For instance, your beneficiaries might receive a lump sum such as one year's salary; although it sounds like a lot, that money will in no way protect your dependants in the future. Consider that if you earn $40,000, and have 25 more years of employment, your total gross income in that time will be $1,000,000! And even if your calculations were conservative, to receive $40,000 per year, your beneficiaries would need a lump sum of $500,000 invested at 8 percent per year. Clearly, a lump sum of one year's salary is not nearly enough, and depending solely on employers' plans is not wise.

Now, then, it's time you did an Insurance Needs Analysis. More specifically, you should do a needs analysis for your spouse, who would be left behind if you died. Look at the following worksheet and fill in the appropriate figures.

Present annual income (both spouses)   _____

Multiply above figure by 65%
   (what your spouse would need if
   you were to die)   _____

Subtract government benefits
   (estimate $0 to $9,000 per year)   _____

Subtract your spouse's income
   (on the assumption your spouse would
   continue working after your death)   _____

ADDITIONAL ANNUAL INCOME
   REQUIRED (if negative, your spouse
   wouldn't need any additional income)   _____

Divide above figure by rate of return on
   investment (e.g., 9% or 10%) to obtain
   amount of capital your spouse would
   require to live on   _____

Add short-term expenses
   (funeral, taxes, short-term loans)   _____

TOTAL INSURANCE COVERAGE
   REQUIRED   _____

Subtract current savings and life insurance   _____

NEW LIFE INSURANCE YOU REQUIRE   _____

You should follow the same procedure to figure out what coverage your spouse requires to protect you. Note, however, that these needs analyses are intended to give you only a general idea of how much coverage you will require. Your actual needs may be a little different. Check with an insurance agent or a chartered financial planner for an accurate assessment. Most insurance agents will do a needs analysis for free. But do keep in mind that since agents work on commission, they hope that you will purchase your insurance through them.

Mortgage Life Insurance

Perhaps your life insurance will indeed cover all of your family's needs if you die. Or perhaps it will not. Imagine if the expenses turned out to be so great that your family couldn't make the mortgage payments and had no choice but to sell the house. Hardly the sort of scenario you'd want for your family, I'm sure. But there is one solution: mortgage life insurance.

With this type of insurance, as the name implies, the insurer will pay off the principal balance of your mortgage in one shot if you die. This benefit can be substantial for your family. Recall that over the life of a 25-year mortgage, you would have to pay about one and a half times the initial purchase price of the house in interest alone. The house will have cost you two and a half times its value! As such, while your mortgage insurance policy will pay off your principal balance owing, the policy is worth much more to you. Imagine, for instance, that you suddenly died the day after you bought the house. In that case, the insurer would pay off the house immediately and you would have saved your family 25 years of interest payments. One and a half times the value of the house in interest payments! So, if your regular life insurance won't pay out enough for your family either to cover the mortgage or to have the capital they will require, then I strongly recommend you take out mortgage life insurance. (Incidentally, it's available through your bank.)

Let me give an example of how indispensable mortgage life insurance can be. Two of my clients at the bank, a couple, had just sold their house and were buying a condominium. The mortgage on the house was jointly life insured, meaning that if either spouse died, the insurer would pay off the mortgage. But now they wanted to transfer the coverage to the condominium. Trouble was, the husband had developed heart disease, and the couple were concerned that his condition would bar them from getting mortgage life insurance on the new property. Fortunately, the insurance company did allow them to "port," or transfer, their insurance policy from an old mortgage to a new one—and for the same premiums, too. And it turned out that the husband's medical condition was not an obstacle. Sadly, about two months after the couple had moved into their condo, the husband died. The insurance company paid off the mortgage. Transferring the insurance to the new mortgage had saved the wife; without that mortgage insurance, she would have been unable to keep the condominium.

When you are considering buying mortgage life insurance, keep in mind that the older you are at the time you take out the policy, the bigger the premiums will be, since you'll be that much closer to your final days. As well, remember that over the life of your mortgage the amount of principal you owe will decrease. If you find that the principal is substantially lower than when you first got your mortgage but your monthly insurance premiums have not changed, write to your insurance company and request a reduction in your premiums.

The moral of the story is, make insurance an integral part of your financial plans. It might not be as exciting or sexy as investing in the market, but if you dismiss the need for insurance, you could lead your family to financial ruin. You want to protect yourself and your family from the unexpected, and you want the security. Disability insurance will protect your hard-earned savings from being eaten away. Life insurance, more selfless in purpose, will protect your family from hardship. Mortgage life insurance will keep the roof over their heads.

Before I leave the subject of insurance, here are a few pointers:

- In the case of life and disability insurance, particularly, the cheapest form is often group insurance through your employer or through an organization, such as your university's Alma Mater society or an automobile association. All of these sources can offer competitive rates.
- If you buy term life insurance (which is usually the cheapest) make sure it is renewable for as long as you anticipate you'll need it. Make sure, as well, that it is convertible to whole life insurance if you anticipate that you may later want permanent coverage.
- Purchasing insurance now is always cheaper than purchasing it later. The older you are, the more expensive it gets. And if you wait until the day you need it most—the day you have an illness, for instance—you might not even qualify at all.
- While there are far too many insurance companies in Canada for me to compare rates, I recommend that you consult with an insurance broker who will be able to break it all down for you. (This service might cost you a small fee.) If you're in the market for life insurance, specifically, one alternative is to contact the Canadian Life and Health Insurance Association at (800) 268-8099. The association will send you a free brochure called "A Guide to Buying Life Insurance."
- Don't overinsure. If you have a million dollars in savings and your family requires $40,000 a year to live on, you might not need insurance at all.

EMERGENCY FUNDS
FOR THAT RAINY DAY

Let's say the roof of your house suddenly developed a leak, and you had to have it repaired immediately. What would you do? Cash in your RRSP? You could, of course. But I don't recommend that strategy. For one thing, if you withdrew money from your RRSP, you would have to pay income tax on it. You'd probably also have to pay a withdrawal fee, maybe even a penalty. More important, however, you would lose the tax-sheltered compounding benefits of the RRSP. In other words, you would lose a lot!

I'll say this only once: don't depend on your retirement savings for emergencies. Instead, set up a fund for emergency expenses—now! If you dip into your savings you will ruin the effects of compounding your earnings and you will lengthen—possibly by many years—the amount of time it will take you to achieve your financial independence. I know it sounds harsh, but you have to make sure you can afford not only the good things life has to offer, but also the accidents and emergencies it sometimes brings along. One of my clients at the bank once came in asking for a loan because he needed to fly to India to visit an ailing relative. This would have been a very high risk loan: he had no security, no guarantees, nothing. So, I had to turn him away. What could I do? The lesson is, don't expect your bank to bail you out in an emergency. Start an emergency fund instead.

As a rule, your emergency fund should amount to a minimum of three months of your basic expenses. Take a look at the budget you made on page 27–28, specifically the essential expenses. Now, add up these essential expenses and multiply by three. That amount is how much you should keep in your emergency account at all times. In other words, plan for the worst: plan for the possibility that your income could suddenly stop for three months and you would still have to pay essential bills. Of course, fixing a leak in a roof should cost you a good deal less. But never plan for the minimum. Play it safe.

Where you put this money is also important. The best option is a money market fund, which consists of very low-risk investments such as government treasury bills, banker's acceptances and commercial paper. Most money market funds have a fixed unit value; the only variable is the interest that the fund earns on its investments. I recommend setting up a no-load fund with a mutual fund company or with your bank, trust company or credit union. With a money market fund, you earn high daily interest at very low risk, and your money is usually accessible within 24 hours at no charge.

Obviously, this fund will take time to build up. So, make it a high priority. Once you've made your RRSP contributions and paid your insurance premiums, make a contribution to your emergency fund. One suggestion is to earmark for your fund any tax refund you might receive this year from the government. Put that refund directly into your money market account to build the fund up quickly. The sources of money for your emergency fund are endless. Here's a handful:

- Hold a garage or jumble sale.
- Sell household items you don't need anymore.
- Put any bonuses, extra cheques or small windfalls directly into the account.
- If you already have very liquid investments, such as CSBs or certificates of deposits, include these in your emergency fund to build it up, but make sure you earmark them as such.

Trust me. The efforts you expend in building your fund will be worth it. You will be protected against emergencies, without having to sacrifice your future financial independence.

But beware! This fund is not for "discretionary" or non-essential items. I know that the temptation to spend can be powerful. (You'll recall that as a kid, I couldn't keep money in my bank account.) The latest model car, a new compact-disk player, an exotic vacation, a new spring wardrobe—there are so many ways to spend your money! But while you may deserve all of these niceties, you should never spend either your savings or your emergency fund on non-essentials. You must learn to differentiate between what is an emergency and what isn't. And you must learn to budget for discretionary items and purchase them only once you have saved up the required cash. If the funds for that luxury, non-essential item are not available right now, postpone the purchase—for the sake of future wealth. The dollar you spend today could be worth much more to you in terms of your future comfort. Consider your parents or grandparents, who grew up during the Great Depression and the Second World War. In all likelihood, they had to live frugally during those difficult times. Yet, they might also have accumulated tremendous wealth, which later afforded them a relaxed lifestyle. Some of them may even have passed on untold wealth to later generations. Just think if they'd known some of the wealth-building techniques you've learned in this book: they'd have accumulated even greater wealth.

There are definite benefits to learning how to save, how to be frugal and how to prepare for emergencies. Look at one of the most economically successful cultures today, the Japanese. Japan has one of the highest savings rates in the world, and because of it the Japanese today enjoy tremendous wealth. Japanese banks and corporations, meanwhile, are among the largest and strongest in the world. Granted, this success is the result of extremely hard work and efficient organizational structure, but it is also due to the long-term view that the Japanese take on life. This attitude stands in stark contrast to the short-term "here today, gone tomorrow" attitude that most westerners have. Take the long-term view—for the sake of your future wealth!

YOUR WILL AND YOUR ESTATE

You may not be around forever, but hopefully the memory of you will be! Just make sure that, when you do depart, your financial affairs are in order and that your dependants and beneficiaries receive what you intended for them.

Making a will and planning for the eventual transfer of your estate may not be the most pleasant and interesting of topics, but they make up one of the golden rules of effective financial planning. Think about it. By planning for that fateful day, you are ensuring that Revenue Canada takes as little of your wealth as possible, that your beneficiaries inherit what they should and that no one ends up in court, tearing your wealth to shreds. You're providing protection, not for yourself, but for your family.

I can't begin to count the cases I've encountered in which someone had died "intestate"—without a will. Believe me, this situation is seldom pleasant. You see, if you die without a will, someone has to figure out who should receive your assets, who should assume your debts and what financial shape you're in. Often, the only way to proceed is to have a court, under provincial law, appoint an administrator who will oversee the distribution of your estate, of what you've left behind. Invariably, the process becomes very lengthy—and very costly.

I've seen it often. And when it happens, all you can do is feel sorry for the dependants and beneficiaries. So why would you allow it to happen? Why would you want the courts or the government to decide what happens to your money when you could decide so easily and cheaply by yourself? Make a will!

There are a few ways to make a will, some more expensive than others. The cheapest and easiest way is to visit your local bookstore or stationery store and purchase a book that contains standard wills with blank spaces for you to fill in. Read the instructions, fill in the blanks, and you've got yourself a will. If your will promises to be too complicated for you to handle on your own, consider visiting a trust company, which can offer you advice. Or there's the obvious solution: consult with a lawyer or notary public. If your will is relatively simple, this option should cost you only $100 to $250.

Of course, as time passes and your lifestyle changes, your will may no longer reflect your wishes. For one thing, you'll have more money to leave behind. Then there are details such as marriages, divorces, births and deaths. Indeed, you'll probably encounter enough events in your life that at some point you'll have to make modifications to your will. Then you'll need a "codicil," which is an addendum to a will. In some cases, you might need to draw up a new will.

And what happens once you do pass on? Is it only a matter of digging up your will, sitting the family around the dinner table and distributing your assets? That depends. For instance, say you happen to have entrusted a bank with some of your investments. Obviously, the bank will need a copy of your will before it can transfer the investments to your beneficiaries. Sometimes, however, the investments may be so large that the bank will want incontrovertible proof that this is indeed your final will and testament—and not merely the good word of your beneficiaries. In that case, the bank may request that your will be subject to "probate." When your will is probated, a court has to confirm that the will you drafted is indeed your final will and testament. And you guessed it: this process costs money. Recently, some provinces have increased probate fees. Ontario, for instance, now charges a fee equivalent to 1.5 percent of the assets of an estate. In other words, if you leave behind an estate worth $1,000,000, the courts will take $15,000 of it.

Is there anything you can do to reduce this cost? Yes. What you need to do is reduce the size of your estate that will be subject to probate by making as many of your assets as possible *joint* assets. This way, when you pass on, the co-owner will become the sole owner. And if an asset has two surviving co-owners, they will assume full title of the asset between them—without the intervention of a court.

Obviously, your objective should be to minimize the hassles of distributing your estate, and reducing the number of assets subject to probate is one way. Another way is to choose an executor, who, upon your death, oversees the distribution of your assets.

No doubt, this is a very important appointment, filled with great responsibility. So you have to make sure you pick someone you can trust. It can be an individual or a company, such as a trust company. But bear in mind that being an executor can be very time consuming. Problems can easily arise. As such, having an executor can carry a price tag. In fact, according to provincial laws, an executor is allowed to charge a fee of between 3 and 5 percent of the value of your estate. Even your cousin Bertha can charge the fee, in which case you might be better off appointing a professional. Indeed, you might want an expert if your estate is complicated. At the very least, appoint co-executors, one professional and one family member.

You should know about the tax implications of leaving your estate behind. Canada does not have death taxes as some other countries do. (Note that if you have a winter retirement home in the United States, the state might charge death taxes on the property.) But even without death taxes, when you do pass on, your estate will almost certainly have to pay some taxes. First, there's the question of capital gains. When you die, you are deemed to have disposed of certain assets. If these assets appreciated in value since the time you bought them, whoever handles your estate will have to account for these gains on your final tax return. (In fact, it's possible to have to file up to four separate tax returns for a deceased person.)

Next, there's the question of your RRSPs. You'll recall that when you withdraw money from your RRSPs, you have to pay income tax at your present rate on whatever you take out. The problem is that when you die, you are deemed to have withdrawn all of your funds, and this "withdrawal" can cost a fair bit in taxes. There is one way to ensure your RRSPs aren't subject to taxes upon your death, and that's to arrange for a "roll-over" of your RRSPs. This is just another way of saying that your RRSPs automatically transfer to your spouse tax free or to your children either if they are under the age of 19 or if they are under 25, dependent and attending an educational institution. Make sure you list the names of your beneficiaries on your RRSPs because, depending on the size of your investments and the need for certainty, an institution with which you invested might require a probate of your will.

As for life insurance policies, most are tax exempt, meaning that your beneficiaries get to keep it all. But do make sure that your present insurance policy is tax exempt, so that it won't reduce the size of your estate and create an unwanted tax burden.

Finally, keep in mind that one of the few remaining tax-exempt investments is your principal residence. In death, as in life, when you dispose of your residence, you don't have to pay taxes on any capital gains. If anything, that's one incentive to own a residence in your lifetime.

Since the ins and outs of estate planning are too complex for this book, you should consult a tax planner or at least read a couple of books on the subject. Nevertheless, if you update your will from time to time, list the names of your beneficiaries on your RRSPs and make investments jointly (with a right of survivorship wherever possible), your estate will suffer the smallest financial drain possible.

CHAPTER 12

From Rags to Riches

I F THERE'S ONE THING I HOPE I'VE MADE CLEAR to you in this book, it's the importance of setting goals for yourself. Setting goals and learning to stick to them. And one way to set goals, as you'll recall, is to have a budget for yourself and your family. You need to determine how you will contain your expenses or increase your earnings, or both, so that your savings will add up to that magic number, 15 percent of your gross income. Once you know how much your savings should be, you can set this figure as your annual objective.

But setting goals will only get you so far. You also need to track your progress; you need to know where you are on your path to achieving financial independence. One effective approach to tracking your progress is to analyze your financial situation on a monthly basis. Every month, without fail, check your running tally—your investments, your spending, everything. Some months, you won't meet your goal, but that's okay. Don't despair or feel intimidated. Your financial plan is a long-term one, and the mere fact that you have a plan will put you light years ahead of someone who doesn't.

In practical terms, what I propose is that you set up a 12-month chart and that at the end of each month (or the start of a new month) you calculate the current value of your investments. But don't stop at your obvious investments, such as your RRSP. Look for your "hidden" savings, as well, items such as your monthly contributions to a pension plan at work or even your contributions to a CSB payroll deduction plan. These items are part of your wealth. Your pension plan will contribute to your retirement one day. And so will your CSB payroll deductions because at the end of each year you can expect to receive a savings bond for the year's deductions.

Monthly tracking is a powerful tool. Not only can it help you ascertain whether you're meeting your goals and what steps you should take to remedy any shortfalls, but it is also effective in helping you beat procrastination or a lack of discipline. It forces you to be organized. And in tracking your progress, you should set up files for the following: investments, taxes, RRSPs, mutual funds, house, automobile, home insurance policies, life and disability insurance (from work and private plans), your investment properties, stocks and bonds, your will (the original of which should be in a safe deposit box), bank statements, loan documents, and files for paid and unpaid bills. You have to track the changes in all of these. For one thing, if you need information about a transaction you did some time ago, you will avoid paying the hefty fee charged by financial institutions to find that information for you. Consider, as well, that Revenue Canada could pick your name at random and decide to audit you.

But not only is monthly tracking useful, it can also be a great confidence booster. It's a great feeling to see your nest egg build up month after month. And, come year end, you will get to see how much better off you are compared to the year before. As you meet your goals each year, you will believe more and more in the possibility of achieving financial freedom. All of a sudden, what was once only a vague ambition will start to seem tangible.

Never forget, however, to set goals that are attainable and reasonable because disappointment can be the worst enemy of financial ambition. Your path to financial independence is a gradual slope, and you must learn not to be disheartened if you don't always move as far as you want to.

Now, let's make use of all your new financial knowledge and take a look at a true-to-life example of how a couple could gain their financial independence. We'll start with some assumptions: one spouse earns $20,000 per year; the other, $40,000 per year. These earnings grow at a rate of 2 percent per year, and both individuals save 15 percent of their gross earnings. They earn a return of 10 percent per annum on their savings. Every year, they each get tax refunds on their RRSP deposits: 30 percent of deposits for the lower-income spouse and 35 percent for the higher-income spouse. They both invest 50 percent of their tax refunds. The couple minimizes tax on non-RRSP investments by choosing vehicles that receive favourable tax treatment from Revenue Canada—that is, vehicles that offer such benefits as capital gains and dividends. (Therefore, we can ignore this tax.) Finally, the couple's budget already includes an allowance for taxes.

Now, let's see how this couple would fare over the next few years.

YEAR 1	Spouse #1		Spouse #2	
Income	$20,000		$40,000	
Savings (15%)	$3,000		$6,000	
Investments				
1/3 non-RRSP	$1,000		$2,000	
2/3 RRSP	$2,000		$4,000	
YEAR-END PORTFOLIO	$3,000	+	$6,000	= $9,000

YEAR 2	*Spouse #1*		*Spouse #2*	
Income (up 2%)	$20,400		$40,800	
Savings (15%)	$3,060		$6,120	
Investments				
1/3 non-RRSP	$1,020		$2,040	
2/3 RRSP	$2,040		$4,080	
NEW SAVINGS	$3,060	+	$6,120	= $9,180

PLUS EARNINGS ON
  TOTAL PORTFOLIO AT END OF YEAR 1
  (10% return on $9,000) $900
PLUS INVESTMENT OF 50%
  OF RRSP TAX REFUND $300 + $700 = $1,000
(half of 30% refund on $2,000 RRSP deposit)
(half of 35% refund on $4,000 RRSP deposit)

YEAR 2 ADDITIONS TO PORTFOLIO	$11,080
PLUS PORTFOLIO AT END OF YEAR 1	$9,000
TOTAL PORTFOLIO AT END OF YEAR 2	$20,080

YEAR 3	*Spouse #1*		*Spouse #2*	
Income (up 2%)	$20,808		$41,616	
Savings (15%)	$3,121		$6,242	
Investments				
1/3 non-RRSP	$1,040		$2,080	
2/3 RRSP	$2,081		$4,162	
NEW SAVINGS	$3,121	+	$6,242	= $9,363

PLUS EARNINGS ON TOTAL PORTFOLIO
  AT END OF YEAR 2 (10% return on $20,080) $2,008
PLUS INVESTMENT OF
  50% OF RRSP TAX REFUND $306 + $714 = $1,020
(half of 30% refund on year 2 RRSP deposit of $2,040)
(half of 35% refund on year 2 RRSP deposit of $4,080)

YEAR 3 ADDITIONS TO PORTFOLIO	$12,391
PLUS PORTFOLIO AT END OF YEAR 2	$20,080
TOTAL PORTFOLIO AT END OF YEAR 3	$32,471

TOTAL PORTFOLIO AT END OF YEAR 5	$61,740
TOTAL PORTFOLIO AT END OF YEAR 10	$169,193
TOTAL PORTFOLIO AT END OF YEAR 15	$309,748
TOTAL PORTFOLIO AT END OF YEAR 20	$647,911

Consider that the couple's savings would be even greater if they made their deposits on a monthly basis rather than on a yearly basis (as I've assumed above). Moreover, earning more than 10 percent or investing more than 50 percent of their tax refunds would make their portfolio that much bigger.

In any event, you can clearly see that with a reasonable family income, and in a relatively short period of time, this couple is able to generate incredible wealth with a simple and straightforward plan. If you consider that the average person will work at least 40 years, a family that can achieve financial freedom in no more than 20 or 25 is well ahead of the game!

Consistently saving 15 percent of your gross income is not that difficult if you set your mind to it. In fact, this plan leaves enough room to use extra savings for your shorter-term goals. Many of us will also have other "forced savings" plans, such as pension plans or stock purchase plans. An average employee pension plan might direct 3 percent of an employee's gross pay to the plan, along with a matching contribution from the employer. Thus, another 6 percent of income will accumulate in savings, without the employee feeling the pinch.

The reason so many people find it difficult to build wealth is that they fail to budget and they're not aware that making lifestyle choices today will bring them wealth tomorrow, when they'll really need it.

Financial independence is yours if you want it. Just stay focused and you will succeed! Good luck!

Doing Your Finances on the Internet

THE INTERNET IS POISED TO BECOME THE MEDIUM of communication and the provider of information—even financial information—of the twenty-first century. In fact, some leading-edge financial services companies have already produced excellent web sites. (In the case of a bank, think of its web site as an information counter that you can visit by computer to get brochures and other materials.)

There are now thousands of web sites (or information counters) at which you can get information to help you in your financial planning. The key is to find the web sites that are useful to you. This task is probably easier for Canadians than for Americans because many of our financial institutions are well known to us and most of them have web sites. Of course, to find these sites you will need to have knowledge of the Net or you'll have to find someone who does.

To get you started in finding useful financial planning information on the World Wide Web (WWW), I have compiled a small directory that lists two useful web sites for each of the following six major areas of financial planning: (1) budgeting,

(2) RRSPs, (3) diversifying your investments, (4) estate planning, (5) tax information and (6) credit information and mortgage/loan calculators.

Please note that since new web sites pop up on a daily basis, I can't possibly give you an exhaustive list of the best sites. I'll have to leave that search up to you web surfers.

BUDGETING

The web site of the Toronto Dominion (TD) Bank can be reached at

http://www.tdbank.ca/tdbank/pers/index.html

This site provides a wealth of financial information, including a good budget worksheet. If you fill in all your sources of monthly income and monthly expenses on the on-line budget calculator, choose the Calculate function and wait, the program will tell you if you have a monthly surplus or deficit. You can also calculate how long it will take you to reach your savings target. An added benefit of this site is that it explains how to download the program into your own computer for future use.

The second site is a web page on the web site, which you can reach at

http://www.altamira.com

This site has a household cash management calculator. With it, you can analyze your situation and see what changes may be necessary to keep your family's budget in line.

RRSPs

You can reach the Money Site, a service of the *Financial Post*, which contains plenty of information on taxes, real estate, finances and retirement, at

http://www.canoe.ca/money/home.html

This site includes detailed information on CPP/OAS, RRSPs, Deferred Profit Sharing Plans and Registered Pension Plans. It is also a great educational tool to help you prepare for your retirement. A visit to the site is also an eye-opener in that you get to see how little the government can currently afford to pay in CPP and OAS and how in the future these amounts may be even lower.

The second site is part of the Bank of Montreal web site. You can reach it at

http://www.bmo.ca/RRSP/

This site includes a useful table for determining how much money you will need for your retirement. If you plug in your current income, all your sources of retirement income and the number of years before you want to retire, the program will do the calculations for you, assuming certain interest rates and earning rates.

DIVERSIFYING YOUR INVESTMENTS

Canada Trust has its Interactive Investment Planner at its web site at

http://www.Canadatrust.com (go to the Mutual Funds page and select Investment Profile)

This planner checks your investment profile by asking you such questions as, How familiar are you with investing? How long do you plan to invest the money for? What is your age? What is your household income? Based on your answers, the program suggests a suitably diversified portfolio. Once you know what your suitable portfolio is, you can even determine what proportions of specific (Canada Trust) mutual funds will work for you.

The second site comes from the Fund Library. You can reach it at

http://www.fundlib.com/

This web site includes substantial information on many topics related to mutual funds. The investor profile questionnaire asks about your risk tolerance, investment time horizon and style of investment (how aggressive or conservative you are). Based on your answers, the program will give you a score and suggest the most suitable types of investments.

ESTATE PLANNING

Once again, the TD has an interesting web page. This one outlines many areas of estate planning. You'll find this site at
   http://www.tdbank.ca/tdbank/lifepl/estate
Topics at this site include trusts, power of attorney, choosing an executor and more. Use it to obtain a basic understanding of what is involved in setting up an estate plan for your family.

The second site in this category comes from the accounting firm of Wear & Company. It's located at
   http://www.wearca.com
Besides other useful information, the site provides a list of 22 of the "Best Estate Planning Tips." Follow these tips and you will save time and money when you consult a lawyer!

TAX INFORMATION

You can't go wrong tapping the Revenue Canada site for information on taxes. It is located at
   http://www.revcan.ca
This is a comprehensive site. Looking through the list of contents on the menu, you will see information about Revenue Canada, FAQs (frequently asked questions), Revenue Canada publications, guides and forms, news releases and speech archives, as well as links to other resources, such as the Department of Finance.

For a good second site, look up the accounting firm KPMG at

http://www.kpmg.ca/taxinfo.html

The areas of taxation this site covers include a federal budget analysis, tax breaks, cross-border tax breaks and KPMG's Canadian Tax and Financial Fitness Survey. The site also provides archives on tax information going back to the previous year and even contains numerous informative articles.

CREDIT INFORMATION AND MORTGAGE/LOAN CALCULATORS

The Canadian Imperial Bank of Commerce (CIBC) has a site that helps you calculate mortgage payments. You can reach the CIBC's site at

http://www.cibc.com

This site gives you all the details you need to calculate what you can afford in monthly payments on a mortgage. It also serves as a good primer on mortgages and on the costs involved in purchasing a home.

A second useful resource is the Scotiabank site, which you can find at

http://www.scotiabank.ca.crmort.htm

This site has various calculators that enable you to calculate not only mortgage payments but also savings and investment values. This comprehensive site is also a superb educational tool on many financial planning topics.

OTHER USEFUL FINANCIAL SITES

Maritime Life's needs analyses for life insurance and retirement can be found at

http://www.isisnet.com/mlac/mlac.htm

The Investment Funds Institute of Canada, which provides detailed information on mutual funds and links to mutual fund companies, can be reached at

http://www.mutfunds.com/ific/home.html

All the large banks provide useful, informative sites, which continue to evolve; these sites are well worth a visit.

Royal Bank: http://www.royalbank.com

Bank of Montreal: http://www.bmo.com

Canadian Imperial Bank of Commerce:
   http://www.cibc.com

Scotiabank: http://www.scotiabank.com

Toronto Dominion: http://www.tdbank.ca

Canada Trust: http://www.Canadatrust.com

All these web sites provide some interactive assistance in determining your financial goals and objectives. The Net is such a powerful tool that you can resolve the majority of your financial planning problems by using it, and the cost to you is minimal. However, if you still need the assistance of a financial adviser to ensure your strategy is implemented correctly, don't be afraid to seek out expert advice!

Who Are You Going to Call?

MAKE SURE THE EXPERT YOU CONSULT HAS THE knowledge you need. Here's what you can expect from various experts:

	STRENGTHS	WEAKNESSES	FEES
Accountants	Provide tax advice on setting up a small business and on personal taxes	Provide no specific investment advice	Possible free initial consultation; otherwise, charge by the hour
Bankers	Provide many essential products, including RRSPs and RRIFs	Usually don't provide specific investment advice	Low fees for specific transactions; usually charge per product or service provided

	STRENGTHS	WEAKNESSES	FEES
Financial planners and advisers	Provide you with a road map; very knowledgeable if CFP*, Certified Life Underwriter (CLU) or C.H.F.C.	If working on commission, may push in-house insurance and mutual fund products that are not necessarily the best available	Mixture of salary and commission
Lawyers	Can assist with estate planning	Don't usually give specific investment advice	Flat or variable fees
Realtors	Have excellent knowledge of real estate market	Are not usually tax experts or financial experts	Commission
Stockbrokers	Offer best selection of investments	Might be more interested in the sale than the long-term prospects of the sale	Commission on stock, bond or security transaction

*NOTE ABOUT FINANCIAL ADVISERS: you are best to start off with a certified/chartered financial planner (CFP) or a registered financial planner (RFP), who can then refer you to the appropriate adviser if your situation requires an expert in one of the other fields. A CFP has taken two or three years of courses specifically related to financial planning, including taxes, economics, financial management, Canadian law, life insurance, business structures and estate planning.

List of Mutual Fund "Families"

THIS IS A LIST OF MAJOR MUTUAL FUND COMPANIES that offer a range of funds. The list is not exhaustive, but it will give you more than an adequate selection from which to choose your portfolio. It is recommended that you keep your mutual funds within a maximum of three families, simply for ease of record keeping.

NAME	PHONE NUMBER
AGF/20/20	1-800-520-0620
ADMAX	1-800-667-2369
AIC	1-800-263-2144
All Canadian	1-905-648-2025
Altamira	1-800-263-2824
Atlas	1-800-463-2857
BPI	1-800-263-2427
Bullock	1-800-263-1851
C.I.	1-800-563-5181
CIBC	contact local branch
Cambridge	1-800-663-1003

Canada Life	1-800-387-4447
Cundill Security	1-800-663-0156
Dynamic	1-800-268-8186
Elliot & Page	1-800-363-6647
Empire	1-613-548-1881
Ethical Funds	1-800-267-5019
Equital Life	1-800-265-8878
Everest Funds	contact Canada Trust
First Canadian	contact Bank of Montreal
Global Strategy	1-800-387-1229
Green Line Funds	contact Toronto Dominion Bank
GT Global	1-800-588-4880
Guardian	1-800-668-7327
Hong Kong Bank	1-800-830-8888
Imperial	1-416-324-1617
Industrial Group	1-800-387-0780
Investors Group	1-800-387-0780
Laurentian	contact Laurentian Bank
London Life	1-519-432-5281
ManuLife	1-800-265-7401
Marathon	1-416-869-3707
Montreal Trust	contact local branch
Multiple Opportunities	1-800-663-6370
National Trust	1-800-563-4683
PH & N (Phillips, Hager and North)	1-604-691-6781
Prudential	1-416-296-3395
Royfunds	contact Royal Bank
Royal Trust	contact Royal Bank
Saxon	1-416-979-1818
Scotia Excelsior	contact Scotiabank
Spectrum	1-800-263-1851
Standard Life	1-800-665-6237
Talvest	1-800-268-0081
Templeton	1-800-387-0830
Trimark	1-800-387-9841
United	1-800-263-1867

Financial Formulas

FOR YOU MATHEMATICAL TYPES, ALL THE FORMULAS you could ever need to do any financial calculations are listed below. In all of these,

n = number of periods
r = earnings rate
i = rate of inflation

Use the following formula to calculate the **future value of a present sum of money** (for example, if you want to know what $1,000 will be worth in 20 years assuming a 12 percent rate of return).

Future value = Present value $(1 + r)^n$
In our example,
Future value = $(1 + .12)^{20}$

Use the following formula to calculate the **future value of an annuity** (with payments beginning at the end of Period 1).

Future value = Payment $[(1 + r)^n - 1] \div r$

Use the following formula to calculate the **present value of an annuity**.

Present value = Payment $[1 - (1 + r)^{-n}] \div r$

Use the following formula to calculate the **value of a periodic investment that increases over time** (for instance, if you invest a fixed percentage of your salary and your salary happens to increase at a fixed rate, such as i).

Future value = Payment $(1 + i)^{n-1} \dfrac{[1 - [(1 + r) \div (1 + i)^n]]}{1 - [(1 + r) \div (1 + i)]}$

MORTGAGE SCHEDULE

To calculate your monthly payment on a mortgage of a certain amount, use the table opposite to find the amount of your regular payment on $1,000 worth of mortgage for various interest rates and amortization periods. (For instance, the monthly payment on a $130,000 mortgage amortized over 20 years at 9 percent interest would be 130 times 8.89, which equals approximately $1,155 per month. You can find the value per thousand dollars of mortgage ($8.89) by following the row across from 9 percent to where it intersects the column for 20 years.

Interest Rate	Amortization Period (Years)				
	5	10	15	20	25
5.00	18.85	10.59	7.89	6.58	5.82
5.25	18.97	10.71	8.01	6.71	5.96
5.50	19.08	10.83	8.14	6.85	6.11
5.75	19.19	10.95	8.27	6.99	6.26
6.00	19.30	11.07	8.40	7.13	6.40
6.25	19.42	11.19	8.54	7.27	6.55
6.5	19.53	11.32	8.67	7.41	6.70
6.75	19.64	11.44	8.80	7.55	6.86
7.0	19.76	11.56	8.94	7.70	7.01
7.25	19.87	11.69	9.07	7.84	7.16
7.5	19.99	11.82	9.21	7.99	7.32
7.75	20.20	11.94	9.35	8.14	7.48
8.00	20.22	12.07	9.49	8.29	7.64
8.25	20.33	12.20	9.63	8.44	7.80
8.5	20.45	12.32	9.76	8.59	7.96
8.75	20.57	12.45	9.90	8.74	8.12
9.00	20.68	10.05	10.05	8.89	8.28
9.25	20.80	12.71	10.19	9.05	8.44
9.50	20.92	12.84	10.33	9.20	8.61
9.75	21.04	12.97	10.48	9.36	8.78
10.00	21.15	13.10	10.62	8.52	8.94
10.25	21.27	13.24	10.77	9.68	9.11
10.50	21.39	13.37	10.92	9.83	9.28
10.75	21.51	13.50	11.06	10.00	9.45
11.00	21.63	13.64	11.21	10.16	9.63
11.25	21.74	13.77	11.36	10.32	9.80
11.50	21.86	13.91	11.51	10.48	9.97
11.75	21.98	14.05	11.66	10.65	10.14
12.00	22.10	14.18	11.82	10.81	10.32
13.00	22.59	14.74	12.44	11.48	11.03
14.00	23.07	15.30	13.06	12.16	11.74

Rule of 72 table									
Rate of Return (%)									
4	5	6	7	8	9	10	11	12	13
Years Required to Double Initial Investments									
18.0	14.4	12.0	10.3	9.0	8.0	7.2	6.5	6.0	5.5

RETIREMENT INCOME WORKSHEET
(in current dollars)

65% x (couple's combined gross income)   _____

Subtract any estimated sources of retirement
income, such as employer's pension plans,
rental income, disability income, part-time
business income, etc.   _____

                                     _____

                                     _____

                                          _____

Amount of annual income to be provided
by your savings/accumulated wealth   _____

Divide this amount by what you expect to
earn per year on this accumulated wealth at
retirement (e.g., 7%, 8%, 9%, 10%)   _____

This is the amount of capital you require to produce your retirement
income (in today's dollars)

Now use Tables 8 and 9 in Chapter 6 to calculate how long it will take you
to accumulate this capital in future dollars.

INDEX

italic indicates tables; **boldface** indicates appendices

IBP HANDBOOK No. 2

Methods for Estimating the Primary Production of Forests

P. J. NEWBOULD

SECOND PRINTING

INTERNATIONAL BIOLOGICAL PROGRAMME
7 MARYLEBONE ROAD, LONDON NW1

BLACKWELL SCIENTIFIC PUBLICATIONS
OXFORD AND EDINBURGH

© INTERNATIONAL BIOLOGICAL PROGRAMME 1967

SBN 632 04880 8

FIRST PUBLISHED 1967

REPRINTED 1970

Printed and bound in Great Britain by
WILLMER BROTHERS LIMITED
BIRKENHEAD

Contents

Foreword

The Handbook series of IBP has a specific purpose. It is for volumes which are urgently needed by biologists around the world who wish to participate in the programme. Some volumes, such as No. 1 *Guide to the Human Adaptability Proposals*, deal with a whole section of IBP; others, such as this and a number of others in active preparation (see back cover), deal with methods of research in a comparatively narrow branch of the programme. Some of these handbooks, like this one, are brief, written by one scientist, who has been selected by the international section concerned and has consulted many specialists in the process of drafting. Other volumes will be larger, with chapters written by a number of different specialists under the guidance of a general editor.

It must be emphasized that the methods described in this and other handbooks are *recommended* for the purpose of IBP, not *agreed*. To obtain universal agreement on any particular method, if it could be achieved at all, would take a long time. Moreover, it might retard rather than advance biology, because the methodology in a great many subjects within IBP is evolving rapidly. The methods described in these handbooks are recommended to scientists who themselves do not think they have better methods. They provide some guarantee that the results obtained by their use all over the world will be comparable.

A further point of importance is that all IBP handbooks are to some extent provisional. Those concerned with methodology in particular may need alteration as a result of practical experience and distribution to numerous specialists. Indeed it is hoped that revised and more definitive editions of these books will be called for before the conclusion of IBP in 1972.

The author, P.J. Newbould, has just been elected to the Chair of Biology in the new University of Coleraine in Northern Ireland. He took his first degree at Oxford, his doctorate in London with W.H. Pearsall. For a number of years past, as lecturer in botany at University College, London, he has been in charge of the Conservation Course. This is organized in consultation with the Nature Conservancy of the United Kingdom, in order to train postgraduate students in the sciences which underlie conservation and the rational use of biological resources. Since IBP commenced, Professor Newbould has taken a prominent part in Section PT, both nationally within the UK, and internationally.

E. B. WORTHINGTON
IBP Central Office
7 Marylebone Road
London, N.W.1

August 1967

Preface

This methodological outline for estimating the primary production of forests and woodlands as part of IBP is based on preliminary documents circulated to more than seventy scientists directly concerned with such studies and incorporates many of their comments. The current version undoubtedly could be improved further but revision can be a never ending process. Rather than trying to produce a polished and generally acceptable version which might not have been ready before the end of IBP it was decided to publish at this stage and to issue corrections and revisions later. Suggestions for these should be sent to the author at the address below.

The New University of Ulster,　　　　　　　　　　　　　　　　*P. J. Newbould.*
Coleraine, Co. Londonderry,
N. Ireland.

I have taken the opportunity in this reprint to correct a few minor errors, and to introduce a few more references.

P.J.N.

1

Objectives

The outline of the PT programme in IBP News 9 states: 'General investigations of primary production should be made at a global network of sites'. This Handbook suggests some of the methods that can be used in forests and woodlands to fulfil this aim. Forests and woodlands are here taken as synonymous and the term woodland is generally used. Woodlands include all vegetation in which trees (more than 5 m tall) play a predominant part. These methods would also be applicable to the tree component of vegetation in which the trees have a minor role.

The actual investigations to be carried out within this theme will vary from place to place; precise objectives and the availability of sites, funds and manpower will determine which methods are to be used in any particular investigation. Objectives may include the provision of primary production estimates as a basis for complete ecosystem studies, comparisons (within woodlands) between species, geographical regions, management techniques and comparisons between woodlands and other types of vegetation or systems of agriculture. In general it is difficult to set up meaningful comparisons without proper experimental design. It is essential in these comparisons to reduce the number of independent variables to the absolute minimum, for example by comparing one species over a range of climate but with similar management regimes and soil types.

Woodland production has been measured by foresters for many years, and their current methods are outlined in several textbooks of forest mensuration (Prodan 1965, 1968, Husch 1963, Pardé 1961, Ferat 1958, Spurr 1952). In general they concentrate upon the economic product, stem wood. Studies of biological production are concerned with the whole dry matter production of the trees, shrubs and ground vegetation. The total dry matter production in any ecosystem is a measure of its efficiency of energy fixation. It also represents the energy input to the system; this energy will subsequently be dissipated by the respiration of all the organisms in the ecosystem, the plants themselves, the consumers including carnivores and the decomposers.

This Handbook does not aim to describe the standard mensuration techniques used by foresters; local advice and tables describing the growth of the main tree species will normally be available in each country (e.g. Bradley, Christie & Johnston 1966). What is required is to convert the foresters' production from timber volume to dry weight and to add to it estimates of the production located in the non-useful parts of the tree and in other parts of the ecosystem. The methods for doing this are indicated in this Handbook.

Complete standardization of methods is undesirable and impracticable but wide adoption of certain general principles will help to make the results of different investigations comparable. This Handbook is intended only as a guide from which appropriate methods can be selected and is especially for the use of institutions where productivity studies are not currently in progress. Reference is made to papers which contain further details of suitable methods.

2

Forest Type and Site Selection

2.1 Forest types

The number of forest types chosen for study in a given geographical area may depend upon the amount of funds and manpower available. It is however hoped that all representative or major types of forest found within the area, either natural or artificial, will be covered as far as possible. At the outset it is important to distinguish between two situations. The annual production of uneven-aged 'climax' woodland, although varying from year to year, probably fluctuates about some comparatively steady mean. Current production of a woodland stand, measured over 3–5 years, provides a value genuinely representative of that site and stand.

By contrast an even-aged woodland shows a regular change in production, which increases to a maximum value and then gradually declines (Ovington 1957). Here the most realistic value for annual production is the mean production over a whole rotation or the whole life-span of the stand. This implies making measurements on an age sequence of even-aged stands.

It is important in each region to compare the best available approximation to natural climax woodland with the main types of plantations. It may also be useful for intercontinental comparisons of production to choose plantations of such widely cultivated genera as *Pinus* (especially *P. radiata*), *Larix*, *Eucalyptus*, etc. It is always important to understand as much as possible of the ecology of the system being studied, especially the seasonal changes in activity.

2.2 Site selection

It may be useful to envisage four sorts of areas as shown in Fig. 1.
1. *Sample area*: initially used only for measurements which will not affect it. Climatic measurements and regular growth recording are carried out here. Ultimately it could be felled as a final sample or preferably conserved inviolate as a reference site (0·1–1 ha).

2. *Buffer area*: an area of at least two tree heights in width, around the sample area; not subjected to any disturbance which could affect the sample area.

3. *Measurement area*: large enough to permit felling of trees, digging of soil pits and root trenches; so far as possible felling should not exceed 5% of the trees to minimize effect on sample and buffer areas (1–10 ha).

4. *Study area*: acts mainly as a large scale buffer zone; may be necessary for the associated study of mammals and birds (10–100 ha).

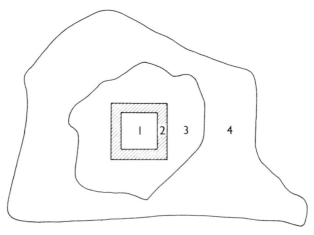

Figure 1. The site: 1, sample area; 2, buffer area; 3, measurement area; 4, study area.

The methods used depend upon the degree of destructive sampling permissible; often one must make non-destructive measurements on a considerable number of trees (perhaps all those in 1) while cutting down a smaller number of trees (from 3) for dry weight determination. Felling should be so organized (possible with reference to the prevailing wind direction) that it does not markedly affect the climate of the sample and buffer areas. The sample area is usually regular in shape, but need not be square. The study and measurement areas need not be regular.

2.21 **The size of the areas** depends upon the sites available, the size of the trees, the structural complexity of the woodland, its general heterogeneity, the accuracy required and the manpower available. No vegetation is homogeneous but the heterogeneity of 1 and 3 should be kept as small as possible while in 4 which may be used for related ecosystem investigations, as for example on vertebrates, more heterogeneity can be accepted. Heterogeneity may involve species composition, age and height structure of the woodland and site conditions, e.g. slope, soil and climate, often indicated by the ground flora. The smaller areas should as far as possible constitute a representative sample of the larger areas (i.e. 1 of 3, and 3 of 4).

The minimum sizes shown above are barely adequate and are intended for areas where woodland sites are small and few and far between. Probably in uneven-aged or mixed woodlands the sample area should not be less than 0·5 ha. In tropical rain forest the areas might have to be as much as five times as large as the maximum sizes given above. Where adequate areas cannot be found, it may be necessary to use measurement areas which are not adjacent to the sample areas, but which are within the same region and are as closely comparable as possible. In some cases more than one sample and measurement area may be located within the same study area, either as replicates, or as an experiment involving different tree species or management regimes.

2.22 Existing research plots should be used wherever possible. In particular it would be of immense value to locate these studies in or adjacent to a mensuration plot on which long term recurrent girth measurements have been made on numbered trees. This will allow much more precision in the estimation of wood production which is the major component. It may also make it possible to relate, (with care and suitable reservations) the total dry matter production (via mensuration data and volume tables where available) to other stands in the same region. The extent to which the stand sampled is thought representative of larger areas of woodland should be stated, giving corroborative detail if possible.

2.23 Replication is highly desirable where comparisons are to be made between stands. In some cases it may be impracticable due to site heterogeneity and shortage of manpower. Replication of non-destructive measurements (girth, height, etc.) may be simpler than replication of destructive measurements and may serve to indicate the amount of variation involved. Subdivision of the sample area and the measurement area will provide additional information on the variability of the stand.

3

Basic Concepts and Terms

3.1 Definitions and the basis of the method

The assimilation of organic matter by a plant community during a certain specified period (e.g. one year), including the amount used up by plant respiration, is called the *gross primary production*. Gross production minus respiration or the formation of plant tissues and reserve substances during the period is the *net primary production*, which may be known simply as primary production. When production is measured as dry weight it includes some mineral salts incorporated into the products of photosynthesis. If ash content is estimated and excluded, or some method is used which estimates only the formation of organic compounds, then *organic production* should be specified. In this Handbook the term production will be used as referring to net annual primary dry matter production unless otherwise specified. The IBP researches to which this Handbook is directed are mainly concerned with net primary production but more developed programmes are likely to involve estimation of other quantities as well.

IBP News 2 (Feb. 1965, p. 12) states: 'A general starting point for comparing photosynthetic primary production is the cumulative course of "net assimilation" (net dry matter production of green parts) over the year(s) or vegetation period(s). This can be determined by the sum total of the following features determined periodically through the year:

(a) Biomass change of photosynthetic plants;

(b) Plant losses by death and the shedding of parts above and below ground;

(c) Man's harvest (in some cases);

(d) Consumption of photosynthesizing plants by animals (botanical and zoological methods will be used to estimate amount lost).'

The unit of study will commonly be a whole biological system, i.e. the sum total of standing crops, which are the populations of living organisms under consideration in a defined area at a defined time. Biomass is the total amount of living matter present at a given moment in a biological system (in this case the photosynthetic plants making up a woodland stand). It is taken to include heartwood and bark (which may no longer be alive) but not dead roots and branches (with no viable buds). In the present context it should be expressed in terms of dry weight, or ash-free dry weight (=organic weight). Biomass may be estimated directly by weighing or indirectly from measurements of the volume and density of the various components concerned.

3.2 Two basic concepts

The basic method quoted from IBP News 2 represents the most fundamental procedure for estimating net production, but another method based on a somewhat different principle may also be used. In terms of mathematical symbols, the two procedures may be expressed as follows (Kira & Shidei 1967). Symbols defined below are used:

B_1 Biomass of a plant community at a certain time t_1

B_2 Biomass of the same community at t_2 ($= t_1 + \Delta t$)

$\Delta B = B_2 - B_1$ Biomass change during the period $t_1 - t_2$

L Plant losses by death and shedding during $t_1 - t_2$

G Plant losses by consumer organisms as herbivorous animals, parasitic plants, etc. during $t_1 - t_2$

P_n Net production by the community during $t_1 - t_2$

If the amounts, ΔB, L and G, are successfully estimated, we can calculate P_n as the sum,

$$P_n = \Delta B + L + G \ (Method\ 1,\ \text{see Fig. 2 (iv)})$$

Instead of measuring the biomass twice at t_1 and t_2, plants may be harvested only once at the end of the growing season (t_2), and by means of stem analysis (4.61) and by separating the plant matter into current year organs and older parts (4.62), we can estimate the amount of plant matter newly formed in the latest one year period (Δt). The amount obtained by this procedure corresponds to ($P_n - L_N - G_N$), the apparent growth increment (B_{2N}). The net production is then estimated as

$$P_n = B_{2N} + L_N + G_N \ (Method\ 2,\ \text{see Fig. 2 (ii)})$$

B

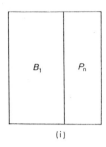

(i)

During the period t_1–t_2, the amount P_n of new plant body is added to the initial biomass B_1.

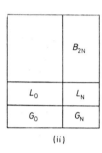

(ii)

On the other hand, a part of B_1, as well as a part of P_n dies and is lost from the biomass. These amounts are respectively designated as L_O and L_N ($L = L_O + L_N$) Similarly G_O and G_N may also be lost by the consumption of heterotrophic organisms from B_1 and P_n respectively ($G = G_O + G_N$). The plant matter newly formed, and remaining to t_2 (i.e. not lost as L_N or G_N), is known as the apparent growth increment B_{2N}.

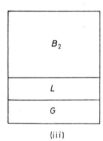

(iii)

Therefore $B_2 = B_1 + P_n - (L + G)$

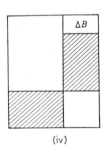

(iv)

or $B_2 - B_1 = P_n - (L + G) = \Delta B$

(The two hatched portions represent equal quantities, a device for subtracting B_1 from B_2, or alternatively $(L + G)$ from P_n.)

Figure 2

The apparent growth increment (B_{2N}) alone is an underestimate of the real net production whereas $(B_{2N} + L + G)$ is an overestimate.

These two methods both have inherent difficulties. In the former the greatest difficulty is that the biomass of the same community must be measured at least twice accurately enough to ensure a reliable estimate of ΔB. In the latter a difficult procedure has to be adopted to separate dead plant material (L) and consumption by heterotrophic organisms (G) into current year and older components.

3.3 Sampling techniques

For either method certain basic principles of sampling apply.

1. Divide the ecosystem into components, such as trees, shrubs, ground vegetation, which can each be considered separately. Within each major physiognomic category, further divisions may include minor layers, species groups or species, and age classes. The intensity of sampling any component should vary according to its importance to the ecosystem as a whole, its inherent variability and the difficulty and cost of sampling.

2. Within each component make some enumeration of what is present. With trees this will involve the measurement of number/unit area, and various dimensions of individual trees of different species (e.g. diameter breast high, DBH or d; canopy area; height; height to first foliage branch). With ground vegetation this may involve estimation of number/unit area, or alternatively frequency of the major species. Where the ground flora is strongly seasonal, this enumeration may have to be repeated in the spring, summer and autumn.

3. Based on this enumeration, design a sampling programme involving three main sorts of samples:

(a) Non-destructive measurements (e.g. measurement of DBH, height, etc.)

(b) Destructive measurements (e.g. cutting of branches or trees, partitioning into leaves, current year's extension growth, main branches, boles, etc. and by use of fresh weights or volumes, with small subsamples for drying, estimating the dry weight of the different components. Partitioning into discrete year's radial growth may often be possible, as suggested for Method 2 above.

(c) Litter fall of various types, see Chapter 6.

4. The object is to obtain correlations (4.8) between a comparatively small destructive sample (which is both time-consuming and destructive of the habitat) with a larger non-destructive sample which is representative of the stand whose production is to be estimated. Often foresters already have a large amount of mensuration data of this non-destructive type which can be used as a basis for production studies. In particular forest plots which have been measured for a good many years are very useful.

3.4   Time scale

Net annual primary production of the tree components of a woodland can be measured on various time scales. Current annual production (which corresponds to the forester's current annual increment, C.A.I.) usually refers to production during the year of study. The actual biomass change over a single year is likely to be small compared with the total biomass present and is therefore difficult to estimate with accuracy. In all woodlands annual production varies greatly from one year to the next, due especially to variation in climate. In even-aged stands production also varies systematically with the age of the stand (as outlined in 2.1).

For purposes of comparison, both within different types of woodland and between woodlands and other types of vegetation, the mean annual production over the whole woodland rotation is the most realistic figure to aim at. This corresponds to the forester's mean annual increment, M.A.I. An alternative value for comparative purposes is the peak mean annual production, which includes the low values early in the rotation, but not those of the senescent stages. This has the advantage of not requiring particularly old stands, and not being dependent upon the length of rotation. In an uneven-aged woodland, the mean periodic annual production, measured over a period of 3–5, or preferably 10, years is probably adequate. In even-aged woodland stands, an age sequence of stands whose thinning history is known can be used to estimate the rate of accumulation of woody biomass through the rotation. It is important to ensure that the stands sampled represent similar species composition on similar sites of similar quality class (Ovington 1957, Cousens & Black 1965). Where this is not possible, estimates of current annual production from one or two stands may be related to a general sequence of production against age of stand for a similar species and region. Foresters are likely to have production tables for different species and site quality classes.

A relatively high degree of accuracy is required in the estimation of stem wood production since this is commonly the largest component of the ecosystem production especially in plantations. In some non-commercial woodlands, although stem wood is still the largest component of biomass, other components of production may sometimes exceed stem production. Annual or rotational variation is taken into account by using radial increments to give average values over the past 5 or 10 years. Branch and large root production can be estimated similarly but separate estimates of leaf, twig and, if methods can be devised, fine root production must be made over at least 3 and preferably 5 seasons.

4

The Estimation of Tree and Shrub Production

The desired estimate of production will be a sum of a number of components, of which the main ones will be:

(a) Bud scales, flowers, fruit and other minor components (Ovington 1963).

(b) Leaves, perhaps with current year's extension growth (twigs).

(c) Branches.

(d) Stems.

(e) Roots.

Ecosystem production will involve the sum of these components for the main layers of the ecosystem, trees, shrubs and ground flora. The annual production of (a) and (b) can either be estimated as litter fall directly in the sample area (Chapter 6) or along with (c) by destructive sampling in the measurement area (4.62, 4.63). Where a good relationship can be obtained between girth or diameter and stem plus branch dry weight, the production of (c) and (d) may be estimated together (4.62). An important new paper (Whittaker & Woodwell 1968), not available when this Handbook was prepared, should be consulted in conjunction with this Chapter.

4.1 The estimation of biomass change

Stem production is the major component, and needs particularly careful attention. The principle of estimation will normally be complete enumeration and measurement of stems within the sample area (4.3), followed by the establishment of a regression between some tree dimension(s) and dry weight. This regression is normally obtained by felling selected trees in the measurement area (4.6). However the actual measurement of biomass change, on which the net production estimate is based may take several forms.

(a) Where it is possible to use a plot on which repeated stem volume estimations have been made over a considerable period, and where good volume tables are available for the species and quality classes concerned, volume increment can be derived accurately from simple DBH and possibly height measurements, and timber volume converted to dry weight by obtaining some values for the specific gravity of the timber concerned.

(b) Where there is no such mensurational framework on which to base the estimates, repeated measurements can be made within the sample plot over a period of 3–5 years. It will then be necessary in effect to construct volume tables and volume/dry weight regressions by felling selected trees in the measurement area. (a) and (b) are versions of Method 1.

(c) If it is necessary to estimate production (albeit less accurately) from a single year's sampling programme, then the estimate of biomass change can be derived from an analysis of the radial increments (for, say, the preceding 5 years) on the stems of the destructive sample taken in the measurement area. The enumeration of the sample area will allow the regressions of dry weight on volume and of dry matter production on some size parameter such as tree volume or DBH, for different species, to be built up into an estimate of stem dry matter production for the sample stand.

(d) If no felling is possible, and there is no mensurational framework, increment cores carefully taken on several radii can be used to obtain an estimate of volume increment over, say, the previous 5 years and also to estimate specific gravity of bark, heartwood and sapwood. (c) and (d) are variants of Method 2.

The principles outlined in (c) and (d) above can only be applied in woodlands where growth is seasonal, and distinct annual rings are formed in the stem timber. Methods (a) and (b) may equally well be applied to seasonal or non-seasonal woodland. Other things being equal (a)–(b)–(c)–(d) represents a series of diminishing accuracy, and (d) should be regarded as a last resort where an inaccurate estimate of production seems better than none at all. There are several basic operations which are common to some or all of these four methods.

4.2 Census of the sample area

Within the sample area the number of living trees of each species are counted and each tree permanently numbered for easy identification. The breast height (1·3 m above ground height on the uphill side of the tree) is permanently marked around each trunk with durable paint.

In all trees the trunk diameter at breast height (DBH) is measured with a steel diameter tape exactly along the paint mark. Diameter tape is better than calipers for the DBH measurements. Each unit graduation measures π cm or π in., so that the value read from the tape represents the circumference of the tree divided by π (3·1416). If a diameter tape is not available, measurements may be made with a normal steel tape and values divided by π. On very small trees a linen tape must be used for circumference or a micrometer type gauge for diameter. Total tree height and tree height to the first major branch (clear-hole height) should also be measured wherever possible, using some optical apparatus (see Hummel 1951, Husch 1963).

In estimating the branch biomass the diameter of the trunk just below the joint of the lowest main branch is often an important measure (see 4.7). This may be measured with tolerable accuracy using a Barr and Stroud Dendrometer* (expensive) based on the rangefinder principle (Jeffers 1956) or some other similar optical instrument (Grosenbaugh 1963). The *Spiegel-relaskop* (see most mensuration textbooks, e.g. Husch 1963, p. 164) may be used. Such instruments also allow direct measurements of taper of the trunk which can be used to give more precision to volume tables. Where the stem is elliptical in section, these optical methods are inevitably inaccurate and a better estimate could be obtained by climbing the tree (with a ladder or a tree bicycle) and measuring girth with a tape.

In multilayered natural forests, the situation of each tree in the stratification is also recorded. The canopy type (dominant, subdominant and suppressed or other convenient grades) is also useful information in forests having relatively simple structure and composition. This inventory can conveniently be mapped on a suitable scale, so that the map shows species, size classes and tree number.

4.3 Recurrent measurements on the sample plot

After the initial census, regular recordings of DBH and height if possible are continued for at least 3–5 years, usually once a year. DBH must always be measured at exactly the same position on each trunk, marked by paint. Greater accuracy can be attained by the use of vernier band dendrometers*, or dendrographs but in quantity these would be expensive and only justifiable where radial growth is very slow, or recurrent measurements are required

---

* The term 'dendrometer' is ambiguous and may refer either to an optical instrument, or to a metal band fixed round the trunk to measure small girth increments.

over short periods such as a week or perhaps a month. The inexpensive pattern described by Liming (1957) might be useful. It consists of a simple aluminium or zinc band with vernier scales on it held tight around the trunk of the tree by a spring. Other patterns are discussed by Husch (1963), Alm & Brown (1964) and Kern (1961).

If the form factor for the species concerned is known, or suitable volume tables are available, bole volume may be estimated from DBH and height. Young *et al.* (1964, 1965) have published volume and dry weight tables for all components separately for many north-east American tree species. From such tables, dry weight increment of all woody parts can be estimated from height and girth alone.

If it is not possible to make recurrent measurements over 3–5 years, similar information (except that it refers to the previous 5 or 10 years) can be gained from increment cores taken with a Pressler type borer (see Heinrichs 1964, Mesavage 1964, Prestemon 1965). Kurth (1963) and Bunce (1961) both discuss some of the precautions necessary in the interpretation of increment cores. Vins (1968) describes an improved version of the core measurer developed by Eklund (1949) at the Swedish Forest Research Institute. This is based on a low-power microscope, and gives automatic recording of the increment measurements.

From increment cores, radial wood increment for the past 5–10 years, and bark thickness are determined and related to the measurements of DBH and height. From these data it is possible to compute basal areas of wood plus bark, and of wood alone, and bole volume if suitable volume tables are available. When they are not available a preliminary approximation of volume can be obtained from Spurr's (1952) volume equations without species corrections, or by the assumption that the bole approaches a paraboloid of rotations for which the volume is represented by

$$V_\mathrm{p} = \frac{\pi r^2 h}{2}$$

in which r is the wood radius at breast height and h is tree height. From the data estimates of tree volume growth are also possible. Basal area increment of a tree may be computed as

$$A_\mathrm{i} = \pi[(r^2 - (r - i)^2)]$$

in which i is the radial wood thickness increment per year (normally based on an average of the thickness of the wood growth for the past 5 or 10 years). One half basal area increment times tree height provides an estimate of stem wood volume growth 'estimated volume increment', V_i.

$$V_i = \tfrac{1}{2}(A_i \times h)$$

In many forest trees thickness of wood increment is greater above and below breast height than it is at breast height. Estimated volume increment is consequently often an underestimate; true wood volume growth is generally 1·0 to 1·5 times the estimated volume increment. This difficulty does not apply providing the growth form is consistent with the volume tables being used, which will themselves be based on DBH.

4.4   Conversion of volume to dry weight

If little or no felling is possible, it will be necessary to convert figures for biomass change, in terms of volumes, to dry weight using values for timber specific gravity. Timber density is commonly expressed as basic specific gravity which is the oven dry weight in grammes of 1 cm^3 volume of fresh timber. Values for this can be obtained from increment borings (though there is some danger of compression) or from any trees which have been felled. It will be important to divide the volume figures into heartwood, sapwood and bark. Carlisle & Brown (1966) found for a particular area of oak (*Quercus petraea*) forest that there was a significant correlation between the specific gravities of heartwood, sapwood and bark at 10% up the tree (specific gravities estimated from cores) and the mean specific gravities of these materials for the whole stem. The use of specific gravity estimates based on breast height increment cores is discussed by Stage (1963). Methods of estimating specific gravity from increment cores are discussed by Walters & Bruckmann (1964).

4.5   Selection of trees for destructive sample

Baskerville (1965) has demonstrated clearly the need to select sample trees for felling on the basis of a stand table. In the highly tolerant species Balsam Fir (*Abies balsamifera*) the proportion of the total tree dry weight contributed by each component (e.g. foliage, branches, cones, stem wood, stem bark, roots) varied markedly with the DBH. To derive a reasonably accurate estimate of total tree dry weight, and dry weight of the separate components, using regressions based on more than 100 felled trees it was necessary to derive a stand table using integral DBH classes (1, 2, 3 . . . . . 10 in. in this case) and to solve each component equation for each diameter class. When this was compared with an every tree summation, in which each component equation was solved for each of the 188 trees in the 0·2 acre plot, the stand table approach underestimated total biomass by 1% and the maximum component error was only 2·9%. Other 'short-cut' approaches, based, e.g. on the tree of mean height, mean diameter, mean basal area, mean volume or the average codominant tree, gave total or component estimates which were as much as 50% too high or too low.

While errors would probably be less where an intolerant tree species was concerned, it seems clear that a stand table approach is necessary. Where computer facilities are readily available it may be possible to use the laborious every tree summation techniques as a matter of routine. Shanks & Clebsch (1962) have demonstrated how it is possible to produce computer programmes (in their case in Fortran language for use in an IBM–1620 computer) for the estimation of forest stand weight and mineral content.

The selection of trees for the destructive sample will therefore involve compromise between the large sample desirable and the available commitment of manpower and money. There is no real short-cut and the trees selected must cover the range of size, form and species of the sample plot.

4.6 Estimating biomass and growth increment in destructive samples

In some circumstances it may be desirable to fell sample trees from the sample area after the period of repeated non-destructive measurements. Using the actual trees which have been measured will increase the accuracy of the dry weight estimates but precludes getting any further information from that sample area. More usually the trees to be felled will come from the measurement area and will be selected as suggested above (4.5) to be representative of the range of size, form and species in the sample area. Methods of dealing with destructive samples are set out by Whittaker, Cohen & Olson (1963).

The time of felling depends upon whether information on leaf biomass is required or not. A single sample time will not give reliable information on leaf production, but combined with some fall-out method the assessment of leaf biomass at sample time is valuable. If leaf biomass information is not required, felling should be done in the winter. If it *is* required then time of felling should preferably be near the end of the growing season in deciduous forest, when the current year's growth has already been completed while the leaves still remain green. Conifers often continue to photosynthesize during the winter at times when conditions are favourable. It would be best to settle on a sampling time when no photosynthesis is occurring; in some cases in the northern hemisphere, January and February are the months of minimum activity.

The following minimum measurements should be made immediately after felling:

    (a) height of top of tree
    (b) crown depth
    (c) crown diameter (when possible this should be measured before felling)
    (d) DBH
    (e) stem diameter just below the lowest living branch
    (f) total fresh weight of leaves
    (g) total fresh weight of branches, current year's extension growth separated
    (h) total fresh weight of trunk.

Certain of these measurements, e.g. (b), (c), (e), may not immediately be used in computation. They do tend however to suggest interesting relationships which may subsequently be used to refine analysis or selection of sample.

Four main tree parts (leaves, branches, trunks, roots) can be treated separately and it is necessary to define them. The border line between trunk and root is usually drawn at ground level. It is not always easy to distinguish branches from trunk. The thickest shoot leading more or less straight to the top of the crown is treated as the main trunk. In cases where the distinction is ambiguous, the criteria of separation should be clearly stated. Leaves include leaf stems (petioles). Fruits and flowers, possibly other minor components such as bud scales and pollen may also be separately weighed when necessary.

4.61 Trunk. The diameter of the trunk is measured at 1–3 m intervals according to tree size, for example at 0, 0·3, 1·3, 2·3 m . . . . and so forth from the trunk base. The bole is then cut into corresponding lengths which are individually weighed. Two sets of stout tripod, chain block and spring balance (probably of the capacity of 500 kg) are sufficient in most cases.

The strain gauge apparatus described by Keen & Weetman (1961) is also convenient. Where a chain saw is used, the cut is wide and it may be desirable to make some allowance for the loss of material as sawdust.

If the bole is too heavy or the measuring gear is not available, the weight may be estimated from stem volume. Wood volume for each log should be computed either from the middle wood diameter of the log or from the square-root mean of the end wood diameters.

$$D_m = \sqrt{\frac{(D_1{}^2 + D_2{}^2)}{2}}$$

Discs cut from each log not only assist in this measurement of log volume but can also be used for estimating wood increment during the previous 5 or 10 years, the proportions of bark, sapwood and heartwood, and the densities of these three components, where this information is required. These discs may be cut either from the centre point of each log, or from the lower end of each log, in which case two discs are used to describe each log.

Values for density of the different components can be used as suggested in 4.4 to convert volume measurements to dry weight, and to validate or invalidate the use of density values obtained from breast height increment cores.

Radial increments during, say, the last 5 years may be read on four radii on each of the discs. The wood volume (excluding bark) at the time of felling (V_S), that n years ago (V_S') and hence the wood volume increment during the period ($V_S - V_S'$) are thereby obtained. The wood increment in the most recent year (ΔV_S) can be estimated on the basis of either linear or exponential growth.

$$\Delta V_S = (V_S - V_S')/n \text{ linear basis}$$

$$\Delta V_S = V_S (1 - e^{-r}), \; r = \frac{1}{n} \log_e (V_S/V_S') \text{ exponential basis.}$$

It is to be noted that the former formula may lead to an appreciable underestimation when trees are in an exponential phase of growth. The volume increment is converted to dry weight using the conversion factors obtained as suggested above (4.4).

4.62 Branches. In some instances it is possible from the felled trees to compute the regression of stem plus branch dry weight on girth or diameter so that stem plus branch dry weight can be predicted with considerable accuracy from girth or diameter measurements. In this case, in a minimum programme, no separate estimate need be made of branch production. Where however branch weight is a variable component, not easily correlated with stem diameter, a separate estimate must be made, as described, e.g. by Whittaker (1965). As with stems it will be necessary to make measurements in the sample area which will be converted to dry weight and dry weight increment using regressions developed on the destructive sample taken from the measurement area.

The single most useful branch measurement is diameter measured just above the basal swell into the stem (Attiwill 1962). This can be measured directly by climbing the trees, or possibly with optical apparatus (Grosenbaugh 1963). If none of these are possible, then a relationship must be established between DBH or stem volume and total branch dry weight but this will lead to inaccuracy.

It may be possible to count the number of branches in each of several arbitrary size classes from the ground, and to determine the dry weight of similarly scored branches on the destructive sample.

There are several ways of dealing with the branches in the destructive sample. The basic essential is to estimate total branch dry weight (from fresh weight and conversion factors derived from dried subsample), branch diameter as described above, and to record position on the tree. Also it will be desirable to partition at least a sample of the branches into such components as wood (or wood and bark separately), current year's twigs, leaves and where appropriate flowers or fruit. The proportions of these components may be determined on subsamples and referred to the main sample. One must discover whether or not the proportions of these components vary with position on the tree.

Wherever possible one must estimate branch age. This can be done either from annual rings (often incomplete or very closely spaced) or from successive girdle scars. A combination of both techniques will probably give the most accurate result.

Then one must develop regressions, using branch age or branch basal diameter as the independent variable (x) and branch (wood and bark or each separately) weight, and current twig (with or without leaves, fruits, etc.) as dependent variables (y).

These regressions will usually be of the form

$$\log y = a + b \log x$$

The samples should always contain one of the biggest branches on the sample tree. It is important also to express the results graphically since some of the relationships may not be of this form, and the branches of a particular tree may constitute more than one population (e.g. Whittaker's (1965) branches of fast, medium and slow growth).

The regression above assumes branch growth at the rate

$$\Delta y = by/x$$

and branch production, Δy, can be estimated by multiplying branch dry weight by b/x and summing the results for a given tree.

When stem and branch biomass, and annual stem wood production are known a crude estimate of branch production is possible from the relation

$$\Delta B/B = k(\Delta S/S)$$

where B and ΔB are branch weight and production, S and ΔS are stem weight and production. Whittaker (1965) gives a range of values for k.

There are likely to be greater errors in the estimation of branch production than stem production. However its contribution to the production of the whole woodland ecosystem is smaller than that of the stems so the larger proportional error is tolerable.

4.63 Leaves. There are basically two methods of estimating leaf biomass and production, as part of the branch component (4.62) and as litter fall (Chapter 6). There are also two ways of regarding leaf production:

(a) The maximum dry weight of foliage present on the tree during the year less the minimum quantity. For deciduous species this minimum will be zero (or nearly so as a few leaves may remain).

(b) The dry weight of the tree leaves at the end of the growing season when translocation from leaf to branch has ceased.

The maximum dry weight, (a), is a true measure of leaf production *per se* and represents the quantity of foliage available for phytophagous fauna. Leaf dry weight (g per n leaves) however varies with season, often decreasing before leaf fall. Decreases in leaf dry weight may be due to translocation losses, leaching by rainfall, consumption by insects, and to respiration exceeding assimilation. It is doubtful if this maximum dry weight can be used in calculating the total annual net production (tree stem + branch + root + leaves + etc.) as some of the leaf components become branch components. The better additive value is (b), the dry weight of the leaves at the end of the season. If measurements of leaves and branches are made at the same time, there cannot be translocation from one component to another between measurements.

Maximum leaf production, (a), can be measured by taking representative sample leaves from different parts of the canopy at regular intervals throughout the year, and calculating the maximum dry weight per n leaves. For deciduous trees this can be combined with an estimate of the maximum number of leaves in the stand, derived either from a branch sample (which gives good differentiation of 'sun' and 'shade' leaves) or from litter fall.

Regular measurements of litter fall (collected every 1–4 weeks through the year, see Chapter 6) will give an indication of the total number of leaves or parts of leaves shed throughout the year. Over a period of one year in a deciduous woodland and over a period of 3–5 years in an evergreen woodland this should near enough equal the number of leaves produced. Regular litter and rain wash collections will indicate which causes of leaf loss (e.g. consumption by caterpillars, other invertebrates, aphid dew, wash-out of organic compounds by rain, immature leaf fall, etc. etc.) are important in the particular stand under study. These all represent losses of leaf production, causing leaf fall to be an underestimate of leaf production. It is therefore important to make accurate measurements of any losses which seem to be quantitatively important. Methods of litter collection are discussed in Chapter 6.

When taking the destructive sample, leaves may either be included with the current year's twigs, and the proportion of twig and leaf dry weight determined in subsamples. Or the leaves may all be clipped off and weighed, keeping those from each major branch separate. Weetman & Harland (1964) store the branches and needles at room temperature for some months until they are dry enough for the needles to fall off when shaken; the needles and twigs can then be separated in a mechanical sieve. A dry weight conversion is obtained from representative subsamples. A regression is then calculated for leaf dry weight on branch basal diameter, which will allow estimation of the leaf biomass in the sample area (e.g. Rothacher, Blow & Potts 1954, Holland 1968). Subsamples of fresh leaves may also be taken for subsequent estimation of leaf area and chlorophyll content (7.1).

Leaves are sorted into age groups where appropriate. In certain evergreen trees such as pines, an age-leaf survival curve is constructed by which the average longevity of leaf as well as the annual amount of leaf shedding is calculated. Leaf retention may vary from tree to tree and in Scots pine, for example, shoots bearing male inflorescences may retain their leaves for 2–3 times as long as female shoots (Steven & Carlisle 1959).

The estimation of leaf production is complicated where there is lammas growth or where severe defoliation by caterpillars encourages a late flush of resting buds (Carlisle, Brown & White 1966a). This is just one instance where it is important to understand the general ecology and biology of the system under study.

4.64 Estimation of root biomass. The sampling of tree roots is tedious but reasonably reliable estimates of biomass can be obtained. Methods are reviewed by Schuurmann & Goedewaagen (1965), Lieth (1968). The roots with a diameter over 0·5 cm or over 1 cm may be dug or winched or hosed out and weighed (Ovington 1957, Singer & Hutnik 1965, Baskerville 1966). Whittaker (1962) uses regressions of root dry weight on root diameter for sample roots, applied to the broken ends of roots on the root crown to correct for root loss on excavation.

An additional estimate of fine roots can be obtained either by excavation of soil monoliths, or by taking soil cores (e.g. Bray, Lawrence & Pearson 1959) down to a depth of at least 50 cm and washing out the fine roots over a sieve. So far as is possible only live roots should be included. Roots larger than 0·5 cm (or whatever limit was employed) are rejected from these samples as they will have been estimated by excavation. The fine roots will include those of trees, shrubs and ground flora and should therefore be included in the estimate of *stand* biomass. Washed root samples frequently contain mineral soil particles. This can be allowed for by determining the ash content of subsamples in a muffle furnace and correcting the root dry weight estimate to a value (say, 5 % ash appropriate to the species and site. Extensive data on the weights of tree roots were compiled by Ovington (1962), and by Bray (1963). Whittaker (1962) has given some shrub root data.

4.65 Attempts to estimate root production. There is however no generally acceptable method for estimating root production (Newbould 1968) and it is only possible to suggest some of the directions in which research is, or might be, proceeding and hope that some technique will emerge from IBP initiatives. If it does it may be possible to use subsequent determinations to find a relationship between root biomass and root production, so that meanwhile it is important to estimate root biomass for all stands studied.

The problem is to estimate the turnover of fine roots (Orlov 1955). This

c

turnover is due to organic root secretions, death and decay, consumption, and losses via mycorrhizal fungi. An additional problem, especially in stands which have been thinned, is the presence of root grafts.

One overall simplification would be the assumption that

$$\frac{\text{Above-ground production}}{\text{Above-ground biomass}} = k \times \frac{\text{Below-ground production}}{\text{Below-ground biomass}}$$

Since no accurate figures have yet been obtained for below-ground production, it is difficult to estimate k, though one could simplify further and assume it to be unity.

The production of large roots can be estimated like that of branches (4.62) using radial growth increments where these are visible. However G. C. Head (*in litt*) reports that extra thickening does not occur on all woody roots, and annual rings are not a reliable guide to root age. Many thickish roots do not thicken at all in some years. A root may show, for example, six annual rings but it is not clear to which six years these rings refer. In apple trees secondary thickening of roots is more abundant close to the tree trunk, i.e. roots taper sharply after leaving the trunk.

Other methods which may be worth pursuing are set out below:

(a) Root biomass samples taken by corer at regular time intervals, say once a month, may be sorted into categories (diameter classes; brown, yellow, white; living, dead, perhaps using a vital stain). This should reveal the annual pattern of root development, and it might be possible to deduce root production from the biomass change of particular categories of root. To get enough cores would be laborious and for this method to yield useful results would need a fair degree of mechanization in the coring, washing, sorting and scoring of roots (Fehrenbacher & Alexander 1955, Newman 1966).

(b) Roots can be studied and their elongation growth and thickening measured in a glass-sided root trench (Rogers & Head 1963, Head 1965). The soil/glass interface and the installation of the trench introduce artificial features into the measurement. It is difficult to convert these measurements (mm root extension/m^2 glass wall per time) into dry matter production per unit area of land. The measurement can be made in terms of mm root extension/mm fine root visible. Measurements of root biomass as in (a) above would give values for mm of fine root in the soil below 1 m^2 stratified by depth, so that root extension data could be converted to root production per unit area.

Rates of root browning determined by this method would help in estimating the ages of roots sampled by method (a). Rates of root thickening can also be measured. This method could also suggest but not measure the importance of the loss of cortical tissue from all new roots, the complete rotting away of roots, and losses by consumption. Root extension of seedlings can similarly be studied non-destructively by growing them in glass-sided containers.

(c) Conventional growth analysis of comparatively small plants in containers gives information on root production/shoot production ratios under conditions which can be varied to relate to field problems (e.g. light, mineral nutrients, temperature). This method should be combined with the use of glass-sided containers. There must be many estimates in the literature for the root/shoot ratios of annual or short-lived plants, and a comprehensive review of these would be valuable. Growth analysis experiments lasting more than a couple of years are less numerous and where harvests are infrequent root production cannot be calculated.

(d) The use of radioactive tracers has been suggested, but it is difficult to see how they could be used effectively for estimating production. They are undoubtedly useful for measuring the extent of root systems (Lott, Satchell & Hall 1950, Boggie, Hunter & Knight 1958) Carbon-14 labelling could possibly be used to measure organic root secretions over short periods of time. Such secretions can also be measured in sterile sand or water culture easily enough, and although unnatural may serve to provide maximal values.

An indirect method of measuring translocation of photosynthate to the roots, and thus root production is via the analogue computer models proposed by Olson (1964). Thus gas exchange measurements, combined with information on the rhythms of root and shoot extension and thickening would suggest what proportions of photosynthate were moving to root and shoot respectively at any particular season.

Further suggestions on root production and biomass are in the USSR Academy of Sciences symposium volume on the subject (1968).

4.7   Correlation between destructive and non-destructive sample

If then we have a suitable estimate of volume change, or even DBH change, and regressions relating these external measurement parameters to total dry weight, or component dry weight, these two sets of information can be combined to develop the estimate of stand production.

The precision of this operation depends markedly on the size and selection of the destructive sample as suggested above.

Kittredge (1944) and Satoo *et al.* (1955–9) proposed the use of the allometric regression on DBH of the weight of different tree components,

$$\log w = a + b \log d$$

in which *w* stands for the weight of a certain tree component and *d* for DBH. Once the regression is established from the destructive sample, it is easy to calculate the biomass on the sample area by combining it with the result of the DBH census.

Though this type of regression has proved useful in a number of different forest types (Ovington & Madgwick 1959a, Kimura 1960, Tadaki *et al.* 1960–5, Nomoto 1964, Ogino *et al.* 1964) more accurate estimation can be expected by using d^2h in place of *d* where *h* is the tree height (Ogawa *et al.* 1961, 1965a, 1965b, Whittaker *in litt*). However Bunce (1968) showed that the inclusion of height only marginally improved his estimate of tree dry weight. In some cases the expression $(d^2 + h + d^2h)$ is to be preferred (Dawkins *in litt*). If tree height is not available for calculation, it may be estimated from the *d–h* curve empirically obtained by destructive measurements with considerable accuracy (Ogawa *et al.* 1965b, Muller & Nielsen 1965).

Generally trunk weight can be most accurately estimated by such a method. There are indications that this is also true for the root weight (Tadaki & Shidei 1960, Ogawa *et al.* 1965b). As for the weight of branch or leaf, the regression is usually consistent within a stand, but it may vary not only with species but between stands of a single species where age or density of stems is variable (Satoo *et al.* 1958, 1959, Satoo 1962). In such cases the diameter of trunk or the area of trunk cross section at the height just below the joint of the lowest branch is often very useful as a universal parameter, because the weight of leaf or branch per tree tends to be proportional to the area of cross-section of this part of the trunk (Shinozaki *et al.* 1964, Loomis, Phares & Crosby 1966). Its measurement in non-destructive samples is discussed in 4.2.

The change of the foliage amount with tree size is sometimes less regular than in other tree components. The leaf amount per tree tends to approach a ceiling value as trees grow to a very large size. When the regression mentioned above is applied to trees bigger than the sample trees actually felled the amount of their foliage is therefore most likely to be overestimated. This could be avoided by making the estimation graphically, based on the leaf amount—D^2H (or trunk weight) curve (Muller & Nielsen 1965). The curve may also be formulated by a hyperbolic equation (Ogawa *et al.* 1965).

These regressions or empirical curves are not necessarily peculiar to a single species. Sometimes several tree species of the same life form growing together in a stand have the same regression in common (Kimura 1960, 1963, Ogino *et al.* 1964, Muller & Nielsen 1965, Ogawa *et al.* 1961); in this case the amount of destructive sample and of calculation may be greatly reduced. Using the common regression for 50 species in a tropical rain forest, Ogawa *et al.* (1965b) could successfully estimate the biomass of the forest with satisfactorily high accuracy.

Measurements of DBH and height in all trees of the sample area, probably at an annual interval for 3–5 years, allow the estimation of biomass change during the period. Each tree component should be separately correlated with DBH or other parameters in the calculation, for the correlation is not the same in trunk, branch, root and leaf. It is generally sufficient to carry out destructive measurements only once at the end of, or during, the period of non-destructive measurement. Where the forest is growing very rapidly, the tree weight–stem size regressions may vary within a few years and the destructive sample should preferably be taken twice, both at the beginning and the end of the study period.

The change of biomass plus the amount of litter fall independently measured in the same period is the estimate of net production by Method 1. One component of production missing in this estimate is the turnover of fine roots, which for the present cannot be exactly determined in the field. Except for this omission it involves all other components including the increments of branch and root biomass which are very difficult to determine by Method 2. However the estimate should be checked by the result of Method 2 because these indirect methods of biomass estimation must always involve a considerable error.

In woodlands without a well-defined growing season, as for example tropical rain forest, where no annual growth rings are formed, Method 2 cannot be applied and only Method 1 can be used. (Muller & Nielsen 1965, Kira *et al.* 1967). In mature and stable stands it is likely that the biomass remains more or less constant from year to year and that total production will therefore equal litter fall including branches and dead stems (Nye 1961, Kira *et al.* 1967). It may be possible to estimate the total amount of leaf, branch and stem litter by sampling in a large area (Chapter 6) which may then be regarded as the estimate of net production. Since such equilibrium of forest biomass can only be recognized on a long term because of the irregular and intermittent death of trees, observations must be maintained for quite a long period before the average death rate of trees is correctly estimated. The upper limits of plot size given in 2.2 may need to be at least trebled for this approach. Another difficulty is that in tropical rain forest a lot of decomposition occurs before material reaches the ground.

4.71 Method 2. Apparent growth increments of respective tree components in a tree estimated by the procedures stated in 4.3 can also be correlated with non-destructive parameters. The allometric regression as used in Method 1 may often be used successfully with stem basal area, or leaf weight per tree as the parameters (Tadaki *et al.* 1961–3). The regressions however tend sometimes to be less simple and the estimation of apparent growth increments from DBH etc. could better be made graphically.

It is necessary in Method 2 to estimate the amount of plant tissues which were newly formed during the study period and died before the end of the period, as pointed out in 3.2. In deciduous forests the leaf component of L_N may easily be estimated as litter fall, whereas in evergreen forests it is hardly possible to classify leaf litter into current and older leaves. The greater part of current year production of evergreen leaves may remain alive in the winter months, and can be measured by destructive sampling, so that a small amount of current year leaves shed during the growing season might be disregarded. The same may also be true for current year branches. It is again emphasized that adding the total amount of litter fall (including both L_N and L_O) to apparent growth increment overestimates the net production.

The result obtained by Method 2 is however likely to be a minimum estimate of net production, because such fractions as growth increments in branch and root, losses of current year tissues including the turnover of fine roots, etc. are often difficult to determine and are therefore excluded from the estimate.

4.8 Shrub production

The estimation of shrub production is similar in principle to that of tree production. Full descriptions of methods are given by Whittaker (1961, 1962), Ovington, Heitkamp & Lawrence (1963) and Gimingham & Miller (1968).

5

The Estimation of Other Components of Ecosystem Production

5.1 Production by ground vegetation

Two main methods are possible for estimating production by the ground vegetation (see also the IBP Handbook No 6 on *Methods for the measurement of the primary production of grassland*, by Milner & Hughes; also Scott 1955).

5.11 The individual plant method. Where distinct plants of a single or only a few species are present, the best procedure will be to collect a number of individual plants of each species (preferably including subterranean organs) at monthly intervals through the year. The collected plants are separated into leaves, flowers, stems and roots, which are dried and weighed. These individual plant data can then be combined with density (number of individual plants/area) data for conversion to an area basis. The sum of (Species A max. biomass − min. biomass) + (Species B max. biomass − min. biomass) + ... gives an estimate of net production.

5.12 The harvested quadrat method. Where this procedure is not appropriate, the ground flora can be sampled monthly by harvesting vegetation from random quadrats.

5.13 Location of samples. The quadrats will normally be located in a few representative plots in the measurement area. The sampling principle may be stratified random, i.e. quadrats placed at random (by random number co-ordinates) within a defined sub-plot. It is important to make the area large enough so that n quadrats can be harvested at each of n' sampling intervals, without this harvesting markedly affecting the growth on quadrats to be harvested subsequently.

5.14 Size of quadrat. The preferred size and shape of quadrat will vary according to the type of vegetation, both mode of growth and uniformity of cover being considered. Suggested sizes range from 100 cm² for mosses,

15 cm × 15 cm (225 cm²) for a uniform fine grass sward to 1 m × 1 m or 0·5 m × 2 m (both = 1 m²). No general statement is possible as to the number of quadrats to be sampled at each sample interval.

5.15 Frequency of sampling. The areas are resampled at intervals during the year, using a different set of random positions. This will demonstrate the pattern of growth and allow estimation of maximum and minimum values. About 8–12 samples a year would be satisfactory, and the sampling interval may be less during periods of rapid change than, e.g. during the winter.

5.16 Harvesting. So far as possible both above-ground and major below-ground parts should be harvested. This can be done either by digging up entire plants or by clipping combined with root cores. The material must be sorted by species or species groups (e.g. in some cases groupings like 'mosses', 'grasses' will suffice) and into components (at least above- and below-ground). It is then dried and weighed, or if bulky, weighed and subsampled for subsequent drying and weighing.

5.17 Interpretation of results. A crude estimate of production can be made from the difference between the seasonal maximum and minimum dry weight figures. This must include at least underground storage organs, if not the whole root system, since apparent above-ground production may simply be attributable to translocation of stored reserves. Not all species reach their maximum biomass at the same time, so a better estimate would be provided by the sum of maximum-minimum biomass for all species individually. The maximum-minimum estimate may neglect some losses by litter fall, but where production by ground vegetation is less than, say, 5% of the ecosystem production, this is unimportant.

5.2 Climbing plants

Climbing plants, especially woody lianes, play an important role in forest types under a warm moist climate. Adequate methods for estimating wood production by lianes have not yet been developed because of the complicated methods of secondary thickening found in their stems. An indirect method for estimating the biomass of lianes in the tropical rain forest was suggested by Ogawa *et al.* (1965b).

5.3 Epiphytes

The biomass of epiphytes will normally be estimated along with the component upon which they are epiphytic. Where it seems likely that their total contribution to ecosystem production is significant, special methods must be devised for dealing with them.

6

Litter Fall

6.1 Leaves and similar litter

Estimates of litter production in the forests of the world are reviewed by Bray & Gorham (1964). There is considerably diversity of opinion as to the best receptacles for catching litter (Thompson & McGinnes 1963). Suggestions include:

(a) Bags suspended from hoops (Ovington & Murray 1964) about 1 m above the soil. The hoops would be at least 0·5 m in diameter. The bag should be freely permeable to water (nylon mesh, cheese cloth, sail cloth, etc.) to reduce moisture and decomposition inside the bag. Care must be taken with this type of litter trap that the hoop does not incline out of the horizontal and the bag must be pegged or weighted to prevent it blowing inside out.

(b) some receptacle like a plastic dustbin or bucket (e.g. 40 cm diameter), perhaps containing a bag made of terylene gauze fixed in position with a sprung steel rim (Carlisle & Brown 1966).

(c) a more elaborate trap designed by Shaw (1968) originally for acorns, proved an effective litter trap.

(d) where there is no tendency for the litter to drift, e.g. some conifers, shallow trays may be adequate. Decomposition will be less in these more open containers. Contamination by soil splash may invalidate subsequent chemical analysis of the samples.

The use of 'Fourdrinier' wire screening as used in paper making machines is recommended. It collects the finest particles, shows very rapid drainage and can often be obtained free.

The precise design to be used depends greatly on local circumstances. It is important that the litter fall should drop into the trap, without any aerodynamic effects preventing this, that it should not drop or blow out again, that material from the ground should not get in, and that litter in the trap should not decompose too much before being collected. Whichever litter trap is used, it is important that it should be large enough and that the

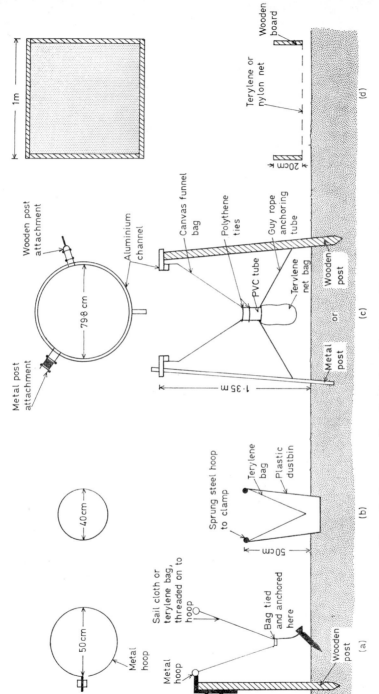

Figure 3. Four suggestions for design of litter trap. For explanation, see text.

rim should be level, and well-defined, and well above the soil surface.

The hoops, buckets or trays should be arranged by some stratified random method (e.g. two or more at random within each square of a grid or along each fixed length of a line. Probably not less than 20 would be needed in one sample area, and providing care is taken not to trample too much of the ground vegetation while emptying them, they can be located in the sample area itself. 20 litter traps may give an acceptably low standard error for the total leaf fall, or total non-branch litter, and also for the major components of leaf fall, i.e. the leaves of the dominant species. The standard error for minor species may be large and the frequency distribution heavily skewed. Where special interest attaches to such minor species, more traps must be used, and the frequency distribution examined to see what statistical technique is appropriate.

For preference they should be emptied once a week throughout the year, especially in the humid tropics and after periods of rain. If this frequency is not possible, they should be emptied at least once a month. The frequency of emptying could well be higher during the main litter fall season and lower at other times of year. Particular care is required in the siting of the trap, and the collection and analysis of the material caught where mineral cycling is being studied (7.3). Where chemical analysis is to be done on litter samples, any metal parts of the litter trap should be coated with inert bitumastic paint. It is also necessary to deter birds from perching on the rim.

The material collected from the litter trap should be sorted into appropriate categories (e.g. leaves by species, bud scales, fruits, twigs and general detritus), dried and weighed. For Method 2 of estimating production it is necessary to sort the material into that derived from current year's production (L_N) and that from previous production (L_O).

6.2   Micro-litter

Some of the smaller components of litter may better be sampled using a smaller receptacle, and not allowing water to drain out, i.e. combining this operation with rainfall sampling. This method is described in 7.2.

6.3   Macro-litter

Large items of litter, e.g. branches, are less regular than leaves in their time and space distribution. The amount of branch fall is most relevant in steady state ecosystems where some sort of equilibrium between dry matter production and its fall-out and decomposition is assumed. Where necessary branch fall should be estimated by recording all the branches from relatively large plots, say 20 m × 20 m as a minimum size, at regular intervals, say monthly. Moderate sized branches can be picked up and weighed on site with a subsample for dry weight conversion. Large branches would have to be measured and marked as recorded, with subsequent regression on dry weight. Where fall-out of branches is to be used, in a supposedly steady state system, to estimate branch production, their weight must be corrected for loss by decomposition (by comparing the dry weight/volume relation of living and fallen branches of similar diameter).

7

The Minimum Programme and
Additional Measurements

The Minimum Programme so far as woodland production is concerned, consists in carrying out the measurements and calculations suggested in Chapters 4, 5 and 6 on a suitable woodland site. There are no acceptable methods for estimating root production and the minimum programme will just involve getting an estimate of root biomass (4.64), without any attempt at measuring production. If subsequently some general relationships emerge between root biomass and root production, the biomass information can be used. Unless it appears from the leaf litter samples (6.1) that there are important micro- or macro-litter components not otherwise estimated, there is no need in the minimum programme to estimate them (i.e. omit 6.2 and 6.3).

In more highly developed programmes a number of additional measurements will be valuable, and some are discussed briefly in this chapter.

7.1 Characteristics of the photosynthetic system

7.11 Leaf area index. The commonest description of the size of the photosynthetic system is the *leaf area index* which is the *area of leaves carried above a unit area of ground*. By convention, where flat leaves are concerned, only the area of one surface is estimated. Where the leaves are not flat, e.g. pine needles, half the total surface area of the leaves is taken. Methods of estimating the surface area of pine needles are discussed by Madgwick (1964). If a measure other than leaf area index is used, it should be clearly stated and a conversion factor to leaf area index, as defined above, should be given.

The estimate of leaf area index will usually be determined from leaf biomass (either from direct sampling or from litter fall) using a dry weight/leaf area conversion factor determined from a subsample of the leaves to which it is to be applied. The dry weight/leaf area conversion varies not only with time of sampling but also with position in the canopy. Methods of measuring leaf area are summarized by Lieth (1965). In the absence of a photoelectric or airflow device for measuring leaf area, it is best to photostat the leaves, using, for example, Ammonax paper, and to measure their areas with a planimeter, or by cutting them out and weighing. It is often convenient to calculate the regression of some transformation of leaf area on leaf length $\times$ width, or length^2, or $\log_{10}$ length and to use this relationship to predict area on subsequent samples. Methods based on punching discs of known area from the leaf, drying and weighing them, tend to be less reliable since the marginal part of the leaf is often under-represented by this procedure.

7.12   Stratified leaf area index. To describe the photosynthetic system further in some detailed studies it is useful to determine the leaf area index as a function of height, and this can be done by dividing the total stand into

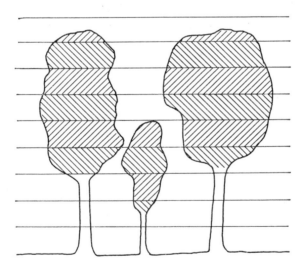

Figure 4. Stratified leaf area index.

ten or more horizontal strata, cutting the canopy of felled sample trees into the parts contained in respective strata as illustrated in Fig. 4 and measuring the leaves from each stratum separately. The interval between the strata may vary according to tree size, but it is best to choose an appropriate

length into which the bole can also be cut for stem analysis (4.61). It would
be valuable if the light profile in the stand is obtained before felling by
recording the relative light intensity at the boundaries between strata (Monsi
& Saeki 1953, Saeki 1963). On regularly growing conifers it may be more
convenient to treat each branch whorl separately.

7.13 Chlorophyll. Another relevant characteristic of the photosynthetic
system is the amount of chlorophyll/unit amount of leaf and stem for
different strata in the canopy. This must be estimated on fresh leaves and
bark, with as little delay as possible. Methods of extraction and analysis
are given, *i.a.*, by Mackinney 1941, Arnon 1949, Whittaker & Garfine 1962,
Bray 1960, Medina & Lieth 1963, 1964. While there is no suggestion that
the amount of chlorophyll limits production, it does represent one measure
of the size of the photosynthetic systems. It is useful in bringing the photosynthetic systems of stem and leaf on to a common basis.

7.14 Canopy photosynthesis. The canopy characteristics described in 7.11,
7.12 and 7.13 can be combined with measurements of the photosynthetic
response curve of individual leaves, and measurements of the radiation
climate, to give a model which can predict total photosynthesis under
defined conditions (de Wit 1965, Monteith 1965, Monsi 1968). Such a
model can be tested against short term estimates of net photosynthesis
based on CO_2 uptake (Monteith 1962, Bourdeau & Woodwell 1965) and
also against long term measurements of production with suitable correction
for stem and root respiration, and other losses. The details of this approach,
which provides a link between Sections PT and PP, lie outside the scope
of this Handbook. Several relevant papers may be found in the UNESCO
Montpellier Symposium (1965) and Copenhagen Symposium (1968).

7.2   Leaf losses

The regular litter fall measurements (Chapter 6, also 4.63) will suggest
which loss components are important in any particular system. Consumption
of attached leaves by invertebrates, especially caterpillars, in some sites
and especially in some years may represent an appreciable amount of the
primary production estimate (3.2, *G*). Methods for estimating consumption
are described fully in IBP Handbook No 13 by Petrusewicz & Macfadyen
(1970). However a few simple suggestions are made here so that the estimate

of primary production may be completed. There are two main methods of measuring consumption. The proportion of hole to entire leaf may be measured in samples taken at intervals through the season (Bray 1961, 1964). Two drawbacks to this are that some leaves may be completely consumed and that holes made in young leaves increase in area as the leaf expands. Alternatively, especially where there are only one or two main defoliating species concerned, frass fall may be collected and counted or

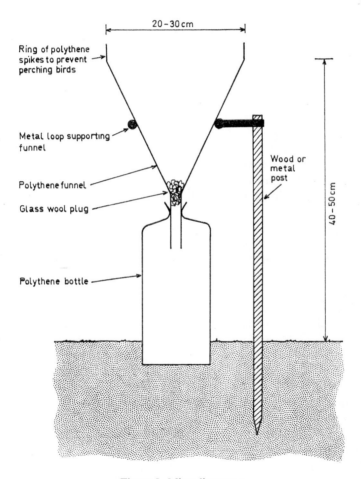

Figure 5. Micro-litter trap.

D

weighed. Simple feeding experiments are carried out on the main defoliating species, in jam jars or beakers, to find out the relationship between weight of leaf consumed and weight or number of frass pellets produced, (values of frass production $= 40 - 50\%$ leaf material are quite common). From this figure and the estimate of frass fall, leaf consumption in the field may be calculated (Carlisle & Brown 1966). Care must be taken to avoid atypical feeding behaviour in these experiments. Further details will be found in IBP Handbook No 13 on *Productivity of Terrestrial Animals: principles and methods* by Macfadyen & Petrusewicz (1970).

Frass fall is best collected in rather smaller containers than are used for leaf litter (Chapter 6). 'Polythene rain-gauges' (Fig. 5) used for measuring rainfall inside the woodland, and providing samples for chemical analysis (7.5) may serve a dual function as traps for frass and other micro-litter (Carlisle, Brown & White 1966b). Fine solid material is caught on a glass wool plug and analysed separately. Other components caught in these small impermeable traps include soluble organic matter washed out of the leaves, fine particles of organic matter including pollen grains and aphid dew (melezitose), Carlisle, Brown & White (1966b). In many cases these minor items will not be significant in the final production estimate, but it is necessary to make approximate estimates of them to ensure that this is the case.

Where plant material is consumed on the tree by, e.g. monkeys or birds, the estimation of loss is difficult and would necessarily be derived from a study of the vertebrates concerned and their average food intake.

Where material largely decomposes before falling to the ground, as is the case in humid tropical forests, these losses will also be difficult to measure. The principle will be to count leaf tips or leaf midribs, to measure twigs, to count seeds, etc. and then to convert these items to the full dry weight of an undecomposed and unconsumed leaf, twig, fruit, etc.

7.3 Chemical and calorific analysis and mineral cycling

Plant samples collected and dried in order to estimate dry matter production often represent a considerable manpower commitment and could yield much additional information on energy flow and mineral cycling if they were subjected to calorific and chemical analysis.

It is especially useful to determine the energy content of the material formed. The annual production expressed in energy units can be compared with records of the available radiation (7.4) to give some estimate of efficiency. Also the annual energy production represents the starting point of ecosystem metabolism and functioning; it is the energy source for all the consumer and decomposer organisms.

In practice the difference between the energy content (cal/g) of different plant components may be small compared with the errors in estimates of production (Ovington & Heitkamp 1960). Where it is not possible to determine energy content, a value of 4700 cal/g dry weight of plant material may be used. The term biocontent is suggested as meaning the total energy content (calorific value) in a standing crop, corresponding to the term for mass, biomass.

Lieth (1968) discusses the precautions necessary in sample preparation (drying, milling and pressing into tablets) and in the calibration and use of the bomb calorimeter.

In some programmes there will be emphasis on the study of mineral cycles (Ovington 1965a, 1965b, Greenland & Kowal 1960, Nye 1961). Details of methods are beyond the scope of this Handbook. In addition to the chemical analysis of samples collected for biomass measurement, it would be necessary to carry out chemical analysis of rainfall penetrating the woodland (7.2), of stem flow and of rainfall collected either outside the woodland or on a tower above the canopy (Carlisle, Brown & White 1966b). Most interest will attach to analysis of N, P, K, Ca and Mg. Where there is no immediate prospect of carrying out chemical or calorific analysis, it may still be worth storing subsamples of all the dry matter components. Components such as leaves, fine roots, twigs, may conveniently be milled before storage, but subsamples of main stem and branches are best stored whole. It may be possible to reduce the number of separate samples by bulking material from several samples. The amount stored can be quite small (10 g dry weight would be enough for most purposes).

7.4 Climate

There will probably be an IBP Handbook on climatological methods. Meanwhile a few comments are added here based on a document entitled 'Climatological Measurements for the International Biological Programme' produced by Dr J. L. Monteith for the British National Committee for IBP.

In general the existing network of climatological stations will provide adequate background information, except that there are insufficient measurements of radiation, especially in the tropics. There are several suitable instruments, e.g. the Kipp's version of the Moll-Gorczynski solarimeter which may be used to give an integrated total (the Siemens electrolytic integrator is suitable) as well as a continuous chart record. Radiation measurements are discussed i.a. by Platt & Griffiths (1964), Gates (1962), Stanhill (1965) and Drummond (1965).

Microclimatological measurements tend to be specialized and expensive and will feature mainly in developed programmes laid on by well-equipped research centres. Records of quantity and quality of rainfall inside and outside woodland areas are useful (7.3).

Similarly information may be needed on the transmission of photosynthetically useful radiation through vegetation, and on the quality and quantity of radiation reaching the woodland floor. There is no agreement about the best and most practical method. Problems include temporal and areal integration, the spectral sensitivity of photocells, and their failure to maintain their calibration. Probably it is best to measure solar energy in the visible spectrum with a thermopile sensitive over the whole solar spectrum ($0 \cdot 4$–2 μ) if necessary using a Schott RG 8 filter to find the amount of infra-red radiation at wavelengths longer than $0 \cdot 7$ μ. In most weather energy within the visible spectrum can be taken as 45% of total solar radiation. Other methods, such as selenium or silicon photocells can be calibrated against these instruments.

8

Results

8.1 Data-recording

A series of fifteen 'woody plant analysis forms' have been developed at Brookhaven National Laboratory by R. H. Whittaker & G. M. Woodwell. They include field recording, laboratory analysis (e.g. of stem discs) and the compilation of data for the whole forest stand. An example is shown as Fig. 6. The forms are printed on thin cards and measure $28 \times 21 \cdot 5$ cm. It is not expected that a given investigator would use all the forms or all the columns on the forms, which allow for a number of special contingencies. They are linked to a programme of computations which is not yet finalized.

The system of analysis involved and full details of the forms are in process of publication (Whittaker & Woodwell 1968). Further details are available from the authors at the Brookhaven National Laboratory, Associated Universities Inc., Upton, Long Island, New York, U.S.A.

8.2 Units

All units should be metric. Dry matter production can be presented as g/m^2 which is the same value as metric tons/km^2, but must be multiplied by 10 to give kg/ha. This latter unit which is generally familiar has the advantage of being quite close to lb/acre (kg/ha $\times$ $0 \cdot 89$ = lb/acre). However since the net annual production of woodlands usually lies between 5,000 and 50,000 kg/ha, and accuracy of estimation seldom permits more than three figures to be significant, there is some advantage in using the unit metric tons/ha or 10^3 kg/ha (i.e. 5–50 for the range above).

The term dry weight is itself imprecise since most biological material retains some bound water even at 105°C. The material should be dried to constant weight, either at 85°C or 105°C and it should be clearly stated which temperature has been used. Many ecologists prefer 105°C at which temperature constant weight is achieved more rapidly, but it can lead to combustion in the drying oven, especially where it is over-filled. It would

STEM ANALYSIS - LOGS

WOODY PLANT ANALYSIS
FORM 1 (STEM DATA 1)

SPECIES ______________

OBSERVER ______________ MONTH ______ DAY ______ YEAR ______ LOCATION ______________

SPECIES (1 2 3) [| |] SIZE RANGE (4) [ ] PLANT NO. (5 6 7) [| |] PLANT PART (8) [1] (STEM)

CARD SERIES: 1. (TERMINAL TWIG, ETC.)
2. (LOGS AND DISC WEIGHTS)

9	10 11 12	13 14	15	16	17	18 19	20 21 22 23 24 25	26 27	28 29 30 31	32 33 34	35 36 37	38 39 40	41 42 43	44 45 46	47 48 49	50 51 52	53 54 55	56 57 58	59 60 61	62 63 64
CARD SERIES	LOCATION	NO. STEMS IN CLUMP	FORM	CONDITION	CLASS	SPECIAL PROGRAM	DATE (DAY MO. YR.)	OBSERVER	SPECIFIC GRAVITY, WOOD 0.001	SPECIFIC GRAVITY, BARK 0.001	TERMINAL TWIG LENGTH MM	DIAM TWIG 1/10MM	LENGTH 2ND YR.	DIAM 2ND YR.	LENGTH 3RD YR.	DIAM 3RD YR.	LENGTH 4TH YR.	DIAM 4TH YR.	LENGTH 5TH YR.	DIAM 5TH YR.
1																				

9	10 11	12 13 14	15 16 17 18	19 20 21 22	23 24 25 26 27	28 29 30 31	32 33 34	35 36 37	38 39 40	41 42	43	44 45 46 47	48 49 50	51 52 53	54 55 56 57	58 59 60 61 62 63 64
										TREE OR SHOOT DATA *						
CARD SERIES	LOG NO.	LOG LENGTH CM	HEIGHT BASAL CUT CM	LOG FRESH WEIGHT (MINUS DISC) 10GR	FRESH WEIGHT BASAL DISC (OR SMALL LOG WHOLE) GR	DRY WEIGHT BASAL DISC (OR SMALL LOG) GR	LOG BASAL DIAMETER (INCL. BARK) MM	LOG BASAL WOOD DIAMETER MM	LOG MID DIAMETER (INCL. BARK) MM	SHOOT NO.	CLASS	HEIGHT CM	BASAL DIAMETER MM	DIAM. AT BREAST HEIGHT MM	AGE YRS	
2	01															
2	02															
2	03															
2	04															
2	05															
2	06															
2	07															
2	08															
2	09															
2	10															
2	19															
2	20															

Alternate size ranges (Dimensions indicated are for range 4, small trees)

SIZE 2	MM	MM	0.1 GR	0.01 GR	0.01 GR	0.1 MM	0.1 MM	0.1 MM			MM	0.1 MM		YRS	
RANGE 3	CM	CM	1.0 GR	0.1 GR	0.1 GR	0.1 MM	0.1 MM	0.1 MM			CM	MM	(MM)	YRS	
5	CM	CM	100 GR	10 GR	10 GR	MM	MM	MM			CM	MM	MM	YRS	
6	DM	DM	1000 GR	100 GR	100 GR	CM	CM	CM			DM	CM	CM	YRS	

*Enter in row for the first log of a tree or shoot.

Figure 6. Sample of the Brookhaven 'woody plant forms'.

be useful in some studies to estimate conversion factors for all types of material from 85°C to 105°C dry weight.

The gram calorie (cal) is the preferred unit of energy despite the adoption by physicists of the joule as the standard unit. The calorie has long been used by biologists and helps, by its association with nutrition, to stress the human welfare aspect of production studies. The solar constant has a convenient value ($2 \cdot 00$ cal cm^{-2} min^{-1}). For energy flow studies cal cm^{-2} day^{-1} is a suitable unit. 1,000 calories = 1 kilocalorie (kcal). Nutritionists commonly use kcal units, often representing them simply as Calories.

8.3 Errors

Three major problems in arriving at a precise and accurate estimate of primary production are errors due to measurement, sampling errors and the effects of climatic variation from year to year. The effects of climatic variation on production are poorly understood and cannot easily be corrected for. It is therefore essential to base the production estimate on a minimum period of three years, with five years being preferable, and ten years quite possible for estimates based on radial increments. This is another argument for using long-established sample plots wherever these are available. Components like litter fall should be estimated over a period of at least three and preferably five years (Carlisle, Brown & White 1966a).

In arriving at acceptable production estimates it is best to direct effort towards minimizing the errors in the major components while tolerating larger (sampling and measurement) errors in the minor components. The largest single component will usually be stem growth, and since this is the component which has been most studied by foresters, use of all available mensuration techniques, volume tables, etc. will help to reduce the error in this estimate. It is estimated that figures for the total volume of boles of trees normally come within about 5% of the true value. The measurement and sampling errors in estimating some of the minor components must be quite large. It is seldom if ever possible to present an estimate of annual production with 95% confidence limits which genuinely represent the likelihood that the true annual production of the community under investigations falls within those limits. It is however often possible to give some estimate of the variability of a particular set of measurements involved in the estimate of community production, as for example the dry weight of trees belonging to the same sample unit, or the dry weight of ground flora quadrats clipped at the same time (Whittaker 1966). In such cases the intensity of sampling should aim at a standard error of the mean of $\pm 5\%$ ($\pm 10\%$ for 95% confidence limits), though in many cases this is unattainable. It would be valuable, in presenting production data, if authors would give some subjective assessment of the main errors involved in their estimate.

In many cases partitioning of material is arbitrary. There is no rigid or general rule for the separation of root and stem, stem and branch, branch and leaf, living and dead. Stoloniferous grasses, stilt roots, deciduous stem spines, all present their own peculiar problems, for which individual solutions must be worked out. The important thing is to *define the criteria used in any separation* and to *be consistent in applying them.*

8.4   Calculations

The general basis for the calculation of net production has been given in 3.1. In production studies the calculations should be clearly laid out and the assumptions involved clearly stated. If possible the validity of these assumptions should be evaluated and the consequences should the assumptions subsequently prove wrong. Sometimes biases may be accepted as the lesser of two evils. This should also be clearly stated and evaluated.

One should define and describe the dimensions of the amounts calculated, e.g. Bunce (1968) says that a tree of 104 cm girth can be felled, weighed and subsampled in two days by three people using a power saw for large branches and trunk sections. Clear distinction should be made between directly measured and indirectly estimated values. It may be possible in tabulation to put actual measurements in bold figures and calculated values in normal type.

Calculations and mathematical treatments are often greatly facilitated by the use of proper symbols. Care should be taken not to use the same symbol, or confusing symbols for different amounts in a series of studies. A system of notations such as were used by Ogawa *et al.* (1965) is recommended.

8.5   Commitment

Since money and manpower are likely to be the main limiting factors in the IBP, any assessment of the commitment involved in obtaining production data would be very useful.

8.6   Publication

Research falling within the scope of this Handbook should be published in the normal and appropriate journals. It would be appreciated if a reprint of all publications could be sent to IBP Central Office (7 Marylebone Road, London, N.W.1., U.K.). Original data, where it is inappropriate to include them in full in a published paper, should be preserved, and duplicated copies made available to those who request them.

Acknowledgements

I would like to acknowledge the help of Prof. J. D. Ovington on whose original draft both the draft circulated in January 1966 and this second version are based.

I would like to thank the following for their helpful comments on the first draft. I have incorporated these comments as far as possible but some proved mutually contradictory.

Mr H.W.B.Barlow, East Malling Research Station, U.K.

Dr W.O.Binns, Forestry Commission, U.K.

Dr J.R.Bray, New Zealand.

Dr M.D.Gwynne, E.A.A.F.R.O., Kenya.

Prof. Dr. Ir. G.Hellinga, Wageningen, Netherlands.

Dr B.Hopkins, Ibadan, Nigeria.

Prof. R.J.Hutnik, Dept. of Forestry, Pennsylvania State University, U.S.A.

Dr J.Kvet, Academy of Sciences, Prague, Czechoslovakia.

Dr H.Lieth, Botanisches Institute, Stuttgart-Hohenheim, Germany.

Prof. H.A.I.Madgwick, Dept. of Forestry, Virginia Polytechnic Institute, U.S.A.

Mr P.H.Nye, Dept. of Agriculture, Oxford University, U.K.

Dr J.S.Olson, Oak Ridge National Laboratory, U.S.A.

Dr M.E.D.Poore, The Nature Conservancy, U.K.

Mr M.W.Shaw, The Nature Conservancy, Bangor, U.K.

Mr R.C.Steele, The Nature Conservancy, Monks Wood, U.K.

Prof. Dr Ir.G.J.Vervelde, Wageningen, Netherlands.

Dr B.Vins, Forestry and Game Management Res. Inst. Zbraslav, Czechoslovakia.

Prof. Dr M.Vyskot, Dept. of Silviculture, Brno University, Czechoslovakia.
Dr G.F.Weetman, Pulp and Paper Research Institute, Montreal, Canada.
Dr P.R.Wycherley, Rubber Research Institute, Kuala Lumpur, Malaya.

I would especially like to thank for their full and extended comments
Prof. T.Kira of Osaka City University, Japan; Dr A.Carlisle and Mr
A.H.F.Brown of the Nature Conservancy Merlewood Research Station,
U.K.; Prof. R.H.Whittaker of the Brookhaven National Laboratory, U.S.A.;
and Dr H.C.Dawkins of the Forestry Dept., Oxford. Carlisle and Brown
produced an extensive duplicated paper on 'The measurement of net primary
production in woodlands'. Prof. Whittaker sent extensive comments and
details of current work at Brookhaven. Prof. Kira forwarded to me extensive
comments which he had summarized, from a meeting of 21 members of the
Japanese Working Group on Terrestrial Productivity. I have drawn heavily
on these three contributions. I must apologize to their authors for any
omissions or misinterpretations which I hope they will correct in due course.

References

Papers included in the symposium on *The Methodology of Plant Ecophysiology*, UNESCO Arid Zone Research 25, held at Montpellier in 1961, and published in Paris in 1965 will be referred to as *UNESCO Montpellier Symposium*.

Papers given at the UNESCO Symposium on the *Functioning of terrestrial ecosystems at the primary production level*, held in Copenhagen in 1965, ed. F.E. ECKHARDT and published in Paris in 1968 will be referred to as *UNESCO Copenhagen Symposium*.

ALM A.A. & BROWN B.A. (1964). Dendrometer bands to measure stand growth. *Minn. For. Note No.* 156, p. 2.

ARNON D.I. (1949). Copper enzymes in isolated chloroplasts. Polyphenoloxidase in *Beta vulgaris*. *Pl. Physiol., Lancaster*, **24**, 1–15.

ATTIWILL P.M. (1962). Estimating branch dry weights and leaf area from measurements of branch girth in *Eucalyptus*. *Forest Sci.* **8**, 132–41.

BASKERVILLE G.L. (1965). Estimation of dry weight of tree components and total standing crop in conifer stands. *Ecology* **46**, 867–9.

BASKERVILLE G.L. (1966). Dry matter production in immature balsam fir stands; roots, lesser vegetation, and total stand. *Forest Sci.* **12**, 49–53.

BOGGIE R., HUNTER R.F. & KNIGHT A.H. (1958). Studies of the root development of plants in the field using radioactive tracers. *J. Ecol.* **46**, 621–39.

BOURDEAU P.F. & WOODWELL G.M. (1965). Measurements of plant CO_2 exchange by infra-red absorption under controlled conditions and in the field. *UNESCO Montpellier Symposium* 283–90.

BRADLEY R.T., CHRISTIE J.M. & JOHNSTON D.R. (1966). *Forest Management Tables. Forestry Commission Booklet* 16, London, H.M.S.O.

BRAY J.R. (1960). The chlorophyll content of some native and managed plant communities in central Minnesota. *Can. J. Bot.* **38**, 313–33.

BRAY J.R. (1961). Measurement of leaf utilization as an index of minimum level of primary consumption. *Oikos* **12**, 70–4.

BRAY J.R. (1963). Root production and the estimation of net productivity. *Can. J. Bot.* **41**, 65-72.

BRAY J.R. (1964). Primary consumption in three forest canopies. *Ecology* **45**, 165–7.

BRAY J.R. & GORHAM E. (1964). Litter production in forests of the world. *Adv. Ecol. Res.* **2**, 101–57.

BRAY J.R., LAWRENCE D.B. & PEARSON L.C. (1959). Primary production in some Minnesota communities for 1957. *Oikos* **10**, 38–49.

BUNCE H. (1961). A correction table for use when taking increment borings of Western Hemlock to determine total age. *For. Chron.* **37**, 158–9.

BUNCE, R.G.H. (1968). Biomass and production of trees in a mixed deciduous woodland. I Girth and height as parameters for the estimation of tree height. *J. Ecol.* **56**, 759–75.

CARLISLE A. & BROWN A.H. (1966). *The measurement of net primary production in woodlands.* Mimeographed.

CARLISLE A., BROWN A.H.F. & WHITE E.J. (1966a). Litter fall, leaf production and the effects of defoliation by *Tortrix viridana* in a sessile oak (*Quercus petraea*) woodland. *J. Ecol.* **54**, 65–85.

CARLISLE A., BROWN A.H.F. & WHITE E.J. (1966b). The organic matter and nutrient elements in the precipitation beneath a sessile oak canopy. *J. Ecol.* **54**, 87–98.

COUSENS J.E. & BLACK J.N. (1965). *Utilization of solar energy by forests.* Mimeographed.

DRUMMOND A.J. (1965). Techniques for the measurement of solar and terrestrial radiation fluxes in plant biological research. A review with special reference to the arid zones. *UNESCO Montpellier Symposium* 13–27.

EKLUND, B. (1949). Skogsforskningsinstitutets årsringmätningsmaskiner: tillkomst, konstruktion och användning. *Meddn St. SkogsförskInst.* **38**, 1–77.

FEHRENBACHER J.B. & ALEXANDER J.D. (1955). A method for studying corn root distribution using a soil-core sampling machine and shaker type washer. *Agron. J.* **47**, 468–72.

FERAT F. (1958). *Dendrometri.* Kutulmus Matbaasi, Istanbul (Turkish).

GATES D.M. (1962). *Energy exchange in the biosphere.* Harper & Row, N.Y.

GIMINGHAM, C.H. & MILLER, G.R. (1968). Measurement of the primary production of dwarf shrub heaths, in MILNER, C. & HUGHES, R.E. *IBP Handbook No. 6*, 43–51.

GREENLAND D.J. & KOWAL J.M.L. (1960). Nutrient content of the moist tropical forest of Ghana. *Pl. Soil* **12**, 154–74.

GROSENBAUGH L.R. (1963). Optical dendrometers for out-of-reach diameters; a conspectus and some new theory. *Forest Sci. Monogr.* **4**, 1–47.

HEAD G.C. (1965). Studies of diurnal changes in cherry root growth and nutational movements of apple root tips by time-lapse cinematography. *Ann. Bot.* **29**, 219–24.

HEINRICHS J.F. (1964). Pocket-sized sharpener for increment borers. *J. For.* **62**, 753.

HOLLAND, D.A. (1968). The estimation of total leaf area on a tree. *Rep. E. Malling Res. Stn. 1966–7*, 101–4.

HUMMEL F.C. (1951). Instruments for the measurement of height, diameter and taper on standing trees. *For. Abstr.* **12**, 261–9.

HUSCH B. (1963). *Forest Mensuration and Statistics.* Ronald Press, N.Y.

JEFFERS J.N.R. (1956). Barr and Stroud dendrometer, Type F.P.7. *Rep. For. Res. For. Comm., London* 1954/5, 127–36.

KEEN R.E. & WEETMAN G.F. (1961). Two methods of weighing trees. *Woodlds Res. Index* **123**, 1–9.

KERN K.G. (1961). Ein Beitrag zur Zuwachsmessung mit dem Arnberg-Mikrodendrometer. *Allg. Forst-u. Jagdztg.* **132**, 206–12.

KIMURA M. (1960). Primary production of the warm-temperate laurel forest in the southern part of Osumi Peninsula, Kyushu, Japan. *Misc. Rep. Res. Inst. nat. Resour., Tokyo* **52–53**, 36–47.

KIMURA M. (1963). Dynamics of vegetation in relation to soil development in northern Yatsugadake Mountains. *Jap. J. Bot.* **18**, 255–87.

KIRA T., OGAWA H., YODA K. & OGINO K. (1967). Comparative ecological studies in three main types of forest vegetation in Thailand. IV. Dry matter production, with special reference to the Khao Chong rain forest. *Nature and Life in S.E. Asia* **5**, 149–74.

KIRA, T. & SHIDEI, T. (1967). Primary production and turnover of organic matter in different forest ecosystems of the western pacific. *Jap. J. Ecol.* **17**, 70–87.

KITTREDGE J. (1944). Estimation of the amount of foliage of trees and stands. *J. For.* **42**, 905–12.

KURTH H. (1963). (Systematic errors in the determination of radial increment from cores). (German). *Arch. Forstw.* **12**, 751–63.

LIETH H. (1965). Indirect measurements of dry matter production. *UNESCO Montpellier Symposium* 513–8.

LIETH, H. (1968). The determination of plant dry-matter production with special emphasis on the underground parts. *UNESCO Copenhagen Symposium* 179–86.

LEITH H. (1968). The measurement of calorific values of biological material and the determination of ecological efficiency. *UNESCO Copenhagen Symposium* 233–42.

LIMING F.G. (1957). Home-made dendrometers. *J. For.* **55**, 575–7.

LOOMIS R.M., PHARES R.E. & CROSBY J.S. (1966). Estimating foliage and branchwood quantities in Shortleaf Pine. *Forest Sci.* **12**, 30–9.

LOTT W.L., SATCHELL D.P. & HALL N.S. (1950). A tracer element technique in the study of root extension. *Proc. Am. Soc. hort. Sci.* **55**, 27–34.

MACKINNEY G. (1941). Absorption of light by chlorophyll solutions. *J. biol. Chem.* **140**, 315–22.

MADGWICK H.A.I. (1964). Estimation of surface area of pine needles with special reference to *Pinus resinosa*. *J. For.* **62**, 636.

MEDINA E. & LIETH H. (1963). Contenido de clorofila de algunas asociaciones vegetales de Europa central y sa relacion con la productividad. *Qualitas Pl. Mater. veg.* **9**, 219–29.

MEDINA E. & LIETH H. (1964). Die Beziehungen Zwischen Chlorophyllgehalt assimilierender Fläche und Trockensubstanzproduktion in einigen Pflanzengemeinschaften. *Beitr. Biol. Pfl.* **40**, 451–94.

MESAVAGE C. (1964). Core examination kit. *J. For.* **62**, 635.

MILNER, C. & HUGHES, R.E. (1968). *Methods of the measurement of the primary production of grassland. IBP Handbook No. 6.* Blackwell, Oxford and Edinburgh.

MONSI M. (1968). Mathematical models of plant communities. *UNESCO Copenhagen Symposium* 131–49.

MONSI M. & SAEKI T. (1953). Über den Lichtfaktor in den Pflanzengesellschaften und seine Bedeutung für die Stoffproduktion. *Jap. J. Bot.* **14**, 22–52.

MONTEITH J.L. (1962). Measurement and interpretation of carbon dioxide fluxes in the field. *Neth. J. agric. Sci.* **10**, 334–46.

MONTEITH J.L. (1965). Light distribution and photosynthesis in field crops. *Ann. Bot.* **29**, 17–37.

MÜLLER D. & NIELSEN J. (1965). Production brute, pertes par respiration et production nette dans la forêt ombrophile tropicale. *Forst. ForsVaes. Danm.* **29**, 69–160.

NEWBOULD P.J. (1968). Methods of estimating root production. *UNESCO Copenhagen Symposium* 187–90.

NEWMAN E.I. (1966). A method of estimating the total length of root in a sample. *J. appl. Ecol.* **3**, 139–45.

NOMOTO N. (1964). Primary productivity of beech forest in Japan. *Jap. J. Bot.* **18**, 385–421.

NYE P.H. (1961). Organic matter and nutrient cycles under moist tropical forest. *Pl. Soil* **13**, 333–46.

OGAWA H., YODA K. & KIRA T. (1961). A preliminary survey on the vegetation of Thailand. *Nature and life in S.E. Asia* **1**, 21–157.

OGAWA H., YODA K, KIRA T., OGINO K., SHIDEI T., RATANAWONGSE D. & APASUTAYA C. (1965). Comparative ecological study on three main types of forest vegetation in Thailand. I Structure and floristic composition. *Nature and Life in S.E. Asia* **4**, 13-48.

OGAWA H., YODA K., OGINO K. & KIRA T. (1965). Comparative ecological studies on three main types of forest vegetation in Thailand. II Plant biomass. *Nature and Life in S.E. Asia* **4**, 49–80.

OGINO K., SABHASRI S. & SHIDEI T. (1964). The estimation of the standing crop of the forest in northern Thailand. *The South-east Asian Studies* **4**, 89–97.

OLSON J.S. (1964). Gross and net production of terrestrial vegetation. *J. Ecol.* **52**, *Suppl.* 99–118.

ORLOV A. (1955). The role of feeding roots of forest vegetation in enriching the soil with organic matter. *Pochvovedenie* **6**, 14–20.

OVINGTON J.D. (1957). Dry-matter production by *Pinus sylvestris* L. *Ann. Bot.* **21**, 287–314.

OVINGTON J.D. (1962). Quantitative ecology and the woodland ecosystem concept *Adv. Ecol. Res.* **1**, 103–92.

OVINGTON J.D. (1963) Flower and seed production. A source of error in estimating woodland production, energy flow and mineral cycling. *Oikos* **14**, 148–53.

OVINGTON J.D. (1965a). Organic production, turnover and mineral cycling in woodlands. *Biol. Rev.* **40**, 295–336.

OVINGTON J.D. (1965b). Nutrient cycling in woodlands. *Experimental Pedology*, ed. E. G. HALLSWORTH & D. V. CRAWFORD, Butterworths, London, 208–18.

OVINGTON J.D. & HEITKAMP D. (1960). The accumulation of energy in forest plantations. *J. Ecol.* **48**, 639–46.

OVINGTON J.D., HEITKAMP D. & LAWRENCE D.B. (1963). Plant biomass and productivity of prairie, savanna, oakwood and maize field ecosytems in central Minnesota. *Ecology* **44**, 52–63.

OVINGTON J.D. & MADGWICK H.A.I. (1959a). Distribution of organic matter and plant nutrients in a plantation of Scots Pine. *Forest Sci.* **5**, 344–55.

OVINGTON J.D. & MADGWICK H.A.I. (1959b). The growth and composition of natural stands of birch. I. Dry-matter production. *Pl. Soil* **10**, 271–88.

OVINGTON J.D. & MURRAY G. (1964). Determination of acorn fall. *Q. Jl. For.* **58**, 152–9.

PARDÉ J. (1961). *Dendrometrie.* Imprimerie Louis-Jean, Paris.

PETRUSEWICZ K. & MACFADYEN A. (1970). *Productivity of Terrestrial Animals: principles and methods.* IBP Handbook No. 13. Blackwell Scientific Publications, Oxford & Edinburgh.

PLATT R.B. & GRIFFITHS J. (1964). *Environmental measurement and interpretation.* Reinhold Publ. Corp. New York.

PRESTEMON D.R. (1965). Improving the power increment borer for hardwoods. *J. For.* **63**, 763–5.

PRODAN M. *Holzmesslehre* (1965). J. D. Sauerlander Verlag, Frankfurt.

PRODAN, M. (1968). *Forest Biometrics.* Pergamon, Oxford.

ROGERS W.S. & HEAD G.C. (1963). A new root-observation laboratory. *Rep. E. Malling Res. Stn. for 1962*, 55–7.

ROTHACHER J.S., BLOW F.E. & POTTS S.M. (1954). Estimating the quantity of tree foliage in oak stands in the Tennessee Valley. *J. For.* **52**, 169–73.

SAEKI T. (1963). Light relations in plant communities. In EVANS L. T. ed. *Environmenta. Control of Plant Growth.* Academic Press, N.Y. & London, 79–92.

SATOO T. *et al.* (1955–9). Materials for the studies of growth in stands. 1–5. *Bull. Tokyo Univ. Forests* **48**, 69–90; **52**, 15–31, 33–51; **54**, 71–100; **55**, 101–23. (Japanese, Eng. summary).

SATOO T. (1962). Notes on Kittredge's method of estimation of amount of leaves of forest stand. *J. Jap. For. Soc.* **44**, 267–72.

SCHUURMANN J.J. & GOEDEWAAGEN M.A.J. (1965). *Methods for the Examination of Root Systems and Roots.* Centre for Agricultural Publications and Documentation. Wageningen.

SPECIAL COMMITTEE FOR THE INTERNATIONAL BIOLOGICAL PROGRAMME. (1965). *I.B.P. News* **2**, Rome.

SCOTT D.R.M. (1955). Amount and chemical composition of the organic matter contributed by overstory and understory vegetation to forest soil. *Yale Univ. Sch. For. Bull.* **62**.

SHANKS R.E. & CLEBSCH E.E.C. (1962). Computer programs for the estimation of forest stand weight and mineral pool. *Ecology* **43**, 339–41.

SHAW, M.W. (1968). Factors affecting the natural regeneration of sessile oak (*Quercus petraea*) in North Wales I A preliminary study of acorn production, viability and losses. *J. Ecol.* **56**, 565–83.

SHINOZAKI K., YODA K., HOZUMI K. & KIRA T. (1964). A quantitative analysis of plant form—the pipe model theory. *Jap. J. Ecol.* **14**, 97–105, 133–9.

SINGER F.P. & HUTNIK R.J. (1965). Excavating roots with water pressure. *J. For.* **63**, 37–8.

SPURR S.H. (1952). *Forest Inventory.* Ronald Press, N.Y.

STAGE A.R. (1963). Specific gravity and tree weight of single tree samples of Grand Fir. *U.S. For Serv. Res. Pap. Intermt. For. Range Exp. Stn. No. INT-4*, pp. 11.

STANHILL G. (1965). A comparison of four methods of estimating solar radiation. *UNESCO Montpellier Symposium* 55–61.

STEVEN H.M. & CARLISLE A. (1959). *The Native Pinewoods of Scotland*, Edinburgh.

TADAKI Y. & SHIDEI T. (1960). Studies on productive structure of forest. 1. The seasonal variation of leaf amount and the dry matter production of deciduous sapling stand (*Ulmus parviflora*). *J. Jap. For. Soc.* **42**, 427–34.

TADAKI Y., SHIDEI T., SAKASEGAWA T. & OGINO K. (1961). Studies on productive structure of forest. 2. Estimation of standing crop and some analyses of productivity of young birch stand (*Betula platyphylla*). *J. Jap. For. Soc.* **43**, 19–26.

TADAKI Y., OGATA N. & TAKAGI T. (1962). Studies on productive structure of forest. 3. Estimation of standing crop and some analyses on productivity of young stands of *Castanopsis cupsidata. J. Jap. For. Soc.* **44**, 350–9.

TADAKI Y. (1963). Studies on production structure of forest. 4. Some studies on leaf amount of stands and individual trees. *J. Jap. For. Soc.* **45**, 249–56.

TADAKI Y., OGATA N. & NAGATOMO T. (1963). Studies on production structure of forest. 5. Some analyses on productivities of artificial stand of *Acacia mollissima. J. Jap. For. Soc.* **45**, 293–301.

TADAKI Y. (1965). Studies on production structure of forests. 7. The primary production of a young stand of *Castanopsis cupsidata. Jap. J. Ecol.* **15**, 142–7.

TADAKI Y. (1965). Studies on production structure of forest. 8. Productivity of an *Acacia mollissima* stand in higher stand density. *J. Jap. For. Soc.* **47**, 384–91.

THOMPSON R.L. & McGINNES B.S. (1963). A comparison of eight types of mast traps. *J. For.* **61**, 679–80.

USSR ACADEMY OF SCIENCES (1968). *Methods of productivity studies in root systems and rhizosphere organisms*. International Symposium USSR, August 28–September 12, 1968. (Reprinted by and available from IBP Central Office.)

VINS B. (in press). Foundations, methods and use of tree-ring analyses on cores extracted by an increment borer. *UNESCO Copenhagen Symposium* 219–27.

WALTERS C.S. & BRUCKMANN G. (1964). A comparison of methods for determining volume of increment cores. *J. For.* **62**, 172–7.

WEETMAN G.F. & HARLAND R. (1964). Foliage and wood production in unthinned Black Spruce in Northern Quebec. *Forest Sci.* **10**, 80–8.

WHITTAKER R.H. (1961). Estimation of net primary production of forest and shrub communities. *Ecology* **42**, 177–80.

WHITTAKER R.H. (1962). Net production relations of shrubs in the Great Smoky Mountains. *Ecology* **43**, 357–77.

WHITTAKER R.H. (1965). Branch dimensions and estimation of branch production. *Ecology* **46**, 365–70.

WHITTAKER R.H. (1966). Forest dimensions and estimated production in the Great Smoky Mountains. *Ecology* **47**, 103–21.

WHITTAKER R.H. & GARFINE V. (1962). Leaf characteristics and chlorophyll in relation to production and exposure in *Rhododendron. Ecology* **43**, 120–5.

WHITTAKER R.H., COHEN N. & OLSON J.S. (1963). Net production relations of three tree species at Oak Ridge, Tennessee. *Ecology* **44**, 806–10.

WHITTAKER R.H. & WOODWELL G.M. (1968). Dimension and production relations of trees and shrubs in the Brookhaven Forest, New York. *J. Ecol.* **56**, 1–25.

WIT, C.T. DE (1965). Photosynthesis of leaf canopies. *Versl. Landbouwk. Onderz.* **663**, 1–57.

YOUNG H.E., STRAND L. & ALTENBERGER R. (1964). Preliminary fresh and dry weight tables for seven tree species in Maine. *Tech. Bull. Me. agric. Exp. Stn, No.* **12**, pp. 76.

YOUNG H.E., HOAR, L. & ASHELEY M. (1965). Weight of wood substance for components of seven tree species. *TAPPI* **48**, 466–9.

Further Reading

AALTONEN V.T. (1920). Uber die Ausbreitung und den Reichtum der Baumwurzeln in den Heidewaldern Lapplands. *Acta for. fenn.* **14**, 1–55.

ANDO T. *et al.* (1959). Estimation of the amount of leaves, twigs and branches of Sugi (*Cryptomeria japonica* D. Don.) by sampling method. *J. Jap. For. Soc.* **41**, 117–24.

ANDO T. (1965). Estimation of dry-matter and growth analysis of the young stand of Japanese Black Pine (*Pinus thunbergii*). *Advanc. Front. Pl. Sci., New Delhi* **10**, 1–10.

ASSMANN E. & FRANZ F. (1963). Vorlaufige Fichten-Ertragstafel für Bayern. *Fortwiss. ZentBl.* **84**, 1–68.

ATTIWILL P.M. (1966). A method for estimating crown weight in *Eucalyptus* and some other implications of relationships between crown weight and stem diameter. *Ecology* **47**, 795–804.

ATTIWILL P.M. & OVINGTON J.D. (1968). Determination of forest biomass. *For. Sci.* **14**, 13–5.

BARGIONI G. (1959). Contributo allo studio del sistema radicale del ciliegio nel Veronese. *Riv. Ortoflorofruttic. ital.* **43**, 3–23.

BASKERVILLE G.L. (1962). Production in forests. *Mimeo, Dept. For. Can.* MD–322–62. 83 pp.

BASKERVILLE G.L. (1965). Dry matter production in immature fir stands. *Forest Sci. Monogr.* **9**, 1–42.

BECKING J.H. (1962). Potential and actual productivity of stem wood in forestry. *Neth. J. agric. Sci.* **10**, 354–60.

BODE R.H. (1959). Über den Zusammenhang zwischen Blattenfaltung und Neubildung der Saugwurzeln bei Juglans. *Ber. dt. bot. Ges.* **73**, 93–8.

BOYSEN-JENSEN P. (1932). *Die Stoffproduktion der Pflanzen.* Jena G. Fischer Verlag.

BRAY J.R. & DUDKIEVICZ L.A. (1963). The composition, biomass and productivity of two *Populus* forests. *Bull. Torrey bot. Club* **90**, 298–308.

BURGER H. (1935–54). Series of papers published under general title of Holz, Blattmenge und Zuwachs. *Mitt. schweiz. Anst. Forstl. VersWes.* **15–31**.

CABLE D.R. (1958). Estimating surface area of ponderosa pine foliage in Central Arizona. *Forest Sci.* **4**, 45–9.

COKER E.G. (1958). Root studies XII: root systems of apple on Malling root stocks on five soil series. *J. hort. Sci.* **33**, 71–9.

DAHLMAN R.C. & KUCERA C.L. (1965). Root productivity and turnover in native prairie. *Ecology* **46**, 84–9.

DUVIGNEAUD P. ed. (1963). *L'écologie, science moderne de synthèse.* Vol. **2**. *Ecosystèmes et biosphère.* Brussels.

EATON F.M. (1931). Root development as related to character of growth and fruitfulness of the cotton plant. *J. Agric. Res.* **43**, 875–83.

ECKHARDT F.E. (1966). Groupe d'Étude de la Productivité Primaire des Ecosystèmes Terrestres. *Enquête sur l'opportunité d'un programme integré de recherches.* Programme Biologique International, Comité François. Montpellier, 1–26.

EIDMANN F.E. (1943). Untersuchungen über die Wurzelatmung und Transpiration unserer Hauptholzkarten. *SchrReihe Akad. dt. Forstw.* **5**, 1–144.

FARRAR J.L. (1961). Longitudinal variation in the thickness of the annual ring. *For. Chron.* **37**, 323–31.

FERRILL M.D. & WOODS F.W. (1966). Root extension in a longleaf pine plantation. *Ecology* **47**, 97–102.

FRITTS H.C. (1962). Multiple regression analysis of radial growth in indivdual trees. *Forest Sci.* **6**, 334–49.

GRIFFITH A.L. & HOWLAND P. (1961). Silviculture research; rate of growth of new roots and new mycorrhiza immediately after planting. *Rep. E. Afr. Agric. For. Res. Org.* 1960, 84–5.

HEIKURAINEN L. (1957). Der Wurzelaufbau der Kiefernbestände auf Reisermoorböden und Seine Beeinflussung durch die Entwässerung. *Acta for. fenn.* **65**, 1–85.

JAPANESE NATIONAL COMMITTEE FOR IBP (1969). *Progress report for 1968 of JIBP.* Tokyo. (Lists on pp. 9–11 42 refs. to Japanese IBP–PT work, of which about half refer to primary production of forests).

KÖHNLEIN J. & VETTER H. (1953). *Enterückstände und Wurzelbild.* Parey Verlag, Hamburg, Berlin.

KOLESNIKOW E.W. (1960). The study of the root system of fruit trees by the use of the absorption method. (Russian). *Izv. timiryazev. sel.-khoz. Akad.* **4**, 34–42.

KOLESNIKOW E.W. (1962). *Wurzelsysteme von Obst- und Beerengehulzen und Methoden zu ihrem studium.* (orig. Russian). 190 pp. Moskau.

KOZLOWSKI T.T. (1949). Light and water in relation to growth and competition of piedmont forest trees. *Ecol. Monogr.* **19**, 207–31.

KOZLOWSKI T.T. & WINGET C.H. (1964). Diurnal and seasonal variation in radii of tree stems. *Ecology* **45**, 149–55.

KRAMER P.J. (1956). Roots as absorbing organs. *Handb. Pflanzenphys. Encyclop. Plant Phys.* **3**, 188–214.

KRAVCENKO V.I. (1964). Dimensions and weight of the aerial and subterranean parts of *Picea abies* trees in stands of different density. (Russian). *Lesn. Z., Arhangel'sk* **7**, 45–7.

KUROIWA S. (1960). Ecological and physiological studies on the vegetation of Mt. Shimagare. V. Intraspecific competition and productivity difference among tree classes in the *Abies* stand. *Bot. Mag., Tokyo* **73**, 165–74.

KUTSCHERA L. (1960). *Wurzelatlas mitteleuropäischer Ackerunkräuter und Kulturpflanzen.* 574 pp. DLG Verlag, Frankfurt.

LAITAKARI E. (1929). Männyn juuristo (the root system of pine, *Pinus sylvestris*). *Acta for. fenn.* **33**, 1–380.

LARSON M.M. (1962). Construction and use of glass-faced boxes to study root development of tree seedlings. *Res. Notes Rocky Mount. Forest Range Exp. Stn.* **73**

LEMKE K. (1956). Untersuchungen über das Wurzelsystem der Roteiche auf diluvialen Standortsformen. *Arch. Forstw.* **5,** 8–48, 161–202.

LIETH H. (1961). La production de sustancia organica por la capa vegetal terrestre y sus problemas. *Acta cient. venez.* **12,** 107–14.

LIETH H. ed. (1962). *Die Stoffproduktion der Pflanzendecke.* Stuttgart, Gustav Fischer Verlag, 156 pp.

LIETH, H. (1964). Versuch einer kartographischen darstellung der Produktivitat der Pflanzendecke auf der Erde. *Geographisches Taschenbuch* 1964/5, 72–80.

LIETH H. (1965) Ökologische Fragestellungen bei der Untersuchung der biologischen Stoffproduktion. *Qualitas Pl. Mater. veg.* **12,** 241–61.

LIETH H., OSSWALD D. & MARTENS H. (1965). Stoffproduktion, Spross/Wurzel verhältnis, Chlorophyllgehalt und Blattfläche von Jungpoppeln. *Mitt. Ver. Forstl. Standortskunde ForstpflZücht.* **15,** 70–4.

LIETH H., OSSWALD D., MARTENS H. & PFLANZ B. (1963). *Das Arbeitsprogramm zur Untersuchung der Stoffproduktion am Botan.* Inst. der Landw. Hochschule Stuttgart-Hohenheim. Mimeographed.

MADGWICK H.A.I. (1968). Seasonal changes in biomass and annual production of an old field *Pinus virginiana* stand. *Ecology* **49,** 149–52.

MARUYAMA I. & SATO T. (1953). Estimation of the amount of foliage of trees and stands (Report 1)—on the Akamatu of Iwate District. *Bull. Govt. Forest Exp. Stn., Meguro.* **65,** 1–10.

MCMINN R.G. (1963). Characteristics of Douglas Fir root systems. *Can. J. Bot.* **41,** 105–22.

MEDWECKA-KORNAS A. ed. (1968). *Contributions from the meeting on primary productivity Krakow—April 1967.* Mimeographed.

MILLER, W.E. (1965). Number of branchlets on Red Pine in young plantations. *Forest Sci.* **11,** 42–9.

MÖLLER C.M. (1947). The effect of thinning, age and site on foliage increment and the loss of dry matter. *J. For.* **45,** 393–404.

MÖLLER C.M., MÜLLER D. & NIELSEN J. (1954). Graphic presentation of dry matter production of European beech. *Forest ForsVaes. Danm.* **21,** 327–35.

MOORE C.S. (1966). The relationship of increment in trunk girth with shoot growth in Apple trees. *Rep. E. Malling Res. Stn.,* 1964/65, 115–9.

NANSON A. (1962). (Some fundamental points concerning the balance of photosynthetic assimilation in a Beech forest of the Ardennes.) (french). *Bull. Inst. agron. Stns. Rech. Gembloux* **30,** 320–31.

NOMOTO N., KASANAGA H. & MONSI M. (1959). Dry matter production by *Chamaecyparis pisifera* in winter. *Bot. Mag., Tokyo,* **72,** 450–5.

ODUM E.P. (1959). *Fundamentals of Ecology.* W. Saunders, Philadelphia, London.

ODUM H.T., COPELAND B.J. & BROWN R.Z. (1963). Direct and optical assay of leaf mass of the lower montane rain forest of Puerto Rico. *Proc. natn. Acad. Sci. U.S.A.* **49,** 429–34.

OLSON, J.S. (1959). Analysis of forest growth. *Health Physics Division Ann. Progr. Rept. ORNL–2806.*

OSSWALD D. (1964). *Das Verhältnis der pflanzlichen Stoffproduktion über und unter der Erde.* Zulassungsarbeit dr T. H. Stuttgart, Unpublished.

OVINGTON J.D. (1956). The forms, weights and productivity of tree species grown in close stands. *New Phytol* **55**, 289–304.

PAVLYCHENKO T.K. (1937). Quantitative study of the entire root systems of weed and crop plants under field conditions. *Ecology* **18**, 62–79.

PETERKEN G.F. & NEWBOULD P.J. (1966). Dry matter production by *Ilex aquifolium* L. in the New Forest. *J. Ecol.* **54**, 143–50.

POLJAKOVA-MINCENKO N.F. (1961). The foliage of broadleaved stands in the steppe zone. (Russian) *Soobshch. Lab. Lesov.* **4**, 40–53.

REES A.R. & TINKER P.B.H. (1963). Dry-matter production and nutrient content of plantation oil palms in Nigeria. I Growth and dry matter production. *Pl. Soil* **19**, 19–32.

REUKEMA D.L. (1961). Crown development and its effect on stem growth of six Douglas-Firs. *J. For.* **59**, 370–1.

RIEDACKER A. (1968). *Methodes indirectes d'estimation de la biomasse des arbres et des peuplements forestiers.* Station de Sylviculture et de Production. Mimeographed.

ROGERS W.S. & BOOTH G.A. (1960). The roots of fruit trees. *Scient. Hort.* **14**, 27–34.

ROGERSON T.L. (1964). Estimating foliage on Loblolly Pine, *U.S. For. Serv. Note Sth. For. Exp. Stn. No* SO—16, pp. 3.

SAITO H., SHIDEI T. & KIRA T. (1965). Dry matter production by *Camellia japonica* stands (Japanese). *Jap. J. Ecol.* **15**, 131–9.

SCHOBER R. (1964). Ertragstafeln und Durchforstung der Fichte. *Allg. Forstz.* **19**, 293–5, 319–22.

SHIDEI T. (1963). Productivity of Haimatsu (*Pinus pumila*) community growing in Alpine zone of Tateyama Range. (Japanese). *J. Jap. For. Soc.* **45**, 169–73.

SIMON W., EICH D. & ZAJONZ A. (1957). Vorläufiger Bericht über Beziehungen zwischen Wurzelmenge und Vorfruchtwert bei versciedenen Klee- und Grasarten als Hauptfrucht auf leichten Böden. *Z. Acker-u. Pflbau.* **104**, 71.

SMIRNOV V.V. (1961). The foliage and the weight of aerial parts of trees in Birch stands of the coniferous/broadleaved forests subzone. (Russian). *Soobshch, Lab. Lesov.* **4**, 86–97.

SMIRNOV V.V. (1963). The quantities of needles in Spruce stands. (Russian). *Lesn. Hoz.* **16**, 17–9.

SMITH W.H., NELSON L.E. & SWITZER G.L. (1963). The characterization of dry matter and nitrogen accumulation by Loblolly Pine (*Pinus taeda* L.) on poor sites. *Proc. Soil Sci. Soc. Am.* **27**, 465–8.

STEPHENS G.R. Jr. (1963). Organic matter production in forests. *Front. Pl. Sci.*, **16**, 6–7.

SWITZER G.L., NELSON L.E. & SMITH W.H. (1966). The characterization of dry matter and nitrogen accumulation by Loblolly Pine (*Pinus taeda* L.). *Proc. Soil Sci. Soc. Am.* **30**, 114–9.

TAKASE G. (1960). On the prediction of the growth of diameter by the increment borer (Japanese). *J. Jap. For. Soc.* **42**, 207–10.

TAMM C.O. (1953). Growth, yield and nutrition in carpets of a forest moss (*Hylocomium splendens*). *Meddn St. SkogsförskInst.* **43**, 1–140.

TAMM C.O. & CARBONNIER C. (1961). Vaxtnaringen som skoglig produktionsfaktor. *K. Skogs-o. LantbrAkad. Tidskr.* **100**, 95–124.

VYSKIT M. (1966). Method of foundation and evaluation of thinning sample plots. *Sb. vys. Sk. zemĕd. les. Fac. Brne C* **35**, 25–58.

WEAVER J.E. (1926). *Root development of field crops.* New York and London.

WEAVER J.E. & KRAMER J. (1932). Root system of *Quercus macrocarpa* in relation to the invasion of prairie. *Bot. Gaz.* **94**, 51–85.

WEAVER J.E. & ZINK E. (1946). Annual increase of underground materials in range grasses. *Ecology* **27**, 115–27.

WEIHE J. (1961). Massen-und Starkenwachstum der Fichte als Funktion des Hohenwachstums. *Allg. Forstz. u. Jagdztg.* **132**, 131–6.

WESTLAKE D.F. (1963). Comparisons of plant productivity. *Biol. Rev.* **38**, 385–425.

WHITTAKER R.H. (1965). Dominance and diversity in land plant communities. *Science, N.Y.,* **147**. 250–60.

WHITTAKER R.H. (1963). Net production of heath balds and forest heaths in the Great Smoky Mountains. *Ecology* **44**, 176–82.

WILL G.M. (1964). Dry matter production and nutrient uptake by *Pinus radiata* in New Zealand. *Commonw. For. Rev.* **43**, 57–70.

WOODWELL G.M. & BOURDEAU P.F. (1965). Measurement of dry matter production of the plant cover. *UNESCO Montpellier Symposium* 519–27.

YOCUM W.W. (1937). Root development of young Delicious apple trees as affected by soils and by cultural treatments. *Nebr. Agr. Exp. Stn. Res. Bull.* **95**, 1–55.

Index